Jessica H

THE MURDER MAZE

First published in 2025
Copyright © Jessica Huntley 2025

Jessica Huntley has asserted her right under the Copyright, Designs and Patents Act 1988 to be identified as the author of the work.

This is a work of fiction. Unless otherwise indicated, all the names, characters, businesses, places, events and incidents in this book are either the product of the author's imagination or used in a fictitious manner. Any resemblance to actual persons, living or dead, or actual events is purely coincidental.

All rights reserved. No part of this publication may be reproduced, transmitted, or copied by any means (electronic, mechanical, photocopying, or otherwise) without the prior permission of the author.

ISBN: 978-1-916827-13-4

First edition
Website: www.jessicahuntleyauthor.com

Cover Design: Get Covers
Edited and proofread by: Jennifer Kay Davies

About Jessica Huntley

Jessica Huntley is an ex-British soldier and Personal Trainer turned author of addictive psychological thriller books. She has spent almost three years writing and is now the author of sixteen books, including two trilogies, six standalone thrillers, two anthologies, a co-written horror novel and a novella.

She writes books for thriller readers who like their stories dark and twisty with complex, yet memorable characters, who often suffer from relatable mental health disorders. When she isn't writing, Jessica is either reading, keeping fit, walking her dog or looking after her young son.

Sign up to her email list to receive news about upcoming book releases and download a FREE thriller short story (You Die...I Die) by visiting her website: www.jessicahuntleyauthor.com

Other Books by Jessica

Published by Inkubator Books

Don't Tell a Soul
Under Her Skin

Published by Joffe Books

Horrible Husbands

The Darkness Series

The Darkness Within Ourselves
The Darkness That Binds Us
The Darkness That Came Before

My ... Self Series

My Bad Self: A Prequel Novella
My Dark Self
My True Self
My Real Self

Standalone Thrillers

Jinx

How to Commit the Perfect Murder in Ten Easy Steps

The Murder Maze

Writing in collaboration with other authors

The Summoning

HorrorScope: A Zodiac Anthology – Vol 1

Bloody Hell: An Anthology of UK Indie Horror

Acknowledgements

This book has taken me so long to finish and it's been a very secretive project along the way, but a few special people have helped me hone, buff and finish it, so that it's finally out in the world.

My two loyal beta readers – Hayley Anderton and Char (@theliteraryreviewjournal) – Thank you so much for reading this book and helping me iron out a few plot holes. It's a rather complicated story, I know!

Thank you to the amazing Candace Fitzgerald and Charlie Albers who are going to be working together to bring this book to audio. I can't wait to hear your voices bringing the characters to life. It's always a "pinch me" moment when I hear my words in audio. It couldn't be in more reliable and talented hands.

Thank you always to my editor and proofreader, Jennifer Kay Davies, who is now so super busy with other projects, I have to book months in advance! Your eye for detail is always appreciated to tidy up my words, ensuring I don't get attacked by readers for my lousy sentence structure.

A big thank you will always go to you - my readers. I can't believe this is my sixteenth book! If you've made it this far and followed me from the start, then thank you. You're super special and I wouldn't be here typing away at my desk without your support.

Connect with Me

To read a FREE short story prequel to The Murder Maze – "You Die...I Die"

Find and connect with me online via the following platforms.

Sign up to my email list via my website to be notified of future books and receive a twice-monthly author newsletter and also receive a **FREE short story – You Die...I Die –** the prequel to The Murder Maze, first published in HorrorScope: A Zodiac Anthology – Vol 1

www.jessicahuntleyauthor.com

Follow me on Facebook: Jessica Huntley - Author - @jessica.reading.writing

Follow me on Instagram: @jessica_reading_writing

Follow me on Twitter: @jess_read_write

Follow me on TikTok: @jessica_reading_writing

Follow me on Goodreads: jessica_reading_writing

CONTENT WARNINGS

Murder. Death. Swearing. Child abduction.

Rape (inferred). Suicide (inferred).

Prologue

A small uninhabited island sits near the eastern tip of Anglesey, Wales. It is the ninth-largest island off the coast of the country and marks the northeastern end of the Menai Strait.

The highest point of the island is 192 feet above sea level and most of it is made from carboniferous limestone and has steep cliffs on all but one side that only an expert climber, or someone with the correct equipment, should attempt. There are rough steps carved into the limestone up the south side of the cliffs, but these are not suitable even for a nifty-footed mountain goat. Appropriate footwear must be worn if attempting to navigate these steps. The approximate diameter of the island is sixty-nine acres. It is privately owned by a mysterious and wealthy estate, having been purchased more than a decade ago from the National Trust, who used it to boost the puffin colonies, hence its nickname of Puffin Island.

The ruin of a large building dominates the centre of the island. This building can be seen from certain points of the mainland using a strong pair of binoculars on a clear day. This building has stood for over two hundred years, rotting and degrading year by year after being left to the brutal elements renowned along the coast of Wales. However, since the island's purchase in 2014, the decrepit building has undergone an extensive renovation, transforming it into a foreboding-looking manor house. As far as anyone is aware, the building does not have electricity running to it, nor any amenities or appropriate plumbing. It is not currently listed on any homeowner registries.

The island is home to numerous bird species, including puffins, guillemot, razorbill, shag, and kittiwake. Even seals can be seen at certain times of the day, sunbathing and resting on the rocks near the shipwreck that was thought to have run adrift a hundred years ago. It might seem like the perfect tourist attraction when visiting Anglesey, but unfortunately, the island is off-limits to tourists. No one has been allowed to set foot on it since it was bought by the unknown estate.

But, if this mysterious island is uninhabited and has no electricity supplied to it, then why can lights be seen from the shore of the mainland after dark? Why is no one allowed within one hundred feet of the shoreline? What's so secretive about the island? And who's renovated the building? Who owns the island now? All these questions and more ensure that the island is at the forefront of tourists' minds when visiting the area.

Perhaps this island is one of those mysteries that are merely there to fascinate and torment the tourists and residents. Perhaps no one will ever really know what goes on there, except for the wildlife. Maybe one day the island will be open to the public. Only time will tell.

Chapter One

The Mastermind – The End

My sides ache from holding back a laugh that's been threatening to erupt since I first started on this journey. Not a normal laugh one uses when they find something funny, but an evil laugh one uses when their diabolical scheme has worked without a hitch. That kind of laugh.

This plan has been so long in the making that I can barely believe it's almost over. A part of me is sad, but then I think of how unbelievably happy I'll be when I have what I want, what I started all this for. Five and a half years of careful manipulation, planning, money and preparation and now it's almost over. It will be worth the sleepless nights, the expense, and the solitude.

Perhaps I'm the dastardly wicked mastermind of every thriller or crime movie. Or perhaps I'm the evil genius in every superhero movie. Whoever I am, I've accomplished what I set out to do. Almost. Yes, I've had help along the way from my family, especially my father. I couldn't have done it without his money and support. All evil geniuses have their loyal followers and sidekicks who will do just about anything to satisfy their master, although I don't think of myself as evil because I'm not the one who has murdered innocent people. I am the innocent victim in all of this. I have never taken a life, nor do I intend to. My hands are clean.

And so, I allow the laugh to escape from my diaphragm, relishing the pure sense of relief as it takes over my body and sends ripples and goosebumps across my skin. It's glorious. There's no other feeling like it in the world, other than maybe a toe-curling orgasm. But if I had the choice, I'd choose this moment every time. Fuck the orgasm.

The two survivors on the viewing screen in front of me are glaring at each other after leaving behind their fallen comrade. I say 'comrade' as if they have all been in it together, as if they're friends who have been helping each other the entire time, but they're not. Nor have they ever been. They're not even close to being friends. They're in it for themselves and they have been all along. That's why there are only two remaining.

They started as four ...

It had all begun so innocently.

Four people were given the chance of a lifetime to win the ultimate prize. They were provided with the chance to redeem themselves and start over.

And now ... two of those people are dead.

The question is ... who's going to be the next to die? Because whoever survives wins the game and, at the end of the day, that's all it's ever been ...

A game.

And I always win …

I always get what I want.

It's time for the final curtain call.

Chapter Two

Jane

The late autumn sun of the afternoon warms her back as she sits in the tiny motorboat on a crudely crafted wooden bench, her clammy hands clenched together on her lap. Her body bobs and jolts as the boat pierces through the chaotic waves. Her bright orange life-vest is miles too big for her so the top of it keeps knocking against her chin whenever the boat crests over a particularly nasty wave. She's already bitten her lip by accident; now she tastes copper as well as the salty sea on her tongue. She's never been a huge fan of water, or boats, or the sea, so every time a wave splashes her, she flinches and wipes her face with the back of her jacket, which seems like a pointless endeavour considering another splash comes along merely seconds afterwards, soaking her again.

The driver of the boat hasn't said a word since she climbed on board. Not a single word. He stares out at the water and expertly navigates them across it. He's wearing a dark green waxed jacket that looks very expensive, possibly a Barbour design. His attire seems oddly posh to Jane, considering they're in rural north Wales. His matching cap is pulled low over his face, obscuring his features, but she guesses him to be around fifty due to the tuffs of grey hair sticking out from underneath it. Before she got on the boat, the man told her in a low, gruff voice that it wouldn't take long to reach their destination and to sit down and not ask questions. She did as she was told and has been sitting quietly ever since.

Jane sees the island in the distance; a huge boulder sticking out of the sea, and she's only been on this boat journey for approximately fifteen minutes. It's hard to tell because her watch is being funny and appears to have stopped working, or it seems to stop and start sporadically. It's not a new watch, but it's never given her any trouble before today and it can't be water-damaged because it's waterproof. The last time she looked at it and knew it was working, the time was 13:01 and that had been as she'd taken her seat in the boat.

The island isn't far from land – about half a mile from the nearest shore – so she doesn't expect to be in this tiny boat for much longer.

Good, the sooner I'm off this thing, the better.

The boat struggles to stay on course, having to be adjusted by the driver every time they crest a wave. Jane swallows, tasting blood and salt again as she cranes her neck to the sky, attempting to distract herself from the deep dark water beneath her. The depths call to her, daring her to dip down beneath the surface. She knows it never does anyone any good to dwell on the past, but sometimes the past doesn't want to be forgotten. It claws its way to the surface like a drowning victim whenever it feels like it, usually when a person is at their most vulnerable, then drags them back down into the dark.

Jane has never felt as vulnerable as she does right now, bouncing across the waves, heading to an uninhabited island with only a piece of paper from an unknown person telling her the reason why she's had to leave her four-year-old son behind.

She is doing this for him. Isn't she?

The engine quietens and the boat bobs to a stop. Jane's stomach lurches.

They have approached the island from the east side from what she can gather, although she's never been great at working out the cardinal points. She looks up. The island seems so much larger now she's here. It hadn't looked this big from the shores of Anglesey.

The driver of the boat turns to her, picks up a backpack that's been hidden under a seat the whole journey, and tosses it to her.

'Good luck,' he says in the same gruff voice and without making eye contact. She still hasn't seen his face properly. 'Remember to leave the bag outside the house when you arrive.'

Jane catches the bag, almost dropping it when she feels how heavy it is. She lifts the flap and peers inside. 'What am I supposed to do with this?'

The driver says nothing.

Figures.

Jane discards her life jacket in the boat before heaving the bag onto her back. The boat is moored precariously next to some smooth grey rocks, so she says a quick prayer before leaping towards them. She lands hard, her left foot slips on the rock covered by slime and bird shit, and she almost lands up sitting in the bubbly water.

Once she's righted herself, she turns back to the boat to ask a question, but it's already motoring away, crashing through the waves at high speed. The driver doesn't look back.

'Great … thanks for the lift!' She mutters a few expletives, adjusting the straps on the bag so that it fits her back and waist better. It weighs a tonne, and the thin straps are already digging into her shoulders. She has on a purple waterproof jacket, but underneath only a T-shirt. It is a warm autumn, and she didn't think she'd need lots of layers. She hopes this is still the case. God knows when she'll be leaving the island.

A piercing shriek makes her jump just as she is about to take her first step across the uneven rocks. She turns towards the sound. A black and white bird squawks at her from a rock, its head held high and its beady eyes focusing directly on her as if it's judging her for being here in its territory. She's heard about the abundance of wildlife and birds on this island.

There are even supposed to be puffins nesting here, a sight she's never seen outside of a zoo.

'What are you looking at?'

The bird squawks once again before taking off into the air, its wings beating effortlessly against the strong wind. Clearly, it doesn't appreciate a strange human encroaching on its land.

Jane did some light research before coming here.

Apparently, no one has set foot on the island for a long time, almost a decade. Tourists are allowed to motor around the island on boats to glimpse the wildlife, but it is forbidden to come ashore. To do so, someone would need special written permission. Many wildlife experts, bird watchers and enthusiasts have tried, but each have been turned down by its mysterious owner.

But now she's here with a written invitation ...

Jane cautiously tiptoes across the rocks, avoiding the wet ones. The heavy bag threatens to throw her off balance, but her sturdy walking boots are already worth their weight in gold, enabling her to cross the rocky beach with relative ease and without falling on her bum.

She reaches the bottom of the cliff face and looks up. It's about thirty feet to the top, give or take, but the edge looms above her like a cloud, forever drifting out of reach.

'There must be another way around,' she says, turning her head to the left and then the right. She sees nothing but water. The tiny rocky outcrop she has landed on is only a few feet wide before it re-joins the sea. Yes, she possibly could wade in the shallows and around the edge of the island, but the risk of slipping and falling in the water is too great a risk. She doesn't want to get soaking wet or be anywhere near the water's edge.

She turns back to the cliff.

The only way is up.

Jane glances at her Garmin watch. It reads 13:15, but it appears to have completely stopped working now. She shakes it and taps the dial. Nothing. She has less than forty-five minutes to reach the top of this cliff. Talk about cutting it close.

Jane sighs as she unclips her backpack and pulls out the climbing gear. It seems whoever has sent her here knew she'd need it. She can't help but think back to three days ago when all of this started.

****

The water was running cold again; the type of cold that made her gasp as she stepped under the steady stream. She'd given the boiler plenty of time to heat up this morning, yet she only had a few glorious seconds of hot water before it turned cold, and she let out a shriek. Just once, she wished things would go right. Just once. Was it too much to ask for a hot shower in the morning?

She'd been up for almost two hours last night with Ben, soothing him to sleep after another nightmare. He kept saying there was a monster under the bed, a classic childhood fear. And then, when he finally drifted off, holding tight to her hand, and she dragged herself back to bed, bleary eyed, she'd been unable to fall back to sleep.

It wasn't an uncommon occurrence though. Her insomnia had started at the beginning of her pregnancy and then, once Ben was born, sleep had been a rarity anyway. He never slept when she wanted him to. She seethed with jealousy when other mum friends exclaimed their child had slept through the night since they were six weeks old, or that they could lay their baby down and they'd soothe themselves to sleep without fuss. Why had Ben screamed whenever she put him down to sleep in his cot as a baby? Why did he continue to wake up every hour through the night wanting her? Even now, at almost five years old, he woke at least four times a night, calling out for her to hold his hand. Granted, she loved holding his warm little hand as his eyes fluttered closed, and it felt nice to be needed by such a precious boy, but at the same time she wanted nothing more than for him to be quiet and go to sleep. Did that make her a bad mum? These hard days and nights wouldn't last forever, and her own mother constantly told her to enjoy these precious moments and the fact he wanted her and that she was his safe space, but it was hard to do on so little sleep.

'Mummy!' The high-pitched voice of her child pierced the sound of running water.

'Yes?' she called out, spitting bubbles out of her mouth.

'Mummy!'

'What?'

'Mummy!'

Jane clenched her teeth, turned off the water and ripped back the shower curtain to find her son standing on the bathmat holding a piece of buttered toast. He stared at her with blue eyes and batted his long eyelashes.

'What is it, Ben?'

'Nothing.' He turned and exited the bathroom, giggling.

Jane took a deep breath, telling herself not to snap. Not today. Not now.

As she climbed out of the shower cubicle, shivering and dripping water over the floor, she glanced down and caught sight of her scar. The caesarean scar across her lower abdomen still looked pink and puckered, but that wasn't the scar she always stared at. She was proud of her caesarean scar, but not the other one.

The now-oddly shaped pattern on her skin, located on her left side a few inches across from her belly button, glared back at her. She closed her eyes against the memory of searing flesh and mind-numbing pain as a red-hot branding iron had been held against her skin.

Five and a half years had passed, but not a day went by when she didn't think about it, didn't smell burning flesh.

Jane grabbed a nearby towel and dried her skin, her hands trembling as she guided them across her body.

'What's that, Mummy?'

Jane looked up and saw her son standing in the doorway of the bathroom, this time holding a cup of milk. Around his mouth was a ring of white residue.

'What's what?' she asked as she quickly stepped into some clean underwear she'd laid out before showering. It wasn't that she didn't want her child to see her naked. She wasn't ashamed of her body, but she always tried to hide the brand on her side.

Ben tottered up to her and pressed a sticky finger to her side, right where the symbol was branded into her. Jane gulped back a lump in her throat. It wasn't time to tell him the truth. How could she? How could she tell her baby boy that she had been tortured by a crazy woman when he'd still been a bundle of cells in her body? At the time, the killer had attempted to brand her stomach, but Jane had turned away at the last moment so that the iron had collided with her side instead; her desperate attempt to shield her unborn child.

'This? It's just a scar, baby.'

'It looks funny.'

'It's a Gemini symbol.'

'Huh?'

Jane smiled as she knelt at his level. She brushed a stray piece of soft hair out of his face and picked a crumb from his lips. 'Gemini is a star sign,' she explained. 'It depends on when you were born as to what star sign you have.' She wasn't about to go into the depths of astrology with a four-year-old.

'What's my star sign?'

'You were born on February the fourteenth. My little valentine. You are an Aquarius.'

Ben stared at her blankly. 'What does that mean?'

Jane smiled again as she stood up and continued to get dressed. 'Nothing, really. It's just a silly thing that grownups sometimes talk about. It doesn't really mean anything.'

'Okay, Mummy.'

Jane leaned forwards and pressed her lips to his soft hair, inhaling his sweet scent. She was taken back to the moment he'd been born when she first encountered his aroma. The moment was unlike any other she'd experienced or would ever experience in her life. His smell was unique to her and every time she held him close, she took the opportunity to inhale because one day he wouldn't let her. One day he'd be grown and gone, and she'd be ... alone.

His father was ... non-existent.

No, now wasn't the time to think about him. Jane had too many things to do today. She had to drop Ben off at preschool, finish her painting for a local exhibition and get to work on time as a waitress.

'Go and finish your breakfast. I'll be there in a minute to get you dressed.'

Ben nodded and left the bathroom, leaving Jane in her underwear. She shivered as she ran her fingers across the puckered skin of the brand.

It was a time in her life she refused to think about.

Jane shut her eyes tight against the vision of blood and clutched her throat, fighting the nausea.

Five minutes later, she arrived in the small lounge to find Ben sitting in front of the television, watching his favourite show. His breakfast plate was clear. The boy loved his food. He may not have ever slept through the night, but at least he wasn't fussy. He'd eat everything and anything she put in front of him and had done so since the first day she started weaning him onto solids. His favourite food was avocado and hummus. How long that would last, she had no idea.

Oliver, her ten-year-old tabby cat, was fast asleep on the arm of the sofa. She'd owned him since he was a kitten. He'd been through some tough times with her, and she couldn't imagine a better companion. He even loved Ben and had often slept in his cot when he was small.

Jane hummed along to Bluey's soundtrack as she tidied a few toys from the living room floor. Her flat was small, but it had two bedrooms and a decent-sized living area. It was all the council could find for her and that was fine. There was a bit of mould growing in the top left corner of the bathroom and all but one plug socket worked in the lounge, which meant she had to overload an extension cable, but at least it was liveable, although the boiler was on the brink again. She'd have to report it. Yet another item to add to her never-ending list of things to do.

Jane paused as she reached the front door of her flat. She bent down to straighten the welcome mat but stopped when she saw a white envelope sitting on top of it. The postman didn't usually deliver letters until around midday and the letter hadn't been there last night when she'd double-checked the door was locked before going to bed.

The envelope had her name on it, but no address, which meant it had been hand-delivered sometime this morning or during the night by someone who knew her.

Jane picked it up and turned it over. It was a perfectly ordinary envelope, nothing remarkable about it at all. Her name was written in black ink using some sort of special calligraphy pen, she assumed, as it was very posh and swirly, barely legible to her.

Curiosity managed to override her need to tidy the flat. She slid her finger into a gap and tore open the top of the envelope, pulling out a piece of card.

It was beautifully embossed with a gold stamp in one corner which said *NV Enterprises* and had been typed with a fancy font, but her name had been handwritten using the same style as the front of the envelope.

As Jane read the words, her eyes grew wide and, as she read the final sentence, she let the card slip from her fingers and drop to the floor.

****

Jane blinks her eyes, sending the memory to the back of her mind so she can concentrate on the task ahead: scaling this almost vertical cliff face with barely any climbing experience. She dabbled in a few climbing wall trips with friends back in her younger days, but that was inside with lots of safety equipment and an instructor telling her exactly what to do and where to place her feet and hands. This is a whole other level of climbing.

Jane maneuvers herself into the climbing harness and adjusts the straps as best she can, then puts her hands on her hips and tilts her head backwards. She spies a fixed bolt in the rock about three feet above her. It seems someone has prepared for her visit because the bolt looks new, as if it's been placed there recently. As she scans the area above the bolt, she sees more scattered about, a few feet in between each one.

But first, she must reach the one above her.

Jane takes out what she needs to make the climb, then puts the backpack on. She rests the rope and the clips over her left shoulder before planting her right foot into a crevice. She presses down on her toes and, using the jagged rock face, pulls herself up, flattening her chest against the damp limestone.

The bolt is still just out of reach as she extends her hand to clip herself in.

Just a little further …

Her left hand, which is anchoring her to the wall, slips and her face smashes into the rock. She bites her lip again, tasting blood. She's missing the tip of her little finger on that hand, and this means her grip and dexterity isn't as good as it could be.

A reminder of that awful time.

Jane flattens herself against the cold cliff again and takes a deep breath. She knows that once she's clipped in it will be easier because she won't have the fear of falling to deal with. Yes, it will still hurt if she slips and falls. She'll probably bang against the rocks a few times, but …

Don't think. Just climb.

Jane grinds her teeth, re-anchors her hand and feet into position and pulls herself up, extending her left hand, which holds the clip towards the bolt.

Three inches …

Two inches …

Just a little further ...

Jane smiles as the clip locks into place, confirming her safety. She tightens the rope, adjusts her backpack once more, and begins to climb, taking each movement steady and double-checking every hand and foot hold.

She doesn't look down. Doesn't want to see the rocky ground far below.

Despite the cool air and the wind, sweat pours off her. She can feel the waxy texture of her jacket clinging to her damp skin. The wind buffets her long, light-brown hair around her face. Now she wishes she'd tied it back in a ponytail before she left.

It's not far to the top now.

Another bird, some sort of gull, screeches at her as she passes its nest, embedded into the side of the rock face. She ignores it and keeps climbing, her breathing laboured.

The waves crash far below, reminding her what awaits if she slips and falls, or any of the clips fail. She pauses to catch her breath and risks a glance behind her. Nothing but water for miles. She turns to face east and sees the mainland of Wales in the distance. Half a mile is a long way across deep water. The only way of getting back to Ben is across it, but not until she's completed her mission. Not until she's solved the mystery of why she's been summoned here.

The muscles in her arms are screaming. She wishes she'd spent a little more time in the gym lifting weights rather than running on the treadmill, but running is the only thing that keeps her sane. She loves to run. She even completed the London Marathon last year in honour of her sister ...

Jane blinks as tears spring from nowhere. Having a breakdown while clinging to a cliff will not help the situation, so she presses on.

She's so close to the top now.

Just a few more feet.

Jane grabs the top of the cliff, shuffling her body upwards as she leans her elbows on the earth and pushes herself up.

And she's done it.

She inhales and smiles at her accomplishment as the salty air fills her lungs. She stares across the sea and then looks down, seeing how far she has climbed. Another wave of pride rushes over her. It's then she realises something.

She is completely alone on this island.

How is she to get back to the mainland? The driver had said nothing about when he'd return to collect her; that's if he was due to return at all.

Before she allows panic to set in, she unclips the ropes and harness and shoves them into the backpack.

Now what?

She glances from left to right, taking in the rocky outcroppings and a barely used path. It looks like that's the only way she can go. She knows there's a building on this island, and that is her next destination. She has the instructions in her pocket. She fishes out the card that arrived mysteriously three days ago and reads it again for clarification.

Her gaze lingers on the last sentence.

Her heart flips in her chest. Someone knows the truth and that same someone has led her here to this island. She could not have come. She could have burned the card, and never thought about it again, but she couldn't. And she didn't.

She's here now and she has to complete this mission.

She needs the money.

She needs to ensure that whoever is blackmailing her never reveals the truth about what happened five and a half years ago.

'Hey!'

Jane almost drops the card as a loud sharp voice booms across the expanse in front of her. She squints her eyes and shields them from the sun using her hand.

A lone dark figure emerges from the south side of the island.

It seems Jane isn't alone on this island after all.

NV Enterprises would like to formally invite you to the opening of our new venture, located on the uninhabited island off the coast of Anglesey.

We can promise it will be an experience you're never likely to forget.

You, Jane Patterson, are the guest of honour.

On 17 October 2024, you are to arrive at the venue no later than 14:00.

You are not to mention this opportunity to anyone.

Further instructions regarding your travel arrangements will follow.

If you are late, you are immediately disqualified.

We know you live in a dingy council flat in Birmingham and your son, Ben, is growing every day and needs new clothes.

Imagine being able to give him the world.

Imagine never having to worry about money again.

£1,000,000. That's what we're offering you.

We expect you to be there.

If you are not, the truth will be revealed.

We know what really happened to you and your sister, Annie Patterson.

Tick Tock.

Chapter Three
Andrew

He hates everything about this situation. He hates the wind, the rain on his face and the God-awful stench of bird shit and salty air. He could be relaxing on a gym tanning bed, preparing for a night out of drinking and partying, not sweating through his T-shirt on a fucking island in Wales, surrounded by nothing but nature, squawking birds and water.

The smallest boat known to man, driven by a less-than-helpful old geezer, dropped him off a few minutes ago and now he's stranded, wishing he'd brought more than a shaker full of energy drink and a protein bar to sustain him. He downs the liquid in one go, burps and then tosses the empty shaker into his shoulder bag, which holds nothing but a spare top and the bar.

He curses the wanker who dropped him here. Barely a word was said between them during the fifteen-minute boat ride where he was tossed about so much his full-English breakfast threatened to come back up on several occasions. Andrew doesn't mind the sea or boats. Hell, he has spent many a day getting drunk or high on boats while on holiday in sunny Magaluf and has even gone scuba diving in the Bahamas while pissed out of his face. However, this situation is about as far from that luxury as he can get. Plus, in Magaluf, he'd been on a million-pound yacht, complete with a serving staff of four, not a tiny dingy that looks as if a man of his size and weight could easily capsize it. No, it's not the water or the boat he hates. It's the sheer isolation of the island he's heading towards. The wind and rain and the fucking Welsh weather. He's heard jokes that it always rains in Wales, and, right now, the country is proving those jokes to be spot on.

Andrew's a posh London boy. From Chelsea. One of *those* rich boys. Thanks to his wealthy father, also called Andrew Carter, he's never had to work a day in his life. He celebrated his thirty-second birthday two weeks ago by going on a weekend bender to Amsterdam where he'd sampled every type of weed he could find, visited more than half a dozen whores, and drank until he passed out or puked.

His father treats him like royalty and gives him whatever he wants, whenever he wants it. He gets an allowance every week and if it runs out then all he has to do is ask his dad and he'll have more money in his account within minutes.

Andrew is not a country boy. He doesn't do fresh air and mud and has never been to Wales before in his life.

'What the fuck am I doing here?' he mutters just as his right foot slips out from underneath him on the wet rocks. He lands hard. All eighty-five kilos of solid muscle slams down, causing his teeth to clench and his vision to blur. He has landed in a puddle too.

Andrew groans as his eyes roll to the back of his head. It takes a few minutes to regain his composure and catch his breath before he's able to haul himself to his feet. He wobbles as he glances at his surroundings.

He appears to have been dropped on the south side of the island. It's not a large pile of rock by any means, but it's hilly and covered with birds which are nesting and squawking and flapping their ugly wings.

He knows he has to get to the main building situated in the middle of the island, but how is he supposed to do that when there's thirty-plus feet of cliff face staring at him? He's no climber, and even if he was, climbing without any ropes or a safety harness is suicide. The old dude who dropped him here didn't give him any provisions, or any guidance on what to do. Useless wanker.

Andrew gingerly tiptoes across the rocks, avoiding the puddles and bird shit. It fucking stinks. He gets to the bottom of the cliff and looks up. There are some rough shapes leading up the side that almost look like ...

Steps.

'Holy shit,' he says as a smug grin crosses his face. He runs his hand over his damp bald head, wishing he'd brought a hat or a jacket with a hood. It's still raining, but barely a drizzle now and his T-shirt is wet through. Ah well, once he's at the top he'll be at the building, which will provide shelter and further information.

He approaches the rocky outcrop. Crude stone steps have been carved into the side of the cliff. The higher he climbs, the more precarious they become. One wrong movement and he could easily slip off the edge and splash down into the water below, no doubt hitting a few rocks on the way. He doubts he'd survive it.

At one point, the steps become so narrow he has to turn his back to the cliff face and shimmy along a rough stone edge. Sweat pours off his head now, further soaking his tight T-shirt, which has a slogan on it saying 'Born to Lift'.

His shoulder bag is sending him off balance, so he takes it off and holds it to his chest instead. The rock is cool against his back, but there are sharp edges that keep catching him as he shuffles along.

Thankfully, the path turns into steps again, some of them so big he has to hoist himself up using his elbows. He's not cut out for this. He's built for lifting weights in a gym, not climbing fucking rocks. He can barely catch his breath, so he decides to have a break on one of the larger flat areas. He sits and takes out his protein bar, chewing with his mouth open as he looks out to the open sea. He knows that time is ticking down. He looks at his watch; a Rolex his father gave him last year.

That's weird. It's not working.

What the hell? It's barely a year old. It was working this morning. He shakes it and holds it up to his ear, listening for a tick, but it's silent. The watch has stopped at fifteen minutes past twelve. Fuck knows what time it is now.

Ignoring his broken watch, he sighs. He thinks back to three days ago when he received his invite to this island. Maybe he should have just thrown the fucking thing in the bin.

Nothing is worth this torture.

****

He stared lovingly at his perfect reflection in the gym mirror as he pumped his biceps with the heaviest weights he could muster. Those veins were popping now! He worked fucking hard to hone his body into something even a god would be proud of. Day in and day out, hardly taking a day off from the discipline it took to look this good all year round. He had the time, the funds and the mentality to stick to a vigorous workout routine every day. Otherwise, he'd be bored. There wasn't much else to do.

Andrew trained in a state-of-the-art gym with the biggest free-weight area in the country. Twenty-seven squat racks. Nineteen deadlift stations. More than 1,500 dumbbells in total, ranging from the pathetic two kilograms to a hefty eighty kilograms. This place was his home. He belonged here, which was why he spent almost two hours a day sculpting his physique. After lifting weights, he'd maybe do a bit of shopping, play video games, smoke some weed or pick up a chick to have some fun with. That was his life. Every day. His father refused to let him help run the car business. Andrew didn't know whether that was because his father didn't trust Andrew or because he thought Andrew should enjoy life and not have to work.

As he dropped the fifty-kilogram dumbbells on the floor after finishing his last rep of shoulder presses, he let out a grunt of triumph, forcing everyone in the vicinity to focus their attention on him for a moment. He loved the attention. Craved it. That was why all the men wanted him to give them tips on training. They wanted to look like him. They craved attention too. He'd once been compared to the great Arnold Schwarzenegger, back in his heyday, back when he'd been competing on the world stage of bodybuilding. But he didn't want to be compared to anyone. Andrew wanted others to be compared *to him*.

'Yo, Andrew!'

Andrew saw his best mate jogging through the gym towards him. They grabbed each other's forearms and Andrew slapped him on the back.

'Good to see you, Rich. What's up?'

'You free for a session tonight?'

'Are we talking lifting or drinking?'

Rich laughed. 'Drinking, man!'

'Yeah, always up for a session. Ah, no, wait … I got a date.'

'A date?'

'Yeah, with that chick from Bill's.'

'The blonde bitch with the huge tits?'

'That's the one.'

'Yo, man! How'd you manage that?'

Andrew shrugged his huge shoulders. 'I finally wore the bitch down.'

Rich and Andrew high-fived.

'Okay, well, if you manage to shag her early and get bored, let me know, yeah?'

'Sure thing.'

Andrew watched Rich as he headed back the way he'd come. Rich trained a lot too, but he trained to feel good rather than look good. He was a loser. A jealous, pathetic loser who didn't like being second-best. He was a good mate, but Andrew didn't really need him. He didn't need anyone. Only his father and his money.

Andrew winked at a young woman who was doing her best not to stare at him as she stretched in preparation for her workout. She was hot. Maybe he'd ask for her number before she left. Every woman he approached in the gym almost always said yes to Andrew. They'd have been crazy not to. The cute woman winked back at him. He was in. Maybe he could have a quickie with her somewhere before his date tonight with Lauren … Laura? … Lucy? … Ah, who cared what her name was. But first, he had another set to finish.

Sweaty, exhausted and pumped, Andrew towelled his head as he entered the changing rooms, ready for a hot shower. Dark rings of sweat coloured his grey tank top, which was two sizes too small, but it made his pecs stand to attention. He pulled the top over his head as he put in the combination on his gym locker padlock.

As he went to reach for his sports bag, he stopped, confused by what was lying on top of it; a clean, white envelope with his name written in squiggly writing he could barely understand.

'What the fuck?' he muttered as he scooped it up in his large, sweaty hand. He tore it open with his teeth and spat out the slither of paper he'd torn off. He read slowly, his eyes growing as big as saucers, like when he was high as a kite. When he reached the end, his mouth dropped open.

****

Finishing his protein bar, Andrew tosses the empty wrapper in front of him and watches as it flutters to the rocks below, finally resting in a puddle of water.

'Right,' he says, dusting off his hands, 'time to get this party started.'

Within a minute, he's scrambling up the steps on his hands and knees, puffing as if he's sprinting on a treadmill.

'Fuck this shit,' he says.

A nearby bird screeches at him. It's mocking him.

He finally drags his body up the last step and collapses onto his back. His chest heaves up and down. He's made it. Thank fuck.

But there's no time to waste. He has to get there on time. He doesn't like to lose. And he doesn't know what the time is because his £150,000 watch is still fucking broken.

Andrew hauls himself to his feet and treks across the uneven ground, breaking into a gentle jog. He can see the large house up ahead, but wait …

'What the fuck?' He raises his hand and uses it as a shield against the sun, squinting to try and make out the shape in front of him.

'Hey!' he shouts.

The shape freezes and stares at him. It's a woman. And she'd be decent looking if it weren't for the bags under her eyes and the slight mum tum. Not that he didn't like a little bit of something to grab on to once and a while. He preferred to be in better shape than the women he shagged because it made them desperate for his approval and attention.

'Who are you?' she asks.

'You first.'

'My name's Jane Patterson.'

Andrew snorts in response.

'Something funny about my name?'

'Nope, just sounds pretentious.'

Jane raises her eyebrows. 'A big word for a big guy who looks like he does nothing but lift weights all day.'

'You calling me dumb?'

'No. I wouldn't dream of doing such a thing. Now, will you tell me your name?'

'Andrew.'

'Do you have a last name?'

'Yeah, but you're not getting it.'

Jane throws her hands up. 'Fine. I don't care. I assume you're here for the same reason I am.'

'And what reason's that then?' Jane fixes him with a glare that makes Andrew scoff. 'I was invited here,' he says.

'So was I,' she responds quickly.

Andrew lifts his head a fraction of an inch. 'Oh yeah, what for?'

'Does it matter? Anyway, my watch isn't working so I have no idea what the time is.' That's weird that her watch is broken too. 'I suggest we get a move on,' she adds.

Jane takes off towards the building without another word.

Andrew glares at her back, wondering what the hell is going on.

He doesn't know what this is all about, but there's only one way he can find out.

And that's to follow Jane up the hill.

NV Enterprises would like to formally invite you to the opening of our new venture, located on the uninhabited island off the coast of Anglesey.

We can promise it will be an experience you're never likely to forget.

You, Andrew Carter, are the guest of honour.

On 17 October 2024, you are to arrive at the venue no later than 14:00.

You are not to mention this opportunity to anyone.

Further instructions regarding your travel arrangements will follow.

If you are late, you are immediately disqualified.

I know you love yourself more than anyone else. I know you already have everything you could possibly ever want, but it's not enough, is it?

£1,000,000. That's what we're offering you. It's not a lot, compared to what you're used to, but this money comes with a lot of extras. There's something else you want, and we know what it is.

We expect you to be there.

If you are not, then the truth will be revealed.

Because we know about your dirty little secret. It would be a shame to ruin your perfect reputation, wouldn't it? I bet Daddy wouldn't approve.

Tick Tock.

Chapter Four
Ryan

He cautiously steps off the small motorboat and onto the tiny jetty that stretches into the water from the shore on the east side of the island. It's only made from a few rotten planks of wood haphazardly nailed together, some on the brink of disintegration from the salt water and constant abuse from the waves, but it's enough to keep his feet dry and save him from having to wade through the water to the land. He turns and waves goodbye to the driver of the boat, an older gentleman by the looks of him, but hard to tell because his facial features are hidden under his flat cap. He had barely made eye contact with Ryan during the short ride to the island and had only uttered two words upon Ryan's departure from the boat: 'good luck'.

Ryan smiles as he takes a deep breath, enjoying the smell of the salty air as it tickles his nostrils. Now the rain clouds have blown away, it feels good to be outside with the warming sun on his back and the gulls squawking overhead. He may have overdressed for the occasion though. He looks down at his smart jeans and navy shirt, which is open at the collar. He's brought a jacket too, but he doesn't need it, so he rolls up his shirt sleeves, showing off his pale arms and tribal tattoo on his left forearm, a token from his wild university days.

Now, only nine years later, a lot has changed for Ryan. *A lot.*

But he can't think about that now.

He needs to hike across the island to the building in the middle before two this afternoon. He checks his watch. It says it's half past one now, but that can't be right. He stares at the second hand on the watch and realises it's not moving. He taps the dial, but nothing happens.

Strange.

Maybe the salt water has got to it. It's not a waterproof watch; it's a rather posh time piece his wife had given him as a wedding gift. He hopes it's not ruined.

Ryan's lost all sense of time now and hadn't thought to take note of when they set off. The driver was late arriving to pick him up at the dock. Then the engine had refused to start again, and the driver had taken almost twenty minutes to get it going. Something about a faulty petrol pipe or the engine overheating.

But Ryan's here now and feeling positive despite the sinking feeling in his heart at leaving his twin girls behind in Manchester. It's only for a few days. They'll be fine. They are in the capable and loving hands of their au pair, Amanda.

Ryan has brought a small bag with him, loaded with water, a few healthy snacks and a first aid kit. He's prepared, probably more so than is needed, but one can never be too careful when arriving onto an uninhabited island with no direct links back to the mainland. It would have been irresponsible to arrive with nothing but the shirt on his back. He doesn't know how long he'll be here. The invitation didn't say.

As Ryan navigates the uneven rocks leading to the main part of the island, he can't help but look around and admire the scenery. He hasn't travelled away from his home in so long. In fact, it's been years since he's even had time alone with his thoughts. There's always so much *noise* going on in his life. Not that he resents the noise, but ...

Ryan stops walking and sighs.

He tilts his head back, closes his eyes and stands still, breathing shallow and steady.

A memory pops into his head. A memory from long ago.

It's not a pleasant one.

The sun on his face feels like ...

Fire. The flames lick at his skin, hot, sizzling ... screaming ...

His eyes fling open.

But the fire isn't real. He's on the island and there's the main building in front of him. He continues walking, looking nowhere but at the large structure.

It's a huge, dilapidated mansion that looks as if it's been here for hundreds of years. The stonework is faded, crumbling in places and covered in moss. It even has turrets and large pillars, making it look like something out of a fantasy film. He knows very little about the place, despite having spent several hours researching it over the past three days since he received his invitation.

There wasn't a great deal of information about the island itself. He assumes it's owned by NV Enterprises because that's who the invite was from. There's no name attached to the house now, but it was owned by the National Trust before it was bought ten years ago. No one has been allowed to step foot on the island since. It's been left to the birds and other wildlife, including large brown rats, which apparently overran the island back in the 1800s when a ship crashed into the rocks. The ship is still there today, or at least what's left of it. If Ryan remembers correctly, it's on the west side of the island. He makes a mental note to visit the wreck when he isn't on a deadline; he enjoys looking at old things. And the mansion before him is drawing his eye also.

It looks like it could be haunted.

But of course, Ryan doesn't believe in ghosts or anything like that. But looking at the ruined building with its blacked-out windows and wrought-iron gates, it's easy to be swayed.

He reaches the gates and pushes them open. An old, rusty padlock drops to the floor with a clang. It seems that whoever owns this place is expecting him.

Now what?

He's here.

Ryan rubs his chin as he stares up at the building. Is he being watched? All the hairs on the back of his neck have sprung to attention and a cold shiver runs up his spine. He thinks back to three days ago when he received the envelope and experienced the same sensation as he opened and read the card inside.

****

He was running late. Again. Time seemed to slip through his fingers like sand every day, especially as an over-worked single dad juggling twin girls with Down's syndrome. Not that he'd change a thing about his life. Well, maybe one thing: to have Lisa there to watch her daughters grow up into the beautiful, cheeky girls they were. Grace and Hope. He was so lucky to have them.

There were days when the grief overwhelmed him so much, he wanted to pull the duvet over his head and block out the world. But then one of the girls would wake up, followed closely by the other, and he knew he couldn't be selfish because they needed him. He didn't have a choice.

So he'd pull the duvet down, slip his feet into his slippers and start the day. Just like he did every single day.

Ryan was twenty-nine and already a widower. A tragic car accident had stolen his wife from him, bringing his entire world to a standstill five years ago. Miraculously, his babies had survived. They had been strapped in their car seats in the back, but his wife hadn't been so lucky. And he'd walked away without a single scratch. Every day he asked himself why he hadn't done more to save her, why he hadn't crawled through the fire to pull her to safety, why he'd let her burn to death before his eyes while his girls screamed beside him, crying for their mother.

He needed help. He needed Lisa.

It wasn't fair. Nothing about his life was fair.

'Mr Neville, did you want me to do a load of washing today?' The sweet voice of Amanda, the girls' au pair, echoed through the halls and up the stairs as Ryan raced around his bedroom, slipping his feet into his black work shoes.

'Yes, thanks, that would be great!' he called back. He tripped over a strewn sock on the floor, scooped it up and chucked it in the washing basket on the landing.

He heard Amanda's footsteps on the stairs and looked up in time to see her arrive at the open bedroom door. She smiled at him with her perfect white, straight teeth. His heart missed a beat as her eyes lit up. Amanda had dark brown, shoulder-length hair with a thick fringe across her forehead. She often wore dark eyeliner. Ryan thought she'd look better without it, but never said anything. It wasn't his place.

She giggled. 'You've got your tie on crooked.'

'Have I?' He looked down and saw his mistake. 'I couldn't seem to get the knot to work this morning.'

'Bad night?'

'The girls were both up a total of eleven times.'

Amanda smiled, taking a step towards him. 'I heard. I could have helped, you know. I'm happy to get up with them.'

'No, no, it's fine. You do enough during the day.'

'Here ... allow me,' said Amanda.

Ryan's breath caught in his throat as she reached out and began to loosen his tie and re-knot it. Every so often her fingers brushed his skin and the hairs on the back of his neck stood up. It was wrong to find her so attractive. His wife had only been gone five years and he wasn't ready to move on. He wasn't even sure how it was possible to move on because he'd loved Lisa with every fibre of his body. Losing her had been the greatest sorrow his heart had ever felt, so opening his dying heart again to someone else was unthinkable. Unfathomable.

'There. All done.' Amanda pressed his tie flat against his chest, her hand remaining there a second longer than was necessary. They held eye contact. She blushed and moved back.

'The girls went into school fine this morning,' she said.

'Great. Thank you. I'll be home at six as normal.'

Amanda nodded. 'See you later, Mr Neville.'

'How many times have I asked you to call me Ryan?'

She blushed an even deeper shade of red. 'Sorry ... Ryan.' The way she said his name made his heart miss a beat again and his breath leave his body.

'Well ... I guess I'll see you tonight then. What are you doing today, besides my washing and picking up my daughters from school and making dinner?'

'I'm going to visit my mum.'

'How is she?'

'She's been having some really good days lately. Sometimes when I see her, she remembers who I am, and we have the most amazing conversations. It's like having the old Mum back.' Amanda forced her lips into a smile, but her eyes told a different story.

Ryan knew her mother had been diagnosed with Alzheimer's last year and was now in a care home because her father wasn't around, and she had no other family to help. Amanda didn't share a great deal about her family and often tried to change the subject whenever it came up. Ryan knew how she felt. He very rarely shared details about his wife either.

'I don't know how you do it,' said Ryan, shrugging into his black jacket. 'You take care of my kids who have Down's syndrome and look after your mum who has Alzheimer's. You're like Superwoman.'

Amanda laughed, seeming to snap out of her melancholy moment. 'Your girls are the most amazing kids on the planet. It's an honour to be their ... au pair.'

Ryan stopped and turned to her. 'You know you're more than their au pair though, right? I mean ... to them, I mean ... You're almost like their ...' Ryan's face flamed hot, and he turned away, attempting to look busy by picking up his laptop shoulder bag. When he turned back to Amanda, she was shuffling her feet from side to side. 'I'm sorry. I didn't mean to make you feel uncomfortable. I just meant that—'

'I know what you meant, Ryan,' she replied softly.

'You're like family,' he said.

'Thank you. I feel the same way.'

They held eye contact again. Ryan could have slapped himself. What was he doing? This gorgeous woman was standing in front of him in his bedroom while his dead wife's belongings were still hanging in the wardrobe next to him.

'I'm sorry, I really must get to work.'

'And I really must get on with the washing.' She smirked at him, alleviating some of the tension. 'Oh, Mr— Sorry ... Ryan ... a letter arrived for you this morning. I've put it on the kitchen table. It doesn't have an address on it, but it does have your name on the front in very fancy lettering.'

Ryan frowned. 'Weird. Did someone drop it off?'

'If they did, I didn't see who it was. I took the girls to school and then, when I came back, it was lying on the doormat.'

'Okay, thanks.'

Ryan left Amanda upstairs to collect the dirty washing and headed to the kitchen. She'd already cleaned in there and done the washing up. He didn't deserve her. She was too good to him. There was no way he'd be able to function without her help. He'd tried. For two long years after Lisa died, he'd suffered single-handedly through the temper tantrums, the bath times, the doctor's appointments, the speech therapy sessions and the birthday parties. But then he'd hit a wall and his body had begun to fail him. His doctor diagnosed him with exhaustion and the beginnings of depression. Ryan joked and told him that he didn't have time to be depressed. But the doctor had helped him open his eyes to the fact that he needed help, and not just from medication.

So he'd asked around his parenting groups for children with disabilities and asked if anyone knew of anyone who'd be willing to move in and help him with a few chores, errands and pick-ups. His demanding job as a car salesman meant he sometimes worked strange hours and he mostly worked on commission, so he needed all the help he could get. Then Amanda contacted him and asked if the position was still available. She'd come for an interview, and he'd hired her there and then because his daughters had taken to her perfectly. She'd sat and played with them on the floor and had even dealt with a tantrum beautifully and patiently.

Three years later, she was still here.

Ryan grabbed the envelope off the kitchen table and opened it. When he finished reading, he stumbled into the nearest chair and sat down, tears streaming from his eyes as a cold shiver ran up his spine.

****

Ryan sets his bag on the ground, unable to bear the weight any longer. It's bad enough he feels as if the whole world is on his shoulders, constantly pressing him into the earth. If only someone were here to help share the load.

He loves his girls, but he feels insignificant, as if he should be doing more. He has Amanda, but without a real mother will the girls flourish with only him to parent them? He worries about it every day, whether he's doing the right thing for them, meeting their extra needs, and ensuring they get the support they require. Amanda is brilliant, but …

It's too much sometimes.

Ryan sits on his bag and covers his face with his hands.

'What have I done?' he asks himself. 'Why am I here?'

But he knows why he's here.

The money.

He's never been a greedy man and has never been wealthy, always scraping by every month to cover the mortgage and the other bills that seem to constantly increase. If he had money, he wouldn't have to worry so much and there would be less of a burden on his shoulders.

That's why he's here.

And that's why he said yes to the invitation to come to this island.

He lifts his head at the sound of voices.

He's not alone on this island after all.

Two people are walking towards him. One is a large man with broad shoulders who looks a lot like a bodybuilder and the other is a petite woman who looks as if she's on a hiking trip. She appears to be a lot more prepared than The Hulk.

He stands. 'Um ... hi?'

'Who the fuck are you?' asks the large man, pointing a finger at him.

'Excuse me?'

'I said, who the fuck are you?'

The woman arrives panting slightly and gives Ryan an eye roll. Ryan smiles back and turns to The Hulk. 'I'm Ryan Neville.'

'Another pretentious name.'

'That's a big word for a big guy.'

'That's what I said!' exclaims the woman. She pushes past The Hulk and extends her hand. 'Hi, Ryan. I'm Jane Patterson.'

Ryan takes her hand and shakes it. 'Nice to meet you, Jane.' He smiles. 'You know, I feel like I've seen you before. You look very familiar.'

Jane blushes. 'Ah, well ... maybe I just have one of those faces.' She nods her head towards The Hulk. 'Our arrogant friend here is called Andrew.'

'Does he have a last name?'

'Apparently not.'

'Why are you two talking about me as if I'm not here?' demands Andrew.

Ryan looks past Jane. 'Because until you can engage in polite conversation, we have nothing to say to you.'

'Whatever,' he mumbles back.

Ryan turns to Jane. 'I thought I was alone on this island.'

Jane nods. 'Same. You can imagine my surprise when I ran into Andrew. Do you think anyone else is coming?'

Ryan looks at his watch. It's still reads half past one. 'No idea. I guess we'll find out soon enough.'

NV Enterprises would like to formally invite you to the opening of our new venture, located on the uninhabited island off the coast of Anglesey.

We can promise it will be an experience you're never likely to forget.

You, Ryan Neville, are the guest of honour.

On 17 October 2024, you are to arrive at the venue no later than 14:00.

You are not to mention this opportunity to anyone.

Further instructions regarding your travel arrangements will follow.

If you are late, you are immediately disqualified.

I know that you miss your wife, and your daughters need you more than ever. Imagine having the money to be able to offer them everything, put them in the best schools and give them the support they need. Imagine not having to work, so you could spend all your time with them.

£1,000,000. That's what we're offering you.

We expect you to be there.

If you are not, then the truth will be revealed.

We know how your wife died ... and we know it was you who killed her.

Tick Tock.

Chapter Five
Christie

She stares in wonder at the large shipwreck that's poking out from the water about fifty feet from the shore of the mysterious island she's just arrived at. The ship itself is on its side, only the port side visible, covered in rust, algae and seaweed. It reminds her of a long-lost pirate ship. Maybe there's hidden treasure on board, or perhaps a map, leading to it.

She's only just been dropped off by a quiet driver with a small motorboat and is glad to be on solid ground. She doesn't like boats, especially the small ones that toss her about like a rag doll. Her stomach is unsettled, and she still feels slightly queasy from bouncing across the choppy waves, but looking at the shipwreck is a welcome distraction. She wonders how long ago it crashed here. Its final resting place isn't far from land, so she assumes the passengers must have survived and then somehow reached the mainland of Wales. It's an interesting story that she reminds herself to look up the next time she has access to the internet.

The shipwreck holds her curiosity until she eventually drags her eyes away to focus on navigating the slippery rocks by the shore. Her boots are already soaking wet, since she had to jump off the boat into knee-deep water. It doesn't help that her right boot has a hole in it, but it's the only pair of shoes she owns. Her blue jumper also has a hole in it and is doing little to keep the chilly wind from brushing against her skin. At least the sun's out now. Back on shore, before she'd climbed aboard the boat, it had been raining, but she's not all that worried about the cold. She's used to it and has been in far worse situations than this.

Christie staggers across the rocks, holding her arms out to the side to steady herself as she makes her way to the flat area of dirty sand. Not exactly an exotic golden beach worthy of cocktails and sunbathing, especially since it's covered in seaweed and bird poo and …

She stops and her mouth drops open.

Is that a seal?

She's never seen one in real life before. Well, she saw loads in a zoo when she was a kid, but never in the wild. There it is, looking like a grey torpedo, sunning itself on a rock, fast asleep, its whiskers twitching. She didn't even know there were seals on this island. It's not something she's ever thought about. She's been living in Leeds for the past six years and hasn't had the opportunity to visit the sea.

Christie stands still and watches the seal as the minutes tick by. She doesn't want to disturb its slumber, but she also must get past it so she can hike up the slope to the main building, which she can just about see in the distance. There's no other way of getting around the seal. She has no idea what the time is because she doesn't own a watch, nor a phone. For all she knows, it's about two in the afternoon. The man who drove her here in the motorboat said she had an hour just before she'd jumped off the boat into the shallow water, so she can't waste any more time watching a sleeping seal.

She clears her throat.

The seal doesn't move.

'This is ridiculous,' she mutters.

At the sound of her voice, the seal opens one eye.

'Move!' she shouts. The seal jolts awake and barks at her before flopping sideways into the water and swimming away. Christie sighs as she says, 'Sorry, but needs must.'

Her stomach growls, signalling the fact she hasn't eaten since early this morning when she left Trevor's flat after raiding his cupboards. She'd brought some provisions with her, carrying them in the pack that's now bumping against her back as she walks. She reaches round and pulls out a chocolate bar from a side pocket. It's melted slightly, but still tastes good.

She thinks of Trevor and wonders how he reacted when he found the note she'd left him on the kitchen counter. He probably won't care anyway. Probably be glad to get rid of her. Besides, there's nothing she can do about it now. She'll never have to see him again once she's finished this expedition and gotten off this island.

It's an adventure!

One she so desperately needs.

And the invitation she received three days ago was exactly what she'd been waiting for.

****

The sofa she'd passed out on late last night creaked as she rolled over, pulling the thread-bare blanket further across her shoulders. As far as makeshift beds went, it wasn't the worst she'd endured. In fact, compared to sleeping on the solid concrete streets next to a smelly bin, lying on her ex-boyfriend's old sofa was practically a heavenly dream, but it didn't stop her middle-aged body from groaning in protest.

Her life was not supposed to have ended up this way: homeless and broke. Was it her fault? It was debatable. Sure, she'd made some bad choices over the years, including allowing her father and brother to control her life and money, but thankfully, she'd now dealt with her monumental mistakes. Christie had (the last time she'd counted the loose change in her pocket) £5.67 to her name. Her bank account was empty (but at least she had one) and her overdraft had never been out of the red in the past year. In fact, she couldn't remember the last time she'd paid the overdraft. Plus, there were the credit cards and the bank loans, all of which were well past due and mounting up with every passing day. Luckily, she no longer had a fixed address, so if the companies were sending her warnings, she didn't see them. Therefore, they didn't exist.

Yep, she was flat broke.

And she'd just hit rock bottom by spending three miserable days living on the streets, sleeping on the hard concrete until she'd summoned the courage to knock on her ex-boyfriend's door and ask for a place to stay. She no longer had a mobile phone, having been forced to sell it for money to buy food, which she'd spent on …

Gambling.

Okay, so maybe it was partly her fault that she was jobless, homeless and bankrupt. Her gambling addiction had started so long ago she couldn't even pinpoint the time when it had switched from being a fun hobby to a time-consuming vortex of doom that had emptied her bank account and forced her to take out more loans than she could remember or ever be able to pay back without some sort of miracle.

Her brother had tried to help by going through her accounts, but then it had all gone wrong. He had cut her off, changed the passwords to her bank accounts, saying she was too reckless to be in charge. She didn't know how it had happened. He had told her he was doing it for her own good, but that made no sense. Why had he left her penniless? Why hadn't he given her some money to help her out of the never-ending hole of debt?

She knew why he hadn't helped her by giving her money. Because she'd have taken the money and used it on her favourite gambling site and pressed that play button until her account had run dry. That was why. Now, she didn't even have any money to gamble with. The banks had refused her attempts to take out further loans and she'd lost her job as a receptionist because she kept forgetting to go to work, preferring to spend her time on her phone, gambling her life away. But now she didn't even have a damn phone.

But all it would take was one win.

One big win.

And then all her money troubles would go away.

'Ah, you're awake. How'd you sleep?'

Christie opened her eyes at the sound of Trevor's voice. He was holding a cup of tea, which he handed to her as she shifted her stiff body into a seated position on the sofa. She took it with a smile.

'Thank you. I slept well. Thanks again for putting me up for a while.'

'It's no problem. I can't believe you got evicted, but Chrissy ... why haven't you paid your rent for the past six months?'

Christie took a sip. 'I did, but ... my brother has stopped all the payments going out from my account.'

Trevor's eyes narrowed. 'Right. But how did he get hold of all your accounts?'

'I don't know.'

'Why would he steal all your money and run away?'

Christie sighed. It was a topic of conversation she'd had with a lot of people, and it exhausted her to keep repeating the same thing over and over. She'd twisted the truth so much now that she couldn't remember what was a lie and what was the truth. Even in her own head, nothing made sense, so how it sounded to anyone else she wasn't sure.

Trevor sat on the sofa next to her feet, which were still under the blanket he'd draped across her last night. 'You need help, Chrissy.'

'I know.'

'Does this have anything to do with the gambling?' Trevor knew a little of her addiction, but his knowledge of her debt barely scratched the surface.

'No, it doesn't. I promise. I just need to get a job and then the bank will let me open a new account. I mean, I do have an account, but they won't let me take out a loan because I haven't paid my overdraft in a while. Maybe I'll try another bank. If not, I'll work for cash. Do you know of anywhere that's hiring?'

Trevor sighed and pushed his long hair out of his face. 'No, but I'll ask around. In the meantime, take a shower, there's food in the fridge and the TV works.'

'You're too good to me,' she said as she playfully kicked him with her feet.

Trevor squeezed her ankles, but his lips remained pressed together. He rose to his feet and chucked her the remote control. 'See you later.'

'Have a good day at work.'

'Bye.'

Once Trevor left the flat, Christie kicked off the blanket, sat up and stretched her arms above her head, her T-shirt riding up to reveal her toned midriff. Thanks to her limited food intake over the past few months, her weight had dropped significantly, mainly around her hips and chest. She managed to scrounge some change from passing pedestrians who clearly took pity on her as she sat hunched underneath a shop overhang with her hood pulled up, attempting to keep dry. She'd used the change to buy a sandwich after the first day because her stomach was well on its way to eating itself. But since then, until she'd turned up at Trevor's door last night, she hadn't eaten in two days. Luckily, she'd been able to use a discarded plastic cup as a vessel in which to collect rainwater, but the recent downpour had soaked her to the skin, rendering her almost incapable of functioning. She'd had no other choice but to ask Trevor for help. She would have died on the streets otherwise.

Looking in the fridge, she smiled when she saw some leftover pasta in a Tupperware container. She grabbed it and put it in the microwave to heat up, then wandered around the flat while she waited for the minutes to tick by.

Trevor's place was small but very tidy. Everything had its own place and there was no clutter anywhere. She smiled as she glanced at the few pictures on the side. There was even one of the two of them when they'd been a couple. Christie couldn't quite remember how it had ended between them because it had happened so gradually, she'd barely noticed until one day he turned to her and said, 'It's over, Chrissy. I've met someone else.'

And that had been that.

Trevor was no longer with that *someone else*, so she couldn't have been that special. Christie sometimes got the feeling he'd broken up with her for another reason and had let her down gently. In any case, she'd been heartbroken for a few days and then picked herself up and got on with her life, even though she had nothing to show for it. No qualifications, no proper work experience and no money.

Christie heard the microwave beep and went to walk back to the kitchen area, but a flash of white caught her eye. She turned and saw a white envelope crumpled in the front door letterbox. Trevor clearly hadn't noticed it on his way out. She pulled it out, straightened it flat and lifted her eyebrows when she read her name on the front.

'What the hell?' she said to the empty room. 'Who knows I'm here?'

She opened the envelope as she walked to the kitchen and by the time she'd finished reading the card inside and reached the microwave, her mouth curved into the biggest smile she'd ever beamed. This was the miracle she'd been waiting for.

****

Still unsure what the time is, she increases her speed, pumping her arms and legs as she ascends the hill towards the top of the island. A few birds squawk at her and she sees a large brown rat run across the path, its little pink feet moving at the speed of light. She jumps a foot in the air and squeals. She's always hated rats … or mice … or gerbils … or anything in the rodent family.

Her hatred of them started long ago when she'd been forced to spend many an hour sat in her basement in the dark while they'd scurried around her. Those squeaks. The way their tiny feet pitter-pattered across the floor and their long tails swished against her bare legs …

Christie shudders and forces the memory back down where it belongs.

Now is not the time to dwell on the past because she has her future to look forward to.

The money …

It's all about the money. She needs it more than she needs oxygen.

Her eyes are already alight with the prospect of spending it. Some will go on clothes and food and rent, but most will go probably go towards gambling because it's the only thing that makes sense to her. Maybe she'll take a trip to the gambling capital of the world – Las Vegas. The lights. The sounds. The adrenaline and applause as she pulls the lever on the machine and the bell signals her multi-million-pound win.

But then another thought pops into her head. What if she doesn't gamble the money? What if she invests it properly, buys a house or starts a business? The idea seems ludicrous right now. It's so far from who she is, but perhaps it's an idyllic point of view that she'll never get to see, something she can dream about, but deep down, knows she'll never succeed with; the gambling always takes over. It's a sickness, one that has her in its tight grip.

She breathes in deep, almost able to smell the money now.

Although, in this day and age, it's not as if they give you a suitcase full of cash. It will all be online, so how's she supposed to accept the money if she doesn't have a bank account?

She sighs. Again, now's not the time to worry about things like that. It's a problem she can deal with in the future when she wins the money.

She stops as she hears voices.

Where are they coming from?

As she creeps closer to the building, she sees three people standing in front of it.

What the hell? She assumed it would only be her coming here. Why are there others and, more importantly, who are they? She doesn't recognise any of them.

Christie walks slowly towards the small group. The woman notices her first and then all three turn and face her, looking as shocked as she feels.

'So ... I guess this is where the fun begins,' she says.

NV Enterprises would like to formally invite you to the opening of our new venture, located on the uninhabited island off the coast of Anglesey.

We can promise it will be an experience you're never likely to forget.

You, *Christie Truman*, are the guest of honour.

On 17 October 2024, you are to arrive at the venue no later than 14:00.

You are not to mention this opportunity to anyone.

Further instructions regarding your travel arrangements will follow.

If you are late, you are immediately disqualified.

I know that you have no money. I know you have no job. I know about your debts. Imagine having the money to be able to not only get yourself out of the money pit but also start afresh with your miserable life.

£1,000,000. That's what we're offering you.

We expect you to be there.

If you are not, then the truth will be revealed.

We know about your addiction ... and what really happened to your brother.

Tick Tock.

Chapter Six

Jane

'So ... I guess this is where the fun begins,' says the pale, stick-thin woman who's just approached the group, who are huddled by the front door of the mansion. She looks exhausted already, sickly even, but there's a fire in her eyes that tells Jane she's not here to mess around.

'For fuck's sake!' shouts Andrew, throwing his hands up in the air. 'Now there's four of us? What the fuck is this, some sort of competition to see who finds the money first? My invite didn't say dick about anyone else being here.'

Jane swivels to look at him, hands on her hips. 'Who said anything about money? You don't exactly look like the sort of person who even needs money.'

'How do you know what someone with money looks like?'

'Nice watch,' she says, nodding towards his flashy time piece. A Rolex, if she's not mistaken.

Andrew snorts. 'Yeah, like we'd all come to a deserted island in Wales for any reason other than money.' He doesn't hold her gaze though.

Jane shrugs, unable to offer him a response. He has a point. Although, he is wrong about one thing. Money may be one of the reasons she is here, but it isn't the *only* reason. She can't help but wonder if the other three have received the same invitation she had: with a threat at the end that's individual to them. Perhaps that's why Andrew has used the money as his main reason to be here; his attempt at hiding the truth.

'What's your name?' asks Jane to the new woman, who flinches when she realises Jane is talking to her.

'Christie Truman,' she answers quickly.

'I'm Jane Patterson.'

'Ryan Neville.'

'Andrew.' Everyone looks at him, waiting for him to expand. He rolls his eyes. 'Fine! It's Carter. My last name's Carter.'

Ryan frowns and scratches his head. 'Wait ... your name's Andrew Carter?'

'That's what I said, isn't it? Weren't you listening?'

'You're not related to Andrew Carter who owns Carter Motors, are you?'

This time, it's Jane who frowns, because she recognises the name of the car manufacturing company, the multi-million-pound franchise that seems to have taken over the UK in the past ten years, but she holds her tongue while the men talk, studying their expressions and body language. She's always enjoyed watching people and how they interact. It's fascinating.

Andrew folds his large arms and puffs out his chest, growing several inches in height as he does so. 'Yeah, he's my old man. Why?'

Ryan laughs. 'I work for Carter Motors at their Manchester branch.'

Jane gasps. 'Really?'

'Yeah.'

'So what? Thousands of people work for my dad. He owns the largest chain of car manufacturing warehouses and garages in the UK. Big deal.'

'And yet his son has been invited to a strange island for the chance of winning a load of money, which he clearly doesn't need, along with one of his employees,' says Ryan. 'Weren't you in the papers recently after blowing nearly fifty grand on a house party where someone almost died of a drug overdose?'

'No, you're wrong … it was sixty grand,' snaps Andrew.

'Maybe it's just a strange coincidence,' says Jane.

'If it is then it's one hell of a coincidence. I wonder if the rest of us are connected somehow,' says Ryan.

At this point, Christie clears her throat. Jane had almost forgotten she was here. 'While you've all been chatting, you do realise it's probably gone two o'clock now.'

Jane looks at her watch. 'Does anyone have the time? My watch has stopped working.'

'That's weird. Mine too,' says Ryan.

Everyone looks at Andrew and his expensive watch. 'Mine's busted too.'

Jane raises her eyebrows. 'Okay, now that *can't* be a coincidence. Did they all stop when you first arrived on the island?'

'I think mine stopped around the time I left shore,' says Ryan.

'Same,' adds Jane.

'Why isn't the door open? Is this all just a big joke? Is there even anyone in there?' asks Andrew.

Ryan leaves the group and walks up to the nearest window, which, to Jane, looks like it's blacked out from the inside. He cups his hands around his eyes and presses his face against the glass.

'I can't see through. The windows are completely blacked out.' He moves away from the window and back to the group.

'So, what the fuck are we supposed to do?' says Andrew. 'It's not like we can just catch the next train out of here … We're on a fucking island … unless anyone happens to be a really good swimmer.' He laughs at his attempt at humour, but Jane doesn't find it funny because there's no way she'd be able to swim that far. 'Did anyone else get dropped off by an old geezer?' continues Andrew, ignoring everyone's nervous faces.

'Yeah,' says Ryan. 'He didn't say much, did he?'

'Surely it can't have been the same guy,' says Jane. 'What time were you dropped off?'

Ryan shakes his head. 'Hard to say without knowing exactly what time my watch stopped, but I reckon it was around about one.'

'What about you?' she asks Christie.

'No more than half an hour ago, but I don't have a watch, so I don't know for sure.'

'There's no way it was the same man. He wouldn't have had time to bring us all to the island one by one. He was around fifty, grey hair, cap pulled down over his face,' says Jane.

'Sounds about right,' says Ryan.

Christie nods.

'Yeah, that's the dude.'

'But that's impossible ... How could—'

'Look, can we forget about the old dude and worry about how we're going to get off this shithole island?' snaps Andrew. 'Like I said ... there's no train service, is there, and the old dude didn't say anything about picking us up, did he?'

Jane mirrors his worry. The fact she's surrounded by water with no way off this island is her idea of a nightmare. She pulls out her phone and glances at the screen, tapping it. It's dead. 'What the hell? It was at least eighty percent charged when I last checked.'

Andrew does the same, followed by Ryan. Andrew has a brand new, state-of-the-art iPhone, whereas Ryan has an older version of her phone, a Galaxy.

'Mine's dead too,' says Ryan.

'Useless piece of shit,' mutters Andrew.

'Okay, so what could cause all of our watches and phones to stop working at roughly the same time?' asks Ryan.

Jane puts her phone away. 'Possibly some sort of EMP, or maybe they all got water damage on the boat ride, although that would be a huge coincidence if they did.'

Ryan nods in agreement. 'But why would anyone set off an EMP to disable our devices?'

'Whoever sent us here wants us to be cut off from the outside world.' Jane's stomach does a nervous flip. They are well and truly stranded. She doesn't like the idea of being unable to contact her mother and Ben. How long are they supposed to be here?

Jane approaches the building. It has a large wooden door with a black, wrought-iron handle and strange decorations carved into it. She tries the handle, but it doesn't budge. Next, she knocks on the door and shouts, 'Hello! Is anyone in there?' She presses her ear against the door.

There's a faint noise; a clicking.

She steps away, her heart rate increasing. Is someone really in there?

The door creaks and then slowly opens, inching wider and wider until the doorway is revealed. But there's no one standing there. The door opened by itself, which is another impossibility unless it's somehow hooked up to open automatically at this precise moment.

'What the fuck,' says Andrew.

'This has to be a joke,' says Christie.

Ryan and Jane glance at each other.

'I'm guessing that means it's two o'clock,' says Jane.

She feels the same as when she'd finished reading her invitation three days ago. It hadn't felt real. It felt like it was a strange dream because stuff like this didn't happen to boring people like her. At least, that's what she's always thought.

But she had been abducted by a serial killer five-and-a-half years ago and now she's wondering if maybe she's cursed to live through crazy situations that usually only happen to unfortunate people in movies.

****

Her legs crumpled beneath her, unable to sustain her weight any longer, and she sank to the floor, joining the white card on the doormat.

There was no way this invitation was real.

But it had her name on it.

Someone had pushed it through her front door. Someone who knew her address. Someone who knew about her son ... and her sister and what had happened five-and-a-half years ago. How was that even possible when she was the only person alive who knew the truth?

Jane stared at the card and reached out a shaky hand, brushing her fingertips over the writing. She wasn't imagining it. She picked it up and read it again. The last sentence filled her stomach with butterflies.

We know what really happened to you and your sister, Annie Patterson.

What did that mean? Who knew? And who were NV Enterprises? Chills flowed throughout her body, and she shivered as goosebumps raced up and down her arms.

Surely they didn't know the truth. How could they?

It was impossible.

Jane closed her eyes as a memory formed in her mind. She saw the killer standing before her, removing her freaky mask and revealing a female face with a Gemini symbol branded onto her forehead. Jane had tried her best to block out the memory and forget the face of that woman, the monster who had branded her, but she was always there in her dreams. Hers was a face she'd never forget. Never. And the strange thing was, she didn't even know the name of the serial killer who'd taken her.

It didn't make any sense.

But why her? Why had she been chosen? Why, out of the millions of people who lived in the United Kingdom, had she been selected to be a guest of honour on a random island to win a million pounds? Was she lucky or was there a reason? And what was she supposed to do to get this money? A test, or maybe a competition of some sort? The invitation was vague yet threatening. If she didn't go, then would NV Enterprises (whoever they were) release the truth about what happened?

'Mummy, what are you doing?' Ben wandered over to her.

Jane flinched. She took a deep breath and plastered on a fake smile. 'Nothing, baby. Just ... We have to leave in ten minutes, okay?'

'Okay, Mummy.'

Jane stood, scooping up the invitation in the process, and brushed herself down. She put the card in her bag, then found a hair tie and scraped her long hair into a rough ponytail, but she couldn't take her mind off the prize money.

With that money, she'd be able to set her son up for life. She could buy a proper house for them to live in and a new car. She could even put some money into her art business, set up her own gallery or maybe take that painting course she'd always wanted to do.

And, what, all she had to do was go to a deserted island in Wales? Maybe it was a trap. Maybe some lunatic had sent this as a joke and was setting her up somehow, but for what reason?

Instead of helping her son clean his teeth, Jane used her phone and googled NV Enterprises and was shocked when several pages of results came back. She clicked on the top one, which was the main website of the company, and read the tagline.

NV Enterprises is a multi-million-pound company, which focuses on building renovations and buying and selling failing companies, redesigning them, selling them and making a large profit.

Okay, so the company was real. Or was it? Just because they had a webpage, it didn't mean anything. Jane knew all about scammers and the lengths they often went to fool unsuspecting people into handing over money or whatever it was they were after. It was usually money. Almost everything these days was about money. Anyone could have written and designed this website. It didn't mean it was real.

'Ready, Mummy!'

Jane almost dropped the phone. 'Sorry, right, let's go.'

Jane ushered her child out the door and strapped him into his car seat. The drive to his preschool only took a few minutes and they arrived with two minutes to spare. Jane waved goodbye to Ben at the door after planting a kiss on his cheek and then got back into her car. She stared straight ahead for several seconds before nodding her head, her decision made.

Fifteen minutes later, she pulled up and parked in the small car park next to the local graveyard and then made her way down the gravel path towards the far end. She stopped when she reached her sister's headstone and crouched to clear a few weeds that had sprung up since her last visit a few weeks ago.

'Hey, sis.' A fresh bouquet of red roses had been placed recently. The card told her they were from Annie's old detective colleagues. 'I wanted to ask you a question.' Jane took a seat on the ground next to the grave and began plucking random pieces of grass and fiddling with them.

'So ... this morning I received a random invitation to an uninhabited island off the coast of Wales. I know, I know, it sounds strange, but bear with me here. All it says is that I have to go to this island and they're offering me a million quid. There's not much information to go on other than the fact NV Enterprises have orchestrated this thing.' She stopped and thought for a moment. 'What would you do? As a cop, you'd probably think it some sort of prank or something, right? Do you think I should do it? But who would look after Ben? I guess I could ask Mum ... I don't know how long I'd be away. It's scary, you know ... but ... I also feel like I've been given a chance to change my future, to change Ben's future even if it is a bit ... strange.'

Jane allowed the silence to develop. The birds were singing in the trees around her, and a dog barked in the distance.

'They know what happened,' she continued, 'but I don't know what that means exactly. I'm afraid they know the truth. They say that if I don't show up then ... I think I'm being blackmailed. What if this is a trap to expose everything that happened five years ago? I barely managed to escape back then. What if this whole thing is designed to lead me back into the darkness to reveal the truth?' Jane thought for a second and then let out a short laugh. 'Listen to me, I'm being so dramatic. This isn't about me, is it? Maybe they chose me because they think I deserve a chance at a better life. I feel like I need to do this for Ben. I need to give this a chance ... and find out what they know. I can't let the truth get out. Not now. I've got too much to lose.' Jane tipped her face to the sky and allowed the sun to warm her skin for several seconds.

'I'm going to do it ... I'm going to go to the island.'

Chapter Seven
Andrew

'This has to be a joke,' says the most recent woman who joined the group. He's forgotten her name. She's too skinny for his liking. Her hip bones are practically poking through her thin skin. She looks like she needs a decent meal. He likes a bit of meat on his women; something to grab on to.

'What the fuck?' he says.

The group stare at the open doorway where no one is standing waiting for them. Andrew looks up at the sky, a growing sense of nausea forming in the pit of his stomach like the impending doom after eating a dodgy takeaway following a night on the lash. The sun has disappeared behind the grey clouds and the air pressure feels heavy; there's a storm on the way. The temperature has dropped at least five degrees within the past few minutes. Fucking Wales and its constant changing weather.

'Did that door just open by itself?' asks Jane.

'That's what it looks like,' replies the bloke who Andrew has already taken a dislike to. Ryan Somebody. He's well-dressed and perfectly groomed, like he's trying too hard. He's a pretty boy, and Andrew hates blokes like that. His roommate was one of them and look how well things ended for him. Yes, Andrew likes to look good and spends a lot of money to keep himself looking top notch, but he's not what most people would consider as *handsome*. He has to work for his looks, unlike pretty boy here, who appears to be naturally blessed. Just like all those wankers in Hollywood. Who's he got to look so good for?

Andrew can't help but notice no one has taken the first step through the doorway, but he's not about to do it. Fuck that. No, let the pretty boy go in first.

'I'll go in first,' says Ryan.

Andrew snorts. Typical. He probably thinks the chicks will see him as some sort of brave hero by taking the first step. The clouds are darkening by the minute and despite it being two in the afternoon, it now looks closer to six in the evening. Andrew doesn't like the look of those clouds, nor the feel of the wind as it rips across the island.

'Can we hurry up and get on with it? Unless you all want to get caught in a downpour,' he snaps.

Jane looks up. 'The weather has changed quickly.'

Andrew bites his lip to stop himself from saying something sarcastic back to her. These people are just getting in his way. He wishes he was alone here. It would be easier if he were.

Ryan walks across the threshold into the house and then beckons them to follow. Andrew enters last. He's never one to usually feel uneasy, but that's exactly how he feels as he enters the main foyer. As soon as he's past the door, it slams shut, sending a loud echo around the room.

One of the women (the skinny one) shrieks and jumps.

'Calm down,' says Andrew. He walks up to the door and grabs the handle. 'The wind just blew it closed.' He pulls on the handle, but the door doesn't open. He yanks again, using his big muscles, props a foot on the wall to use as leverage and heaves again. 'Fuck,' he says. 'They've locked us in here.'

'And who are *they* exactly?' asks Jane.

'NV Enterprises,' says Ryan.

'Yes, but … *who are they*? Has anyone ever heard of them before? I did a bit of research, but there's not much out there other than a quick explanation on a website.'

'NV Enterprises designed and created an escape room a long time ago.' Everyone turns and stares at the woman who isn't Jane. 'What?' she asks with a shrug.

'I'm sorry,' says Jane. 'Did you just say *escape room*?'

Andrew's heart sinks to the bottom of his large chest and his lungs constrict. Is the air getting thinner in here? He's struggling to breathe. He tries to clear his head of dark thoughts by thinking back to the excitement he felt when he first found the invitation resting on top of his gym bag. If he'd known this whole thing was regarding an escape room, then no amount of money, fame or blackmail would have lured him here.

****

Because we know about your dirty little secret. It would be a shame to ruin your perfect reputation, wouldn't it? I bet Daddy wouldn't approve.

He didn't see the number of zeros on the invitation. They meant nothing to him. He had money. Maybe not that much, not yet. Not until his old man croaked, but it wasn't the money that sent his pulse racing and gave him a funny taste at the back of his mouth.

His dirty little secret.

Daddy wouldn't approve.

Shit.

As soon as he'd finished reading the invite, he yelled at the top of his lungs and punched the gym locker beside him, startling several gym members who'd been changing nearby and causing a dent in the locker door.

It was impossible. Who would know about it?

He'd never told anyone, and no one had ever caught him. He'd got away with it.

His father would forgive and forget a lot of things, but not that.

But someone knew and someone was going to tell if he didn't go to a random island in Wales. What the hell was that about?

Maybe he could go, confront whoever the fuck it was who was blackmailing him, grab the money and get out of there. A million quid would come in handy. The most his father had ever given him was about a hundred grand and that hadn't lasted long. A million quid of his own would mean he could buy his own place and do whatever the hell he wanted without the say-so from his old man.

He couldn't tell anyone about the invite. It was one of the stipulations and he wouldn't have told anyone anyway because then he'd have to show them what the invite said, and his mates would want him to share the money around. The world was full of greedy vultures and if anyone got a whiff of money, they went crazy. He had many so-called friends who only hung out with him because he was loaded. Including Rich, who always knew he could score some weed or something stronger from Andrew.

He'd be keeping the secret visit to the island to himself.

And who the hell were NV Enterprises? He'd never heard of them. Perhaps a business who his father dealt with ... That was why they'd mentioned his father in the blackmail.

The uneasy feeling was still there in his gut, twisting and gnawing at him. Someone knew what he'd done all those years ago.

He needed to let loose and release the building pressure.

He shook off the tension creeping over his broad shoulders. Nope. It was nothing to worry about. No way would they know about *that* particular dirty little secret. No way in hell. Besides, even if they did, once he won the million quid, he'd disappear to a remote island somewhere and live it large for as long as he could until it all blew over and his father sorted it out. Andrew wanted to enjoy himself and live life to its full potential and with a million bucks, the sky was the limit. He wouldn't need Daddy's permission. Of course, that sort of money didn't last long these days, not in London anyway. He'd barely be able to afford a decent house for that price in the city, but it could buy a whole heap of other shit. Cars. Booze. Drugs. Women …

Andrew stuffed the invite into his gym bag and took a shower. When he returned to his locker with a towel around his waist, he found Rich standing next to it.

'I thought you left,' said Andrew. He whipped the towel off, not shy in showing off his body.

'I forgot to ask you something,' replied his friend.

'Couldn't have texted me?'

'I didn't want a paper trail, if you know what I mean.'

Andrew nodded as he pulled on his boxers. 'How much you need?'

'A pack.'

'When?'

'Tomorrow.'

Andrew snorted. He remained silent as another man entered the changing rooms and placed a bag in a nearby locker. Andrew and Rich watched him until he'd left the area. 'Come to mine at nine tonight.'

'I'll be there.'

'And then we're going out,' added Andrew.

'I thought you said you couldn't tonight.'

'Changed my mind. I want to get wasted and celebrate.'

Rich's eyebrows shot up. 'Celebrate what?'

'None of your business.'

'Fine. Whatever, man. I don't need to know the reason. I'm there. You want me to call Dan and Steve?'

'Yeah. Call everyone. Tonight's going to be one hell of a party.'

The music was thumping, the ground shaking, his back sweating. He loved a bit of drum and base. The drink in his hand was a Jack Daniels and Coke, his favourite drink. The dancefloor was heaving. Sweaty, half-naked chicks everywhere. Some skanky bitch was practically dry humping his leg and he had another pressing her bum against him, grinding like she was on a pole.

He downed the last of his drink, now needing a re-fill. He pushed his way through the crowds, leaving the women behind him sulking. He didn't care. They were only a six at best even with layers of make-up. He didn't need women; not right now. Maybe later.

He needed a hit.

He thought he'd be able to control his urges, but it had been too long.

And so he made his way to the bar.

It was gone midnight. Rich was off somewhere probably banging a chick in the filthy toilets out the back. He'd lost sight of Dan and Steve hours ago.

The withdrawals were too strong to ignore; too strong to push down this time. He didn't have a choice. It was now or never.

Chapter Eight
Ryan

Ryan, along with Andrew and Jane, stare at Christie as if she's spoken in a different language. *An escape room?* It makes no sense. He's never done an escape room. They aren't really his thing, nor are mazes or those spooky horror houses kids usually do at Halloween. A dozen questions race through his mind, but before he can open his mouth to ask them, Jane speaks.

'How do you know that? It didn't say anything about an escape room on the website.'

Christie smirks, seemingly quite pleased that she's finally able to offer some value to the group. 'Let me guess, you only clicked on the top search result.'

Jane shakes her head, a slight flush appearing on her cheeks. 'No, I did look through a few other results, but they all said the same thing. NV Enterprises buys and sells companies and does building renovations.'

'Yeah. In general, they do. Several years ago, they renovated a building and turned it into a state-of-the-art escape room that was only accessible to certain people at the time.' Christie sounds certain. Jane blushes even redder and clenches her jaw, looking as if she wants to argue.

Ryan puts his hand up before anyone says anything else. 'What do you mean by *certain people*? Who?'

'The super rich with nothing better to do.'

Ryan rubs his chin; his beard growth is starting to get to the itchy phase. He likes to grow it from time to time, as long as it's neat and tidy. 'Okay, so what does this mean? We've won some sort of competition to take part in a new escape room or something?'

'Maybe he'll know,' says Andrew, pointing towards the spiral staircase in the middle of the foyer.

Jane screams and covers her mouth with her hands.

Christie takes several steps backwards, her eyes wide.

Ryan freezes as he sees a person dressed in black walking down the stairs towards them. Where did they come from all of a sudden? It's hard to distinguish whether the person is male or female because they are dressed in a long black cape with a large hood, covering almost all their face and the shape of their body. The figure reminds Ryan of that television show everyone was addicted too earlier in the year.

'What the hell?' whispers Jane.

The person is now standing at the bottom of the stairs and they haven't uttered a single word yet. They're just standing there, as if waiting for a signal to begin.

'Okay, is anyone else a little freaked out right now?' asks Jane. 'Why aren't they saying anything?'

'Are we supposed to ask them questions?' pipes up Christie.

Ryan swallows a lump in his throat and approaches the dark figure, ignoring the twisting of his stomach. 'Excuse me? But can you explain what—'

'Welcome to The Murder Maze,' says the figure in a deep, eerie voice.

At the sound of the word 'murder', Ryan's heart leaps in his chest. He already wishes he could take it all back and not set foot on this island, but Amanda had encouraged him and now he realises he shouldn't have listened to her. He should have trusted his instincts.

****

Ryan didn't hear Amanda's footsteps behind him so when she placed a hand gently on his shoulder, he jumped in his chair, which caused her to leap away too.

'Sorry, Amanda, you scared me!'

She clutched a hand to her heart. 'I didn't mean to. You looked as if you were a million miles away. Are you okay? I thought you'd have left for work already.'

'I ... Yes, I mean ... No, I'm sorry. I've just received something in the post that ... It's nothing. Never mind.'

'What's happened? Is that the envelope I told you about just now?'

'Y-Yes.'

Ryan thought about following the invitation's instructions, but he couldn't make this decision alone. Amanda was the most trustworthy person he knew. How could NV Enterprises possibly know if he told her or not? He'd felt the same about his wife. He'd always told her everything. Every single boring detail, and she'd always listened, no matter what it was.

He gestured to the card lying on the kitchen table in front of him. Amanda's eyes widened as she picked it up and began to read. But it was when she read the last sentence her mouth dropped open, and she gasped.

We know how your wife died ... and we know it was you who killed her.

'I ... I don't understand. Are they threatening you?' she asked.

Ryan shook his head and wiped away a stray tear from his left eye. 'I don't know. It seems like it. It's not true though ... what it says. I didn't kill my wife. She died in a terrible car accident when the girls were just babies.'

Amanda lowered herself onto the chair next to him and placed a hand on his arm. 'I know. I remember you telling me. Just awful.'

Ryan smiled. 'Thank you.'

'But why would they say such an awful thing? And how do they know so much about you and your girls?'

'I don't know,' he said. 'I don't even know if this invitation is real. I mean ... it sounds too good to be true, doesn't it? Why me? Why would anyone offer me a million pounds?'

'Either you've been targeted for a reason or you're just very lucky.'

'Clearly, I've been targeted in this ... scam, or whatever it is. They've found out all about me. They know about Hope and Grace and the fact they need extra support. They know about my wife and that she's ... not here anymore.' Ryan leaned across the table, shaking his head, and then buried his face in his hands. He took a deep breath. 'Besides, it doesn't matter that I've been chosen for this opportunity. I can't do it, can I? I can't just drop everything and go. I have the girls. There's no one to look after them. I don't know how long I'll be away.'

There was a long silence and then Amanda said, 'Um ... hello?'

Ryan looked up at her. 'What ... No ... No, Amanda, I couldn't possibly let you look after the girls all by yourself. Not that I don't want you to look after them, but you do so much for them and for me already. I couldn't ask that of you.'

'I want to do it. I already live here with them. Their routine won't change at all. It's just that you won't be here for a few days or however long you're away. I don't care if it's a week. Ryan, you have to do this. You *need* to do this. And besides, when was the last time you had an adventure or any fun or went out and spoke to other people besides me and the people you work with?'

Ryan sighed and stared down at his hands, now clenched together in front of him. His palms were sweating, and he had a feeling he'd have to go and change his shirt before he went to work as his armpits were clammy too.

'I can't,' he said.

'Give me one good reason why not. And just forget about the girls for a moment. I've got them covered.'

Ryan continued to stare at his hands, but he couldn't come up with a suitable answer for Amanda. Every time something did pop into his head, he knew what she would say. It wasn't a good enough reason. The truth was, he'd trust Amanda one hundred percent to look after the girls while he was away, but what if they needed him in the middle of the night? Amanda had never tended to their needs in the dark of night. She wasn't used to the lack of sleep she was no doubt going to get. But she seemed adamant that she wanted to do it and she was right. He hadn't done anything fun or adventurous since Lisa had died. The last holiday he'd had was before they'd found out they were expecting twins. Maybe it was time to have a few days to be adventurous.

A million pounds? If that wasn't an incentive to do it, then he didn't know what was. But what was involved exactly? The invitation offered no insight into how he would receive the money. Would he be pitted against others somehow? Back in his young and carefree days, he'd been exceptionally competitive. In fact, his university pals used to call him Ruthless Ryan because he'd always put one hundred percent of his efforts into everything he set his mind to and would often not care if others dropped by the wayside. He wasn't like that now. Life and marriage and having twin girls with learning difficulties had changed him, but could Ruthless Ryan come out to play again?

Plus, there was nothing to lose. Even if he came away with nothing, he wouldn't have lost anything. In fact, he would have gained a fun experience and a little break from his daily struggles in life. It felt wrong, selfish almost, but if his wife had been here, she would have been saying the exact same thing as Amanda. She would have been packing his bags and pushing him out the door, telling him to live a little and take a risk.

'Okay,' he said quietly as he lifted his head. He grabbed his phone from the laptop bag. 'Let's do it.'

Chapter Nine
The Mastermind - Now

My body is practically fizzing with excitement and adrenaline as I watch the four unsuspecting strangers unite in front of the mansion, huddling together like lost sheep. They have never met, yet they all have one thing in common: me.

Tensions are high; I can tell. No one knows exactly why they are here and that's what I want. I want them to be confused. I need them to be worried and snap at each other. Hell, if a fight broke out, I wouldn't stop it.

Jane seems the most in control, which doesn't surprise me. I know a great deal about her, more than she realises. She's a strong woman, despite what's happened to her in the past. In fact, I believe it's made her stronger. She can easily handle the other three. I'm not worried about her. If I had to put my money on anyone to walk out of here with the money, she'd have my bet.

It's going to be interesting to see how they react as time moves on. Already, they are going to be feeling disorientated from not knowing what the time is, thanks to a small electromagnetic pulse that was administered in the motorboat when they first climbed aboard. Plus, there's a pulse that continually transmits in this house, meaning they won't have access to their precious devices until they get back to the mainland – if they ever get back, that is.

This house has been masterfully designed and built to test each of them to their limits and beyond. Just how far are they willing to go to keep their truths hidden?

Only time will tell.

It's time to greet my guests.

'Welcome to The Murder Maze.'

Chapter Ten
Christie

'*Welcome to The Murder Maze.*'

A ball of fire erupts in the pit of her stomach, and she fights the urge to bend over against the pain. The word *murder* seems to echo for longer around the spacious entrance hall. All four of them look at each other in turn, waiting for the stranger in black to continue in its strange, creepy voice.

'*This is a fully immersive escape room-type experience,*' continues the figure. '*But it is unlike anything you will have done before. You are here to solve a murder. The first one of you to solve it, complete the tasks and escape will win the money.*' The figure stops talking. They are keeping their head bowed so that their face is hidden, but Christie does spy a hint of light skin.

Christie's stomach flips over on itself. She's got to hold it together. She believes she knows where this is going.

'What the fuck?' says Andrew. 'What murder? Is this a game or what?'

'*Solve the clues. Complete the tasks. Solve the murder. Win the money.*'

Ryan clears his throat. 'Okay, but whose murder are we solving? Do we get some sort of breakdown on the case?

I'm assuming it's a made-up case and murder, like a murder mystery game.'

The figure shakes its head. *'That is for you to find out.'*

Andrew laughs. 'This is making no sense! What kind of fucked-up escape room is this? We don't know who the victim is so how are we supposed to solve their murder?'

'The victim will be revealed in due time.'

Andrew snorts.

'You will now all leave your bags and possessions inside that box.' The figure points to a black box about the size of a coffin in the far corner of the room.

'No way,' says Jane. 'I'm not doing that.'

'Then you are to go no further.'

Jane stares at the box. 'When will we get them back? Why aren't our phones working? I have a young son,' she says.

Ryan smiles. 'And I have twin girls. I need to call and check on them.'

'That isn't necessary. Your possessions will be returned at the end.'

Christie watches while Andrew, Jane and Ryan approach the box, remove their bags from their shoulders and place them inside. She doesn't have anything on her to place in there. She notices that the stranger doesn't explain why their watches and phones all seemed to have stopped working.

'*Good luck*,' says the figure as it turns and begins walking back up the stairs. Each step is slow and deliberate, and the length of the cloak makes it look as if they are gliding.

'Wait!' shouts Jane. 'What's the next step? There's always a sequence to these escape rooms. You haven't given us any sort of clue as to how to progress.'

The figure doesn't turn around or stop walking as it says, '*All four of you have received the clue, but only one of you can read it.*'

Christie doesn't know what that means, but all she can think about is the money. It's why she's here. It's all she's ever cared about, and nothing is going to get in her way. If there's a fake murder to solve, she's going to be the one to solve it. She's seen enough detective shows to know the basics. This will be easy, especially since the other three don't seem to believe that this is happening. Oh, it's happening. And she knows exactly how she's going to play this game.

She doesn't even care about the blackmail, which she notices the figure hasn't mentioned either. Maybe they all have something to hide.

****

The hairs on the back of her neck tingled, as did every other part of her body, even her toes. She could taste the money already; although *taste* was an odd expression to use, it was true. Money was better than sex, better than the most delicious ice cream, better than the most extravagant meal. To her, money was everything and, without it, she was empty, and her life was meaningless.

One million pounds.

Oh, yes, it tasted good.

Ignoring the heated-up food now cooling in the microwave, Christie headed for Trevor's laptop and switched it on. She didn't have a phone, so would have to use it to have access to the internet.

She instinctively navigated to her emails and put in her password. Numerous reminders popped up about overdue bills and payments to various gambling sites. She deleted every single one, then deleted her whole account. There was no point in keeping it. Once she had the money, she could start again with a new one.

Next, she typed *NV Enterprises* into Google. Nothing came up. Nothing hugely relevant anyway, other than a website that was clearly fake as it had only been created less than a year ago. It said something about the business buying and selling other businesses. It also sent alarm bells ringing. Someone had created a fake website for NV Enterprises and then sent her an invitation to a remote island.

She leaned back in her chair, eyeing the invitation on the side. There was a reason she'd been invited to the island. There had to be.

Something nagged away in the back of her mind. She's seen something like this before. Was it on television, a gameshow, perhaps? No, not a game show. Some sort of experience, like a haunted house maze, a fairground attraction. Or maybe it was a documentary.

That was it.

She grabbed the laptop again and typed in a few words into the search engine, eventually finding a small Reddit article, buried deep in the search results.

Ten years ago, a Netflix documentary had appeared. NV Enterprises had created a brand-new escape room back in the eighties, but there had been an accident and a person had been killed. After that, all traces of the company and their link to escape rooms had been removed from the internet, but there were still a few Reddit posts buried somewhere that talked about the whole ordeal. Plus, the Netflix show had been removed within a day, but in that time, it had been viewed thousands of times.

User345: You guys remember that escape room that opened in 1988?

PinkGirlBunny: Ah, yeah. The one where that kid died.

User345: Whatever happened to the bloke who ran the company?

Escape12: Who says they were a bloke? No one ever found out who owned and built the escape room. But it was huge back then, wasn't it? It was before its time. Tragic about the kid though.

User345: What happened exactly?

Escape12: No one knows for sure. It's a conspiracy. It happened before everything was filmed and uploaded online, so there's hardly any info about it. Even the death of the kid was buried. Don't even know the kid's name. Netflix attempted to do a documentary a few years ago, but it was deleted from the platform within twenty-four hours.

PinkGirlBunny: Are you some sort of escape room enthusiast or something?

Escape12: Something like that.

Christie checked the date of the post. It was from five years ago. She clicked on Escape12's profile and attempted to send them a quick message, but the profile had been removed. Strange. In fact, all the users were now gone. Someone wanted whatever happened in 1988 to remain hidden. Who would have that sort of power?

She closed her eyes, thinking. Her ex-lover popped into her head. Not Trevor. No. Before him there had been someone else and now she was gone. Victoria's death had ripped Christie to pieces. She missed her every day. She longed to stroke her hair and kiss her lips, but her death had stolen all those precious memories. Victoria had died in a boating accident while holidaying with her family. Christie hadn't even had the chance to say goodbye.

Now, all Christie had left was a hole in her heart, and nothing would ever fill it except for one thing and one thing only.

Money.

Or revenge.

But since revenge wasn't an option, money would have to suffice.

How was she supposed to get to Wales though? She had no money for travel, no clean clothes and no food and water. And the invite said further instructions to follow, so how were they going to contact her if she didn't have a phone?

Should she tell Trevor about it? He'd probably try and convince her it was a scam, some sort of hoax. Plus, what about the thinly veiled threat? They said they knew about her brother. What did that mean? Did they know he'd stolen all her money and left her homeless? Is that what it meant?

Christie had nothing to hide. As far as she was concerned, the blackmail meant nothing. She'd go to this island and get the money. She didn't have any choice. She had nothing to lose and almost everything to gain. Whoever this person was who was attempting to blackmail her, had got it wrong.

Chapter Eleven

Jane

Her hands haven't stopped trembling since the dark figure who gave them the foreboding message disappeared up the flight of stairs. Nothing makes sense. Not that any of this made sense before, but now she has more questions than answers. Blood is thumping through her veins so hard she can hear it, feel it. She wishes there was a chair behind her because her legs are like jelly, threatening to collapse at any moment.

An escape room.

They were taking part in an escape room.

And now she's had to give up her bag and phone. That hadn't been mentioned in the invitation, although the man who had brought her to the island had said something about dropping her bag somewhere. Granted, the phone is useless since it is dead, but it still provides her a sense of safety and security.

The whole idea of taking part in an escape room didn't sound too bad in the grand scheme of things. Some people would even go so far as to say it's an adventure and to enjoy the experience, but something about this whole thing is setting her teeth on edge. Something is making her skin crawl to the point she wants to scratch so hard she bleeds.

They are locked inside this building on a remote island with no means of getting off until they solve the clues to a fake murder. Plus, they have no way of contacting the mainland. But the underlying question she keeps asking herself is why is she here? Why are any of them here?

Jane has taken part in an escape room before, several years ago for a friend's hen do. It had been quite a challenge for the group, but whether that was due to the severity of the clues and puzzles or the amount of alcohol they'd ingested was another matter. They'd had to solve combinations, find secret doors and, eventually, after much laughing and messing around, they'd made it out with only a minute to spare. Their prize had been nothing more than the experience and pride of completing and winning the escape room mystery.

But back then she'd been childless and carefree. Now, she just wanted to get home to Ben, preferably with the money.

It isn't that she's worried about Ben … Okay, maybe a little, but her mother had jumped at the chance of moving in and staying with him for a few days. She'd told Jane it would do him good to spend time away from her, but as she'd hugged him, breathed in his scent and said her goodbyes, it felt as if her heart was being ripped from her chest. She's never been away from him. Never. Other than the few hours he was at preschool during the week.

Is she being selfish by coming here? Is it too late to change her mind and go home? Is there some sort of 'get out' clause in this escape room thing?

The money.

She is doing this for the money and nothing more. Also, there's the small matter of the blackmail at the end of the invitation she'd received. Someone here knows about her sister and what happened to her.

'Is someone going to say anything?' asks Andrew. He stomps up the stairs, sending dust flying, and stops at the top. 'Did the guy we just saw vanish into thin air?'

'What makes you so sure it was a man?' asks Christie.

Andrew sniffs loudly. 'I'm guessing.'

'None of us could see their face, but the voice ... it sounded a bit distorted, right?' Ryan looks at Jane and she nods in agreement.

'Whoever they were, they gave me the creeps.'

'Let me get this straight,' says Andrew, stomping back down the stairs. 'We're taking part in an escape room to solve a fake murder to win a million quid. Why? What's the catch? What's the deal with NV Enterprises and why isn't this whole thing on the news?'

Jane knows he's making a good point but is utterly relieved it isn't in the media. It would be her worst nightmare to be interviewed. What if someone found out about her? If a journalist dug too deeply into what had happened with her sister ...

Her life would be over.

It's definitely better that this escape room hasn't been in the media.

'Maybe it's some sort of trial period,' says Ryan. 'Businesses test out things all the time, right? Before they release it to the general public.'

There's a murmur of agreement around the room.

'Well,' says Jane. 'I suppose what we need to think about it figuring out the first clue. Any ideas?'

'Do you think we're on some sort of time limit?' asks Christie.

Jane bites her tongue. Had Christie purposefully ignored her question? There's something about Christie she doesn't like. There's mistrust behind her eyes, like she's hiding something.

'I don't know, but I'd like to get off this island as soon as possible,' says Ryan. 'I have to get back to my girls.'

Jane raises her eyebrows. 'What are their names?'

'Hope and Grace.'

'I have a son who's four. His name's Ben.'

'My girls are five.'

She smiles and something inside her relaxes when he smiles back. Out of the two other people, he seems the most down-to-earth and approachable. Plus, he's a parent himself, so he knows the trauma and anxiety that comes with leaving his child (or children, in his case) behind to take part in this mental ordeal. No mention of a wife though, she notices.

Andrew, on the other hand, has irritated her from the start. If this truly is a competition, she knows who she wants on her side and it's certainly not Andrew.

'It's the first time I've ever left them,' he says.

'Same,' says Jane.

'I practically made myself sick this morning when I had to say goodbye to the girls and leave the house. Although, they were buzzing with excitement about the prospect of Amanda staying over and looking after them.'

'Amanda?'

'Oh, sorry, she's my ... I mean, she's sort of like their live-in nanny, I guess.'

A fizz of relief flutters in her stomach. Yes, she's attracted to Ryan, but how can she be thinking about him like that at a time like this?

'Ah. My mother is staying with Ben. No doubt she'll feed him loads of chocolate and fizzy drinks and teach him all sorts of bad habits.'

'I'm sure he'll have a great time.'

'Hello!' shouts Andrew.

Jane jumps and turns to him. Ryan's so easy to talk to, she'd forgotten about Andrew and Christie being in the room and listening to their conversation.

'Maybe you two can eye-fuck some other time, yeah?'

Jane feels her face heat up. She turns away, so Ryan doesn't see.

'Unless you've forgotten already, this is a competition, so all of us are against each other. Therefore, we aren't here to make friends.'

Ryan scoffs. 'That's a relief, because you're about as friendly as a rattlesnake bite.'

'Fuck off, pretty boy.'

'Hey, now listen—'

Jane clears her throat. 'Guys, we can't turn against each other. Remember what the person in the cloak said ... the clue. All of us have received the clue, but only one of us can read it. Let's focus on what's important and, right now, that's solving the first clue.'

'Yeah, but what does it mean?' asks Ryan. He walks towards her and stands close, as if signalling that he's on her side. A whiff of aftershave tickles her nostrils. It's pleasant and she quickly allows herself to study the man standing next to her, who is, whether she likes it or not and for all intents and purposes, her competition. His thick black hair is slicked back, and his stubble is in that spiky phase. All she wants to do is feel it against her fingers. Her eyes land on a small scar across his neck. As soon as she sees it, she looks away. Does he have more on his body somewhere? The man intrigues her. His eyes are kind and warm, but they also seem to hold a silent sadness. She wonders what has made them that way.

'Isn't it obvious?' asks Christie.

Jane looks at her. 'What?'

'The clue. Don't tell me I've figured it out and you haven't. Looks like I'm winning already.'

'Care to share with the rest of us?'

'Hell no. This is a competition, right?'

'Yes, but the clue seems to suggest that we have to work together to figure it out. If only one of us can read it, then how is that fair? That person will have to share it with the rest of us.'

'Maybe it's somewhere in this room,' says Ryan.

Christie rolls her eyes. 'No, it can't have already been here. The clue says we already received it. We all did.'

'That makes no fucking sense,' says Andrew.

Jane bristles at his tone and choice of language. She attempts to hide the shudder that envelopes her as her stomach turns over on itself. Where is the nearest bathroom? A raging heat spreads through her body, causing her upper lip to sweat. She wipes her lip and forehead with the sleeve of her jacket, hoping no one notices her unease. She doesn't want to appear weak.

'Do you know the answer to the clue or not?' asks Jane. She's beginning to think that Christie is just pretending she knows to mess with their heads.

Christie shrugs her shoulders.

'So, basically, you said you know, but you actually don't,' says Andrew. 'Looks like we're shit out of luck then, doesn't it?'

Chapter Twelve
Andrew

His head is pounding like a drum-and-base solo. He's regretting those Jaeger bombs last night, but people had been buying him drinks for hours. Not only friends but strangers too. That's just the type of guy he is. He told them some spiel about his dad gifting him a large sum of money and they lapped it up. People are always attracted to money because money is power. And he's feeling powerful right now despite his sore head.

However, what he really needs to do is get the hell out of this dump and back to the mainland. But first, he must win the game and to do that he has to beat the three losers in front of him. Jane has rubbed him up the wrong way from the start. She may act all shy and serious, but he knows her type. She fucking loves the attention. In fact, she looks vaguely familiar, but he can't be bothered to waste his brainpower on trying to remember where he knows her from. Maybe he shagged her once. She's not bad looking. Then again, if she had slept with him, surely she'd have remembered him.

As for the pretty boy, he's just as bad with his slicked back dark hair and gentle attitude. Andrew wants to roll his eyes every time he opens his mouth. The man can stand to benefit from lifting a weight once and a while too. Andrew feels sorry for him really.

Then there's the other chick. Christie, he thinks her name is. She's the only interesting one out of the three of them. Despite being skinny and pale, she looks as if she could hold her own. Plus, she seems to have a half a brain on her.

None of them will be a problem for him.

Andrew lets out a long sigh and turns to look at Jane, smirking as she averts her eyes. 'So ... what now?'

'Has anyone ever done an escape room before?' asks Ryan. 'Is there a certain way they're done? Clearly, we need to figure out the first clue to get started, but what happens if no one can solve the first clue? Do we get given hints or something?'

Christie shakes her head, but Jane nods. 'Yes, I did one, but it was a very long time ago. I was on a hen do. It was just a bit of fun really. But what I do know is that escape rooms are designed to be beaten, otherwise there's no point in doing it. I can guarantee you that we have everything we need to move forwards with the maze in this room or on our person right now.'

'But the point of this escape room isn't to actually escape, is it?' says Christie.

Everyone looks at her.

'It's called The Murder Maze. We're here to solve a murder, not escape.'

'Perhaps it's merely a turn of phrase,' says Ryan. 'Solve the murder and then you'll be able to escape.'

'Are you saying we're properly trapped on this island?' asks Jane with a gasp. She's panicking. Good. As long as he remains calm, then it's all good. They can freak out as much as they want. Once he has the money, he'll swim to shore if he has to. He was a decent swimmer back in his school days.

Christie shrugs. 'I didn't say that, but the aim of the game is to solve a murder. I'm sure, as we go through the maze, that we'll be provided with means of escape … eventually.'

'Right, but first we need to figure out this clue,' says Jane. 'Any ideas?'

A silence follows.

'Fuck this,' says Andrew. He marches up the stairs where the dude in the cloak disappeared and starts searching around for something, anything, that looks like it could help him.

'What are you looking for?' asks Christie.

'I'll know when I find it.'

Another long silence.

'Oh my God,' says Jane.

Andrew turns around. 'What?' She's got her hand in her pocket.

'I think I might know the answer … The invitations we received. We all received one, right?'

Ryan claps his hands together. 'Of course! That's it. Great work, Jane.'

Andrew scoffs. 'But we can all read, right? The clue was that only one of us could read it.'

'Yes,' says Jane, 'But perhaps the clue is only on one of them. Only one of us can read it. I reckon that one of the invitations has something on it that the others don't.'

At this point, Andrew turns and looks down the stairs towards the group. The woman might be on to something. Maybe she has a brain after all. He's noticed that pretty boy hasn't said much lately. What's the point of him even being here? He's fucking useless.

Christie nods. 'You're right. Can anyone remember anything about their invite? Something that maybe stood out.'

Andrew knows the answer almost immediately. Because he knows it's him who is the special one. He's the only one that can read the clue because it's his invitation that's different. He grins and places his hands on his hips.

'What are you smiling at?' asks Ryan. He takes a step towards him.

'None of your damn business.'

'It's you, isn't it? You know what the clue is.'

'Maybe I do and maybe I don't.' Ryan then surprises him by rushing up the stairs towards him, clenching his fists. Andrew puffs out his chest and assumes a defensive position. 'Yeah, come on then ... What are you going to do about it?'

Ryan's face is level with Andrew's chest, and he knows he has about fifty kilograms over him. He can easily throw Ryan across the room without breaking a sweat.

Andrew's eyes widen and his nostrils flare as Ryan shifts backwards. 'That's what I thought.'

'Are you going to tell us or not?' asks Ryan in a calmer voice.

Andrew smiles to himself. He's got them rattled and that's his intention because if they are on edge, they won't be focusing on winning. He hasn't come here to make friends and allies. They are his competition. His enemies. And nothing is going to stand in the way of him winning the money. Nothing.

Chapter Thirteen
Ryan

The tension in the room is frosty at best. He can't believe the audacity of the man standing in front of him. Plus, Ryan has a feeling that Andrew has a hangover, which probably isn't helping his mood. The obvious signs are there; puffy, red eyes, sallow skin. In fact, Ryan's almost convinced Andrew may even be under the influence of drugs, which makes him not only a loose cannon but a dangerous one. Ryan's had his fair share of dealing with people like him. He already knows he has to keep away from him, but the fact he knows something about the clue and refuses to share the details with anyone else is enough to make his blood boil. He needs to get home to the girls and this big brute is standing in his way. But he should have known better than to attack him out of the blue. The vile man is clearly only trying to wind him up and cause him to lose focus. And he's doing a good job too.

'Don't worry, mate, I'll tell you eventually.'

Ryan relaxes his balled-up fists. 'I am not your mate.'

'You got that right. Listen, I don't trust a single one of you, so why the hell should I share the clue with you?'

'Because it's the right thing to do,' says Jane. 'We can't move forwards without it.'

'We need a game plan,' says Christie.

'I have one already,' replies Andrew. 'Win.'

Christie rolls her eyes. 'I think out of the four of us, I'm the one who needs the money the most. Until a few days ago, I was living on the streets.'

'I'm sorry,' says Ryan.

'I don't need your pity.'

Ryan sighs. 'Look, we all have our reasons for being here. We all received an invitation and I'm betting we all need the money ... except for Andrew ... Why the hell did you even come? Aren't you rich?'

Andrew shrugs his huge shoulders. 'Could always use more money. Plus, my old man would never give me a million quid. I could do a lot with that money.'

Ryan tries not to show his annoyance. There's no way Andrew needs the money that badly. He only wants it for purely selfish reasons. Ryan is determined to stop him at all costs.

'Right, but to progress in this escape room, we need to trust each other,' he continues. 'At least, for this first part. We might not like it, but it's what needs to happen.'

'Whatever,' mutters Andrew.

Ryan starts walking back down the stairs towards Jane, who is giving him a look that tells him to keep going with his speech. 'None of us have any idea about what is going to happen. Hopefully, when we get past this first bit, we'll have more of an idea about whose murder we're solving and go from there.'

'Yeah, the person in the cloak was a bit vague on the details,' replies Jane.

'Maybe that's the whole point,' says Christie. 'We're supposed to work out the clues and puzzles on our own, right? No point giving the game away at the start.'

No one answers.

Ryan has the sudden urge to run and hide. If the front door was open, he'd probably turn and sprint out of the building, down to the dock and swim back to shore. His nerves are getting the better of him and he just wants to give both of his girls a big squeeze and never let them go. He doesn't want to spend time with a bunch of self-absorbed strangers. Although Jane is making the experience more bearable, but there will come a time when he'll have to cut all friendly ties with her and focus on his own goal of winning the money. It's the only thing keeping him sane right now.

He also keeps thinking about his girls and whether they'll be okay without him, but Amanda had been brilliant, as always, and hadn't seemed at all nervous or phased about looking after them by herself. He reminds himself to offer her a raise when he returns and buy her the biggest bouquet of flowers and, if he wins the money, send her off on an all-expenses paid holiday to a destination of her choice. She deserves it.

'Fine,' says Andrew. Ryan snaps his head round, wondering if he'd misheard him. 'I'll tell you what I think the clue is, but I have no idea if it's correct or not, though it makes sense to me.'

Chapter Fourteen
Christie

Christie's shoulders relax as Andrew says he'll share what he knows, but just as he's about to open his mouth, the hooded figure they saw earlier steps out from the shadows on the lower floor. Jane is standing closest to them, and she screams, leaping towards Ryan, who immediately does the whole hero thing and puts himself between her and the creepy person in a robe.

'Where the hell did he come from?' shouts Andrew, who jogs down the stairs and joins them on the bottom floor. Now all four of them are standing in a line facing the figure, who hasn't said anything yet and is merely standing still, looking freaky. Its head is lowered to the floor.

'Why isn't he saying anything?' asks Jane.

'So we're still going with the assumption it's a man then?' replies Ryan.

No one directly replies.

Then, the figure begins talking again in a distorted, deep voice. It's louder than before, as if the voice is being said over speakers. Is it even the figure who's talking?

'Congratulations on passing the first stage.'

'What first stage?' asks Andrew. 'We haven't figured out the first clue yet.'

'The first stage was not about figuring out the clue but deciding to trust each other.'

Andrew has the decency to look guilty while Ryan shoots him a look that says *I told you so*.

The hooded figure continues. *'Therefore, I can now reveal more details about the murders you will be solving. You will still need to work out the first clue in order to progress in the maze.'*

Jane clears her throat. 'I'm sorry, did you say *murders*? I thought you said there was only one murder to solve?'

'There is.'

'Will you stop talking in fucking riddles!' screams Andrew.

The hooded figure turns directly towards him. *'You will be solving one murder ... each.'*

Christie frowns as she looks around the group, who are mirroring her facial expressions.

'How is that fair?' snaps Andrew. 'What if one murder is harder to solve than another? What about the clues and puzzles? You mean to tell me that they're all different too?'

The figure continues. *'You will each be solving a different murder using different clues and puzzles and will be interrogating the suspects to gain the information needed to proceed.'*

Ryan holds his hand up as if he's in school. 'Wait ... we have to interrogate people? Like ... *real* people?'

'That is correct.'

'You never mentioned anything about live-action role play,' says Christie.

'The suspects are not role playing.'

The silence that follows is filled by the pounding in Christie's ears. Her heart is beating so hard against her chest she fears it might explode at any second. Andrew looks as if he wants to punch his fist through the nearest wall. Jane's eyes are wide, and her shoulders are trembling whereas Ryan is perfectly still. He's the first to speak.

'Forgive me, but I'm not sure I understand what you're getting at here.'

'The murders you will be solving within The Murder Maze are real-life cases.'

Chapter Fifteen
Jane

Jane can't help herself. An audible gasp escapes her lips as her hand flies to her mouth to cover it. She manages to stifle a whimper.

No, no, no.

This can't be happening. She doesn't want to solve a real murder. What the hell is NV Enterprises playing at? Haven't they heard of the police before? Surely the professionals are better equipped to deal with these murders than four unsuspecting people. The word *murder* itself is enough to set her stomach in a knot and break her out in a cold sweat. She's not qualified to solve one. That was her sister's domain, her career. Annie solved multiple murders during her time as a detective, but Jane had never heard about any of her cases because they'd been estranged since Annie first went into the police force.

Jane shakes her head and moves backwards, wishing the ground would open up and swallow her whole or a side door would reveal itself so she could sprint to safety and back to her baby. This is all a big mistake. She shouldn't have come.

Ryan is the only person able to utter any words. 'Are you being serious?' he asks, sounding as if he were telling off a child rather than addressing a creepy figure, who still hasn't revealed their identity.

'I can assure you that I am being one hundred percent serious.'

Ryan lets out a laugh that sounds close to being fake. It's the first time Jane's heard any sort of anger in his tone. 'But that's ridiculous. Why can't you have the police, whose job it is to *solve* murders, do it?'

'The four murders you are about to solve are not currently active within the police system. The cases have been closed.'

'Then why the fuck are we having to solve them?' asks Andrew.

'Because they have been solved incorrectly and the people responsible for the deaths are still free and have not paid for their crimes ... and that's where you all come in.'

'But we're stuck in this house, this murder maze, so how can we solve a real murder from in here?' Ryan's voice has risen a few octaves. Jane can tell he no longer wants to be here, the same as her. The tension in the room is practically pulsing with nervous energy.

'Rest assured you will have all the necessary items, information and abilities to solve these murders from within The Murder Maze. All you have to do is solve the clues, investigate the deaths, talk to the suspects and witnesses and come up with the answer as to who killed the victim at the end.

If your answer is deemed acceptable then you will be pitted against each other for one final challenge.'

'And what happens when we get out and solve these murders? Or what happens if we can't solve them?' Jane has so many questions piling into her brain that she can barely make sense of any of them. She doesn't know how to ask them properly or in which order.

The figure laughs and it makes every hair on the back of her neck stand on end. Her skin crawls as she fights back a full-body shudder. It's the creepiest laugh she's ever heard, a mix between a witch's cackle and an evil spirit.

'I promise you that all will be revealed as you progress through the maze. Now ... are you all happy to proceed?'

'Do we even have a choice?' snaps Ryan.

'You always have a choice.'

'What about the money?' asks Jane. 'Whoever wins this maze, whoever solves their murder first, gets the money, right?'

'That is correct.'

Jane looks at Ryan, who holds her stare for several seconds. She's certain he is thinking the same thing – that they want to go home – but neither of them says so.

The money is keeping them here, otherwise there would have been no point in them leaving their children behind.

'Fuck it, I'm in! I've always been in,' exclaims Andrew, rubbing his large hands together. 'It's exciting, right?'

'Once you have figured out the first clue, just head through those doors.' The figure extends a long arm, pointing towards the corner of the room where a black door opens. Everyone swivels their head to look at it.

'What's back there?' asks Jane, turning to look back at the figure.

But they're already gone, disappearing into thin air like a puff of black smoke.

Chapter Sixteen
The Mastermind – Now

It's glorious to watch my little puppets squirm under pressure. All of them have severe control issues. Perhaps it's something they should see a professional about. They don't like to feel as if they have no control over their lives and, right now, that's exactly what's happening. I love twisting the metaphorical knife in deeper with every piece of information I provide them. They're lucky I've given them any information at all. I could have easily trapped them inside the house with nothing but the clothes on their backs, but I have to give them a chance to redeem themselves, otherwise it doesn't seem fair.

I'm looking forward to seeing how long it takes Andrew to share the information he has. He's already said he would, but I wonder if he'll change his mind. He's an interesting one because he's such a loose cannon. Anything could set him off, especially since he has no access to drugs or alcohol, and I reckon he'll be getting hungry soon too. A man that size is used to eating every couple of hours. Sooner or later, his energy stores will deplete, and he'll want a hit of something. Whereas Christie is used to surviving on an empty stomach with little access to food and water. Perhaps she has the most advantage when it comes to lack of nutrition.

I have done my bit for the time being. I may as well make myself comfortable behind the desk of computer monitors. Perhaps a cup of tea is in order. It's going to be a long night. They don't even realise that they've been inside this house for several hours already. It's amazing how time flies when you're having fun. Well, I'm having fun. I don't know about them.

Lifting my phone from the desk, I press the call button. 'Everything okay at home?' I ask.

'Yes, all fine. Everything good there?'

'All running on target.'

'Great. I'll join you in a couple of hours as planned.'

'No rush. Everything's under control. Thanks again for setting this up.'

'I'd do anything for you, you know that.'

I smile as I hang up and a photo appears on my screen. I can't be distracted, so I place the phone in a drawer and shut it, turning back to the screens where my little puppets are pacing frantically. None of them have gone through the open door yet.

I wonder who will be the first one …

Chapter Seventeen
Andrew

Blood boils in his veins, froths and bubbles like he's injected himself with something potent. Maybe it's the lingering hangover or the onset of withdrawals, or perhaps it's the fact he has to work with these pathetic people, or a combination of all three. Andrew has never worked well with others. Never been a team player. It's why he's avoided having proper friends and why his father doesn't trust him to run the company. The old man is bound to hand over the reins one day, but until that day comes, Andrew will continue to be a one-man band.

Why bother to work with people? It's a known fact everyone lets you down. It doesn't matter if they are family or a close friend. At some point or another, they will always let someone else down. It's merely a matter of *when*.

The open door in the corner is calling his name. It's the way to freedom, to riches and glory, but now he knows he must work with these idiots, so he can't leave them behind. Not yet anyway. He's sure there will come a time when he can ditch them and stride off into the sunset with his head held high.

'I guess we should go through,' says Christie, walking up to the door.

'Wait,' says Ryan. 'Before this escape room officially starts, can we all agree to not keep things from each other? We need all of us to escape.'

Andrew sighs. 'Whatever,' he snaps as he rubs his temples. He wishes this headache would fuck off so he can concentrate. Yep, he is regretting the alcohol-and-drug-fuelled bender he'd gone on with his mates last night … and the night before … and the night before. Withdrawals are a bitch at the best of times and being stranded on a remote island with no way off and no access to his sweet fix is the worst situation to be in.

Ryan approaches Jane and stands next to her. 'This isn't what I was expecting.'

'Tell me about it,' she replies.

'What were you expecting, huh? It's a fucking escape room. There are supposed to be clues and puzzles to solve,' says Andrew.

'Yes, but not real murders! This is way of out my league. In fact, I'm certain it's out of all our leagues. We're not qualified to solve murders. This is ridiculous.'

'And yet, here we are.' Andrew takes a deep breath and holds it before letting it out slowly.

'Okay … so the creepy figure said that all four of us already hold the first clue. We also figured out it could possibly be the invitations. Andrew, you said you think you figured it out. Are you going to share it with us now?' asks Jane.

Ryan nods in agreement. It seems she and him are joined at the hip now, both drawn to each other just because they have kids and something in common.

Christie is pale, and it looks as if she wants to cry. Is she afraid of something?

'I said I think I know what it is,' he says. 'I might be wrong.'

'No ... You? Wrong? Never.'

Andrew snaps his head round to look at Ryan. 'Watch it, pretty boy.'

Ryan clamps his mouth shut.

'Is anyone going to go through the door first?' asks Christie.

'Ladies first,' replies Andrew, holding out his hand towards the door.

Christie locks eyes with him and as she walks past, he swears he hears her mutter, 'Dick.'

Christie disappears through the door, leaving the room in silence. What are they waiting for? A shout for help? A scream?

'Guys, come on in!'

Andrew legs it before Jane and Ryan have even moved a muscle. He strides to the open door and emerges into another room, this one quite bare apart from one thing.

A metal table in the middle with four glasses on it and a jug full of water.

'Thank fuck,' he says as he runs to the table, pours himself a glass of water and chugs it. The cool water hits his stomach, his thirst instantly quenched. It's only a matter of seconds before the others join him. They each pour a glass and drink the water. The only sound is the glugging of the liquid as it travels from their mouths, down their throats and into their stomachs.

Thirst quenched for the time being, Andrew takes the opportunity to look around the new room. It's completely void of any decoration, not even anything on the walls, which are completely white. There are no windows and no other doors leading out of the room.

The only way out is back the way they—

The door slams shut.

'Fuck!' he shouts, rushing to the door, but there's no handle on this side and no way of opening it. They're sealed inside this room. He gulps and fights back the rising anxiety as stars dance in front of his eyes. Is the oxygen disappearing again? He can barely take a breath.

'There must be some other way out. What do we think?' asks Ryan when he's finished his glass of water.

'Well,' replies Jane. 'Let's think about the invitations again, since Andrew still seems to be keeping his idea to himself.' She shoots Andrew a dark look.

Andrew has worked out the clue already, but he wants to see how long the pretty boy and the girls take to figure it out. It's clear that Andrew is smarter than all three of them put together, but he can't reveal his secret weapon too soon. He'll bide his time.

Jane appears to be enjoying the challenge. She's pacing up and down in front of Ryan while taking small sips of water. Ryan has a frown on his face.

'Did anyone bring their invite with them?' he asks.

Jane shakes her head, and blushes.

Christie says, 'No.'

Ryan takes a deep breath. 'Me neither. Whoever designed the game must have realised there was a chance we wouldn't bring them. They must have left us a way to solve this clue or else the game would already be over. Can anyone remember anything specific about their invitations? Mine was addressed to me personally and it had no address on the envelope. There were also things in the invite that were personal only to me.'

Christie nods. 'Same.'

'Yes, same,' replies Jane. 'But there were no clues on it. Not that I could tell anyway.'

'Oh, for crying out loud,' snaps Andrew, fed up with their slow minds. 'You guys are useless. Fine, I'll tell you. It's the letters.'

The other three turn to him.

'What letters?' asks Jane.

Andrew sighs. 'The random letters that were in a different font to everything else.' Confused faces stare back at him. 'Are you saying that my invitation was the only one that had random letters of each word in a different font?'

Ryan shrugs. 'The only letters or words that were different on my invite was my name. It was handwritten.'

'Same,' replies Jane and Christie in unison.

'Why would you receive a different invite to everyone else?' asks Ryan.

'Because whoever has set all this shit up knew I'd be the only one who'd be able to solve it, especially if I happened to leave it behind,' replies Andrew. He rubs his hands over his face to wake up his internal thoughts. 'These people know details about us, stuff even our closest friends and family don't know. They must have been watching us for a while.'

Whoever owns NV Enterprises is a sneaky bastard, that's for sure, because not many people know Andrew has a photographic memory.

Chapter Eighteen

Ryan

Ryan stares at Andrew, who's got his eyes tight shut and is massaging his temples as if he's attempting to summon a memory from deep in his subconscious. There's something he's hiding from the others. Ryan hopes the arrogant twat sees sense soon and shares his knowledge with them, otherwise they could be stuck here forever. Too much time has already passed. It feels like it anyway. It's very disconcerting not knowing what the time is or having any idea of a time scale as to when this nightmare island visit will end.

Andrew eventually faces the others. 'I have a photographic memory.'

'A what?' asks Christie.

'Didn't you hear me? A photographic memory! It's when someone can remember things even if they've only seen something for a moment. It's also called an eidetic memory. I've always had it, but never really told anyone. I used to call it my secret superpower when I was a kid.'

'You can't be serious,' says Jane with a laugh.

Andrew glares at her and she takes a step closer to Ryan, who clears his throat, holding up his hands. 'Okay, great,' he says. 'So somehow the person who set all this up knew about this and has orchestrated the first clue so that only Andrew can solve it.'

All eyes turn to Andrew.

'Well?' asks Christie.

'I'm thinking! It's not like I use it all the time. I didn't know I was supposed to be remembering and studying the fucking invite, did I? I only read it once or twice. I noticed some of the letters of the words were in a different font, but I thought it was maybe a typing error or something.'

'This is impossible,' says Jane, shaking her head. 'We're screwed. Why didn't you bring it with you?'

'I could ask you the same question.'

Jane's cheeks turned slightly red. 'I didn't think I'd need it.'

'There's your answer. Just give me a minute,' mutters Andrew as he turns his back on the group and walks to the nearest corner of the room. Ryan studies the way his shoulders hunch forwards and his head hangs down, and he feels a momentary pang of sympathy for the man. He is a brute, there's no doubt about that, but now the ability to proceed in the maze rests solely on his broad shoulders, and he can see the stress building behind the tough exterior.

Jane leans towards Ryan and keeps her voice low. 'Andrew could easily tell us a lie and keep the real answer for himself. We can't trust him as far as any of us could throw him and that's not very far at all considering his size.'

'I don't think he will. I mean, I agree with you about not being able to trust him as far as we can throw him, but we all need the clue to move forwards, including him. There's nowhere for him to hide in this room. To get out and move on, he'll have to allow us to come too. He needs us and we need him.'

Jane presses her lips together. 'I don't like this. It feels as if we've all been deceived from the start.'

Ryan silently agrees. This experience has already taken a serious and sinister turn. It's no longer a fun game of solving puzzles and racing to the finish line to win a cash prize. Now they have real murders to solve. The families of the real victims are waiting for their response and help to bring the killers to justice. Ryan doubts the police have been informed about this little experiment either. Maybe the families haven't even been contacted. Who are these murder victims anyway? Why is the owner of NV Enterprises so invested in finding the real killers? And, more importantly, who's gone down for the murders if not the real killers? Is the creepy figure they've been seeing the owner of the business or a mere pawn in the game too?

'Do you think the victims are related to the owner of the company in some way?' asks Jane.

Ryan turns to her. 'You must have been reading my mind because I was just thinking along the same lines. Why does he or she care so much about them?'

'It certainly is something to think about. Or ... and this is probably even more disturbing ... maybe they just picked four random murders that have happened and thought it would make for an entertaining experience.'

'If that's true then this person is severely unstable and disturbed. What kind of person thinks it's entertaining to throw a bunch of people together and force them to solve some murders?'

'Well, there have been lots of television shows over the past few years that have pushed boundaries, haven't there? The public just lap it up when they see people on screen suffering and making difficult decisions.'

'You don't think we're being filmed, do you?' Ryan automatically looks up, checking for cameras.

'It would be illegal for them to film us without our consent,' replies Jane, although by the low tone of her voice, Ryan reckons she's not overly convinced. None of this experience screams like it's all above board.

Ryan sighs and runs his fingers through his hair, causing it to lose its slicked-back sleekness. A few strands escape and stick up, but he doesn't attempt to flatten them. He catches Jane looking at him out of the corner of her eye and she quickly looks away and wanders over to Christie, who has taken a seat on the floor and is staring at Andrew while he's figuring out the clue. He still has his back to the group and is muttering to himself.

Ryan stares at the floor, wishing he could transport himself back home, back to his girls, back to Amanda. He misses them all. He wants to wrap his arms around all three and give them a hug. It surprises him that Amanda keeps cropping up in his thoughts. Yes, she's attractive and young, and the girls adore her, and she is kind and considerate, but ... she isn't Lisa. She isn't his wife, and she isn't the girls' mother.

Lisa had been so adventurous and daring. She'd even begged him to take her rock climbing in the Lake District while she'd been in the early stages of pregnancy, whereas he'd wanted to wrap her up in cotton wool and protect her from everything that could possibly cause her and the babies' harm. That was just who she was though. She loved life. The thought made him smile, but he's quickly interrupted by Andrew, who has stomped back to the group.

'Okay ... I think I remember the letters that were different.'

'Let me jot them down in my phone ... Oh, wait, we handed them over, didn't we, and even if we hadn't, it was dead,' says Jane.

'We still have no idea how all of our devices have died at the same time,' says Ryan.

'It might explain how we were brought to the island by the same guy in the same boat though,' says Jane. 'Perhaps, somehow, they were able to alter the times on our devices or turn them off and on, so we all thought we were leaving the mainland at around one, when in fact it would have been at least half an hour apart, over the space of two hours.'

Ryan bites his lip, thinking about Jane's explanation. It seems rather far-fetched, but then this whole thing could be considered far-fetched, so it makes sense in a twisted way. They wanted them all disorientated. Well, they'd succeeded.

'We'll just have to try and remember the letters. Go ahead, Andrew,' continues Jane when no one responds to her directly.

Andrew sniffs loudly, closes his eyes and speaks slowly. 'B ... F ... W ... S ... L ... I ... A ... P ... O ... R ... T ... A ... O ... E ... E ... C ... D ... R ... E.'

The room is silent for several seconds after he's finished, each of them staring at one another as if waiting for someone to reveal the answer. To Ryan, they are merely jumbled up letters.

'B-But that doesn't make sense,' says Christie. 'They are just random letters.'

'Maybe it's an anagram,' says Ryan. 'Anyone any good at them? Andrew, you must be with your photographic memory.'

'Am I supposed to do all the fucking work here?' he snaps back.

'You're the one with the brilliant mind,' replies Ryan. 'Without writing it down I'm afraid I'm no help. I can't even remember the first five letters you just said.'

'I can help,' says Jane, moving forwards. 'Andrew, can you repeat the letters again slowly?' Ryan watches Jane as she closes her eyes and listens to Andrew again.

'It could be any number of phrases,' she says once he's finished. 'There are nineteen letters. I highly doubt it's a single word. I can't think of any nineteen-letter words, so it must be a phrase using several words.'

Andrew puts his hand up. 'Wait ... I got this ...' All eyes turn on him. 'This room, it's practically empty, right? Apart from that water table.'

Jane gasps. 'The word *water* fits with those letters.'

'So, what's left over?' asks Ryan.

Andrew grins from ear to ear. 'I've got it ... There are four of us. There are four words. Blood. Fire. Water. Space.'

Chapter Nineteen
Christie

Blood. Fire. Water. Space.

The words snap into focus in Christie's head, but she still can't quite separate the letters and make them fit. She's mildly impressed by how Andrew has worked out the clue so fast. For a meathead who looks as if he has more brawn than brains, he's certainly made himself useful over the last few minutes, despite his constant vile behaviour and attitude. She can do without that. But something tells her he's more on her side than anyone else, so maybe she can persuade him to join her. Not that there are official sides or teams, but Ryan and Jane seem to have automatically joined together since the start. Their body language tells her they are more comfortable near each other than anyone else.

'Okay ... so we possibly have the words. Now what?' asks Ryan.

'Do any of the words mean anything to anyone?' asks Jane.

She's met with silence.

Christie feels her stomach flip. One of those words does mean something to her, but she doesn't want to go first.

'I'm afraid of water,' says Jane, raising her hand. 'I almost drowned when I was a kid.'

Christie glances at Ryan, who gulps and scratches the back of his neck. 'I mean … if we're going down that road, then … I have a fear of fire.'

Andrew snorts with laughter. Ryan doesn't give the reason why.

Christie clears her throat. 'I feel weird when I see blood.'

Everyone turns to Andrew. 'What?' he snaps.

'Are you afraid of space?'

'Maybe.'

This time, Ryan snorts with laughter. 'Why are you afraid of space? It's not like you're ever going to go there.'

'Shut it, pretty boy.'

'Are we supposed to do something relating to what we're afraid of?' asks Jane. 'I don't get it.'

Christie leaves the others to talk amongst themselves and heads to the water table for another drink. Her mouth is dry and perhaps some water will settle her stomach, which is determined to keep doing backflips. She takes a sip as she listens to them squabble. Listening is a good skill of hers that she's honed over the years. It's amazing how much information she can glean from merely listening and never opening her mouth. So far, everyone has weighed in and helped to solve the clue except for her. She can't help but feel a bit useless, standing with her hands in her pockets while the others use their brains. This type of thing isn't her strong point, which is exactly why she needs to allow them to lead.

Christie replaces the empty glass on the table, but as she lowers it, she notices something on the surface of the metal. 'Um ... guys ... you might want to come check this out.'

No one answers her.

She glances over at the group, but they are too busy arguing over what the words might mean. Christie sighs as she pushes her empty glass of water into the middle of the table where there's a slight indentation in the metal.

Nothing happens, but then she realises that there are three further indentations in the surface of the table. She takes the glass out of the divot and picks up the water jug instead, pouring some into the empty space.

A loud click echoes around the room, signifying that something is happening.

'What the hell?' says Andrew, running to stand beside her. 'What did you just do?'

Ryan and Jane join them.

Christie takes a step back. 'I just ... poured some water in that depression in the table. Look, there are three others too.'

Jane bends down so her eyeline is level with the surface of the table. 'There's some sort of mechanism inside, I think. If water activated one of them then that means that blood, fire and space must activate the others.'

'Great,' mutters Andrew. 'Anyone happen to have a lighter?'

Christie can tell he's being sarcastic by the tone of his voice, but as she dips her hand into the pocket of her trousers and brings out a small lighter, Andrew's smirk disappears.

'Weren't we supposed to empty our pockets back in the other room and hand everything in?' asks Ryan.

'If I did then we'd be pretty screwed right about now, wouldn't we?' Christie replies coolly. 'Besides, it's one of the only things I own.'

Christie clicks the lighter and lowers the flame to the closest divot on the table. The metal catches alight and continues to burn, flickering orange and yellow. 'Must be some sort of flammable coating on the metal,' she says.

'Right ... blood ... who's up?' says Andrew.

Christie's stomach flips again.

Jane approaches the table, running her hands along the sides. She stops when she gets to the corner. 'This should be sharp enough.'

Christie flinches as Jane digs the sharp corner into the palm of her hand and a pinprick of blood beads on her skin. Christie swallows back bile and turns away, unable to look at the glowing red blood any longer.

'What's the deal with space then?' asks Andrew.

'How should I know?' replies Ryan.

'Maybe we should just leave the space as it is,' suggests Jane.

Christie turns around and sees that Jane has finished squeezing blood into the depression. There's a small round puddle of blood on the table. But it appears Jane is right about leaving the fourth hole as it is.

Within seconds, a fourth click sounds.

Everyone freezes as the table jolts and sinks into the floor, its legs disappearing through narrow holes the same diameter as the legs. The table stops moving after several seconds, leaving it several inches shorter than its original position.

'What ... the fuck,' says Andrew.

Ryan runs his hands along the table. 'I think it might be some sort of counterweight that's been activated. Why's it stopped? We must be missing something.'

'Oh shit,' says Jane. 'I think I know what we are supposed to do.'

'What?'

Jane points at each corner of the table where four round, coloured spots have appeared on the surface. 'If we place the glasses full of water on each of the four corners and fill them up with the right amount of water ...'

'Wait ... but we've all had a drink. What if we've drunk too much?'

'Then we're screwed,' adds Andrew.

'We need to work out how much water to use in each glass. It's the only thing that makes sense,' says Jane.

'How? There are no sums or numbers or anything around here. Are we just supposed to guess?' asks Andrew.

'Was there anything else about your invitation that was different to ours, Andrew?' asks Ryan.

'Without seeing yours how am I supposed to know?'

'Okay, but your name was handwritten, right? The same as ours.'

'Yeah.'

'What if the letters in our names make a number?'

'You've lost me.'

'A = 1, B = 2, C = 3 and so on. Look …' Ryan picks up one of the glasses and holds it up. 'These glasses all have units of measurement on them in millilitres. Everyone, start adding up the letters in your name.'

Christie's face burns hot as she watches the others focus on counting in their heads. What if they're going off on a completely wrong tangent? Is her secret about to be revealed? She quickly adds up the numbers for her name and says a secret prayer, hoping no one will second-guess her answer.

'Everyone got their number?' asks Ryan.

'Yes. Mine is sixty-eight,' says Jane as she bends down so her eye line is level with the glass on the table. Her hand trembles as she pours the water up to sixty-eight millilitres.

She then stands and hands the jug to Ryan, who pours his amount. Christie breathes out a sigh as she realises that they aren't all saying their numbers out loud. She bends down and pours the water up to eighty-four millilitres before placing her glass in the third corner.

She glances at the others, checking for their reaction. Andrew holds her stare. She gulps back the lump in her throat as he narrows his eyes at her. Has he added up the numbers in her name too? Does he realise that the number is wrong and therefore her real name isn't Christie Truman?

Chapter Twenty
Jane

Andrew is the last to fill up his glass, but as the last few droplets splash into it, it's obvious there isn't enough water to reach the desired mark.

'Fuck sake!' he shouts. 'You guys drank all the water!'

'Um, I think you'll find that you drank the most out of all of us,' answers Ryan.

'Whatever. Looks like I'll have to improvise.' Without turning around to shield himself, Andrew yanks his flies open and reaches into his boxer shorts.

Jane gasps and turns around as she listens to the trickle of urine splashing into the glass.

'Didn't take you as a prude, Jane,' says Andrew with a laugh. 'Look, Christie's taking a good look.'

Christie scoffs. 'I'm just fascinated. I've never seen one so small before.'

Jane can't hold back a snort of laughter.

Andrew mutters incoherently as he finishes shaking. Jane turns around just as he places the glass of urine and water on the table, the pale-yellow liquid sloshing over the edge.

As soon as the four glasses are sitting at each corner of the table, everyone steps back as if expecting something dramatic to happen, but nothing does. Nothing at all. No one says a word or even breathes for several seconds before Jane lets out her breath in one big whoosh.

'Well, so much for that working. Are we missing something?'

Christie clears her throat. 'Maybe they are in the wrong order. Maybe each glass needs to be in a certain corner.' Everyone stares at her. 'What?'

'How many different combinations could there be?' asks Jane.

'Twenty-four,' replies Andrew without missing a beat.

'Are you like some sort of maths genius as well as someone who has an eidetic memory?' Jane raises her eyebrows.

Andrew shrugs his enormous shoulders. 'Hey, at least I'm being fucking useful.'

'What's that supposed to mean?'

'Just that some of us, not naming names, have been more useful than others so far.' He swivels his eyes towards Christie, who narrows hers at him. There's a tension there, bubbling under the surface, but Jane can't quite pinpoint the exact reason why.

Ryan picks up one of the glasses. 'Look, the sooner we get out of this room the sooner we can start to solve these murders and, by the sounds of it, we'll be working independently on different ones, so it'll all work out for the best for everyone here. This could take a while. Andrew, whether you like it or not, your memory is going to come in handy with this part of the game too, otherwise we'll end up repeating patterns over and over. You can move your own glass. I'm not touching anything you've pissed in.'

Andrew huffs, but nods, taking a stand next to Ryan at the table. Jane contemplates offering to help, but she has a feeling that the more people involved, the more likely they are to get confused and mess up. Andrew, despite his faults and horrible attitude, is obviously the best man for the job, and Ryan seems to have a sensible head on his shoulders and has taken control of the situation. She likes that.

In fact, she likes him a lot. She's never fallen for someone so quickly before. Maybe it's the fact she knows he's a good father that drew her to him like a moth to a flame. It doesn't hurt that he is also kind, considerate and handsome too.

He reminds her a bit of Ben's father in the looks department. Jane hasn't thought about him in so long. She doesn't even remember his name. He'd been a random one-night stand she met on a night out when she was celebrating finishing an art project she'd been working on. Her friends had got her wasted on flavoured vodka shots and she'd ended up in some guy's bed. When she woke up, he was gone. He hadn't left a note or anything. Too ashamed to stick around and wait for him, she'd left his house, which he appeared to share with a few messy mates, and didn't think anything more of it.

Until her period was late six weeks later.

Jane had asked her friends if they remembered him, but no one did. And she'd been too drunk to remember where he lived and hadn't thought to take note of his address when she'd left the next morning.

Of course, she considered having an abortion. She did her research, weighed up the pros and cons of both choices and made her decision. She was single, still young and had a dream of becoming an artist and travelling the world, which would be hard to do with a baby in tow.

She made the appointment.

And then she'd been kidnapped by a deranged serial killer. The rest was history. Her maternal instinct had kicked in. The killer had come at her with a branding iron, ready to burn away the top few layers of skin on her stomach where her baby was currently residing and growing. It was only a few bundles of cells, but a switch inside her flicked on. She fought for her life and for her baby ... and she'd won.

Or had she?

Jane blinks as she returns to reality. Andrew and Ryan are arguing at the water table. She isn't sure how long they've been at it. Without a working watch, it's difficult to tell.

'We've already done that combination,' shouts Andrew.

'No, we haven't.'

'Yes, we fucking have! Who has a photographic memory here … me or you?'

Ryan throws his hands up in surrender. 'Fine. Have it your way.' He glances at Jane and rolls his eyes and she responds with a smirk. Ryan turns and goes back to assisting Andrew.

Jane focuses her attention on Christie, who appears to be a little nervous. She keeps scratching behind her left ear, and dark stains are blooming under her armpits on her T-shirt. Jane smiles as she walks up to her, deciding to try and break the ice a little.

'You okay?'

Christie's eyes widen. 'Yes, fine, why wouldn't I be?'

'Well, we're stuck inside a building on a remote island and the only hope of getting out rests on two men's ability to keep count.' Christie's lips curve into a smile. 'I would offer you some water, but …' Jane's eyes swivel to the water table.

'I'm fine. I could actually do with a wee.'

'Oh my God, me too! I've been dying to say something.'

'Probably best not to squat in front of the men though.'

'Ha, yeah, I'd rather die. I guess we're going to have to hold it for a while.'

Christie's shoulders have visibly relaxed now. 'Thanks,' she says.

'No problem.'

'Sorry I came across as a bit abrupt earlier.'

Jane shakes her head. 'We're all under a bit of pressure. A lot is riding on this ... game. If that's even what we can call it now.'

'Yeah, tell me about it.'

Jane notices that Christie keeps refusing to make eye contact with her, a tell-tale sign she's nervous again or hiding something from her, but Jane doesn't mind. She knows Christie has no reason to share her life story with her. They are strangers after all. And they are against each other in this 'game'. They each have their own reasons for being here and Jane isn't about to let her guard down by sharing her own secrets with Christie either.

'Fuck yeah!' Andrew's sudden shout causes both women to jump.

Jane turns and sees the table moving down into the floor again, but this time, instead of stopping, it continues to sink until there is nothing but a hole in the floor where the table had once been.

It seems the game is truly about to start.

Down into the creepy, dark hole in the floor they go.

Chapter Twenty-One
Andrew

Andrew punches the air and whoops as if he's just beaten his personal best in a heavy lift as the table sinks into the floor, clicking and creaking. He isn't sure what magic or special effects has been orchestrated but watching an actual table disappear is quite something. It sinks further below the floor, revealing a large hole.

No one moves until whatever mechanisms are moving the table stops whirring. Andrew pauses for a moment and then cranes his neck forwards and peers into the hole. It's dark and there doesn't appear to be any steps leading down. It smells musty and damp, but not unpleasant. It reminds him of …

Never mind.

'Ladies first,' he says, extending his hand towards Jane and Christie, both of whom move backwards and shake their heads. They don't notice that his hands are trembling.

'Hell, no, I'm not going first. There could be traps down there,' says Christie.

Andrew rolls his eyes. 'This isn't some horror movie escape room. We aren't all about to be chopped up into little pieces or killed off one by one.'

'How do you know?' snaps Christie.

'I just do.'

'Well, if you're so sure ... after you.' Christie nods at the hole.

Andrew snorts and turns to Ryan, giving him a hard slap on the back. 'There you go, mate. Here's your chance to do the right thing and impress the ladies. Be the big hero man.'

Ryan narrows his eyes. 'I'm not your *mate,* remember, and since you're the one who has practically single-handedly solved this part of the first puzzle, you should be the one to go first.'

Andrew clenches his fists at his sides. 'Bunch of fucking pussies,' he mutters as he steps towards the hole. But as he does, his heart rate increases as if he were doing sprints on a treadmill. He's never been good at cardiovascular exercise. Give him heavy weights over running any day.

He maneuverers himself so he's sitting on the edge with his feet dangling. With the light from above, he can just make out the bottom of the hole, which is the top of the table far below. He uses his strong arms to gently lower himself off the edge, but his feet don't touch anything solid, so he pushes himself away and jumps down.

It's further than he expects, and he lands with a loud thud, knocking over two of the water glasses. Due to his size and weight, his knees buckle underneath him and he falls forwards on his hands and knees. His left hand makes contact with the blood pool on the table. Gross. He fights the urge to swear, not wanting the others above him to think he's a pussy himself.

'You good?' Ryan's voice booms above him.

'Fucking peachy, *mate*,' replies Andrew, pushing himself to his feet and wiping his hands on his trousers.

Above, Ryan helps the women over the edge of the hole. Rather than catching them as they land, Andrew shuffles along the pathway that gradually sinks lower into the floor. Wherever they are going, it's deep underground.

Again, his heart rate pounds erratically like a bass drum, and he has a hard time breathing in. There isn't enough oxygen in the air to satisfy his huge lungs. Is someone sucking out all the air?

As he inches along, a faint light above his head flickers to life, but it's only strong enough to highlight a small area. The light causes random shadows to dance on the walls, like an eerie puppet show.

The pathway leads to steps, which are steep and uneven. Andrew reaches out to the wall for support, but it's smooth, with nothing to grab on to as he descends into the gloomy depths.

The others are coming up behind him, having all now made it to the bottom of the hole. Andrew finds it exceptionally difficult to walk down the steps. His frame is so large that he takes up almost the entire width of the staircase and passageway, whereas the women behind him can walk along it with no problems thanks to their smaller size.

His chest constricts. Are the walls closing in around him?

Andrew places one hand on each wall and pushes, attempting to stop them from squeezing the life out of him. There is no air. There is no room. He's going to be crushed to death ...

'Andrew ... what are you doing?' Ryan's voice echoes somewhere in the back of his mind. It isn't until he feels a hand on his shoulder that Andrew lets go of the walls. He gulps in the air with jagged breaths, turning to face the trio behind him, all of whom seem perfectly fine and aren't freaking out about the walls closing in.

'Are you okay?' asks Jane.

The lights are still very dim, so it's difficult to make out faces, but Andrew nods. 'Yeah. I'm fine.' He laughs and clears his throat.

Ryan squeezes past his massive body. 'How about I lead for a while?'

'Cool. Yeah. Knock yourself out.' The men lock eyes and Andrew gives a slight nod in thanks.

As he follows Ryan further into the dark narrow passageway, he can't help but think that whoever has built this place has built it especially for him, knowing he suffers from severe claustrophobia.

Space.

Now it makes sense.

But how can anyone know about his childhood fear of enclosed spaces and the dark? Only his parents know. He has no siblings or friends from that time in his life. He has no girlfriend. How can anyone else possibly know? Just like how can they know about his photographic memory?

Unless … unless he is being ridiculous and this tight, dark passageway into the ground hasn't been designed to fuck him up and make him look weak. It's merely a coincidence … No one could possibly know that he'd been trapped in a basement for almost two days when he was eight years old. It had been his own fault. He'd gone to explore an abandoned house while on holiday with his parents, had entered the basement and the door had slammed behind him. His parents had been beside themselves, alerting the police to his disappearance. Eventually, someone had been walking past the old house and heard his screams for help. He'd been rescued, but the damage had already been done. Andrew had since been able to put the past behind him and, with the help of a child psychiatrist, has been able to face his crippling fear of enclosed dark spaces and has lived a relatively normal life. Of course, there was also that other thing that happened; the thing he has never talked about, not even to his psychiatrist.

Apart from the fact he still sleeps with a night light. Something his old roommates had taken the piss out of him for, but they'd never known the true reason.

Andrew bumps into the back of Ryan, who has stopped. 'What's up?' he asks.

'There's a door here, but I can't open it.'

'You've got to be fucking kidding me.' Andrew takes a deep breath to try and stop the mounting dread creeping up his spine. They are trapped underground in a tight passageway with no way out but to go back the way they've come. This cannot be happening.

'There's no handle or anything,' says Ryan as he runs his hands over the door.

The light is fading …

'I think the lights are going out,' whispers Jane, who is standing behind Andrew.

'No … no, they can't be,' he replies, his voice rising an octave. 'Out of my way.' He shoves Ryan to the side and angles himself past, so he is facing the door.

The dwindling light is now almost gone.

'There's got to be a way out.' Andrew runs his hands frantically up and down the door, around the edges, searching for some sort of latch or handle.

Then the light goes out. Completely.

And the darkness engulfs him.

Someone, somewhere, begins to scream …

Chapter Twenty-Two
Ryan

The lights going out are enough to unsettle Ryan, to send a flutter of anxiety through his chest, but what sends shivers down his spine are the animalistic screams that suddenly erupt from Andrew. He doesn't expect those sounds at all. It's like nothing he's ever heard before. It all makes sense now.

Space.

It's not outer space that Andrew fears, but enclosed *spaces*. Ryan knows he needs to act fast and get everyone out of this situation. But first, he must get Andrew to stop screaming and calm enough to focus. He reaches out his hands, feeling around in the pitch black, and kneels on the ground next to Andrew, taking a deep breath. Andrew is on the floor like a child, curled up into a ball, shaking like a scared dog. Ryan places a hand on Andrew's broad back.

'Andrew. Listen to my voice. We are safe. Nothing is happening. This is just a psychological trick to try and unsettle us. I know you're afraid, but I need you to stay calm, okay?'

A whimper comes from the large man on the ground.

This feels wrong. He reckons not many things would reduce a man like Andrew to a cowering mess. How does the person who set all this up know their weaknesses? Ryan gulps back a lump in his throat, not willing to think about that right now.

Ryan stands up. He can't see the two women, but he can hear their jagged breaths. Everyone is afraid, but for different reasons.

'There must be something around here that will open this door. Maybe we've missed something,' he says.

'Are we supposed to go back to the previous room?' asks Jane. 'It doesn't make sense that we'd make it this far and then have to turn back.'

'Look!' whispers Christie.

Ryan sees nothing but darkness as he spins in a circle, unsure where he's supposed to be looking. Christie could be pointing at something, but there's no way to see her outstretched arm.

Then he sees it.

Faint green symbols slowly appear on the wall next to him, revealing themselves as if being hand-painted on there and then. The weird green glow is enough to slightly light up the darkness, but not by much.

The symbols are familiar and there are twelve in total.

Behind him, Jane gasps. 'They're zodiac signs!'

'Are you sure?' asks Christie.

'Quite sure. I'd recognise the Gemini symbol anywhere. I'm a Gemini myself.'

'What are we supposed to do with them?' asks Ryan.

'What's everyone's star sign?' continues Jane without answering his question.

'Capricorn,' answers Christie.

'Aries,' says Ryan.

There's a silence while they wait for Andrew's answer. Ryan crouches to his level again and speaks calmly. 'What's your star sign?'

'How the fuck should I know? I don't know any of that star sign crap,' snaps Andrew. His breathing is erratic and loud.

Jane clears her throat. 'When's your birthday?'

'June twelfth.'

'Okay, so you're a Gemini like me, but I was born May thirty-first, so …' Jane approaches the wall with the symbols and stands in front of it, speaking out loud as she pushes against each symbol in turn. 'Aries is first. Then Gemini twice. Then Capricorn.'

As soon as she takes her hand away from the Capricorn symbol, the wall shakes and then starts disappearing, revealing a large bright opening beyond. The bright light makes Ryan shield his eyes and he blinks rapidly.

Andrew staggers to his feet and shoves Jane out of the way, entering the bright hallway first.

Ryan gives Jane a knowing look before letting the women in ahead of him.

The room they find themselves in is the most spectacular room he's ever seen. Rows and rows of books line the left wall, all in colour order, starting with the light colours and ending in the dark. A huge crystal chandelier dangles above their heads, illuminating the area with so much light it's almost blinding.

On the far wall is a large fireplace with huge lion statues on either side, which appear to be either made of gold or at least gold coating. The fire isn't lit, but there's a pile of wood next to it. In the centre of the room are four ordinary-looking chairs, all facing towards each other with a black folder on each of them. On the front of every folder are their names.

Ryan approaches his folder and picks it up. As he does, he experiences a sinking feeling. Something feels very, very wrong.

Chapter Twenty-Three
The Mastermind

Wow. Consider me surprised. No, shocked. They figured it out already and are on to the second stage. This is where shit gets real. I thought they'd be stuck trying to figure out the table puzzle for hours, but maybe I've misjudged them. Andrew performed perfectly. His photographic memory was spot on, and I have to applaud him for it. He's a clever man, encased in a thuggish body. The perfect disguise.

I howled with laughter when he had to piss in the glass to get enough liquid in it for the table puzzle to work. I did not see that coming. Well, I did, because that was the whole point, but it was still funny to watch. If they hadn't drunk so much water in the first place, he wouldn't have had to do it. But that's what I want them to learn; to be less greedy. To think before they act. I'm not just giving them water because I'm a nice person. They have to earn it. There's no food for them, but they'll be okay. Well, most of them will. I doubt Andrew will last long without food. The man eats close to four thousand calories a day.

Seeing him fall to pieces in the dark corridor was pure brilliance. I should have filmed it, then I could have watched it over and over again whenever I wanted. Ah well, I enjoyed it while it lasted. It will be interesting to see how the others cope when they come face to face with their fears. If they think that the table puzzle with the blood, water and fire was their test, they've got another thing coming.

It's going to be a thing of beauty.

This next phase is going to test them to the limit. They no longer have to work together. They are all out for themselves now.

Let the real game commence.

Chapter Twenty-Four
Christie

The room is eerily fascinating. Everywhere she looks, another decoration or feature jumps out at her; the carved lion heads made of plaster on the ceiling, the skulls of dead animals adorning the walls, the intricate patterns on the floor, swirling in every direction. She shudders as she catches sight of a particularly grotesque-looking skull, which looks strangely like a human with horns. Not to mention all the books and random items on all four walls, none of which are modern, but ancient and most likely expensive.

What is this place? And how far underground are they, if at all? Are they not in the main house anymore? How can anyone build a huge room and narrow passageways under a house in the solid rock of an island? Unless it's an illusion and they've somehow worked their way upwards into a room of the house, but she could have sworn they went underground. Is all of this just to mess with their heads, to ensure they are completely distracted and confused?

Unlike the passageway that led them here and the previous white room with the water table, this room is warm and spacious. Andrew clearly had a panic attack in the narrow tunnel on the way here. She doesn't blame him. Seeing him fall apart like that had caused her own bravery to waiver. But it did feel oddly ... personal, like this entire game is somehow designed to reduce even the strongest of them to snivelling children on the ground. Is that what's happening? Is she about to face her worst fear next? Or maybe Jane or Ryan? The puzzle in the previous room had needed blood, water and fire to complete, but it hadn't been anything like what Andrew had experienced. Christie dreads the idea of what could happen to her.

The fear of the unknown is something she's never liked. Even as a child, she'd hated having surprise birthday parties because she liked to know what was coming up so she could prepare herself, but nothing could have prepared her for this. She has to remember she's in this for the money and, now they've entered this room, it means a murder needs to be solved: a real murder. It's up to her now. She really needs a wee though, and her stomach is groaning at her, which is nothing new, but a sandwich wouldn't go amiss right now.

Ryan has already picked up a folder from one of the chairs and is flicking through it, his face contorted into a frown as he studies the pages one by one. Andrew seems to have returned to his normal self after his harrowing experience and is now studying the freaky skulls on the walls, walking up and down with his big arms folded. Whereas Jane is checking out some of the books on the shelves.

Christie joins her. 'Fancy a bit of light reading, do you?' she asks.

Jane continues to read some of the spines. 'Hmm, not really my usual genre to read. This room is weird, right?'

'Weird is an apt word to use,' she replies, turning and watching Ryan, who is now sitting on a chair and has his elbows on his knees, leaning forwards as he continues to read the folder. It doesn't sit well with her that he appears to be ahead of the game already. His face tells her that what he is reading isn't pleasant, so she decides to find out what has his eyes so wide and glued to the page. Christie leaves Jane with the books and walks up to her chair and folder. She takes a seat before flipping to the first page.

Christie,

Welcome to The Murder Maze.

As you already know, to win the prize money you must solve a real-life murder. This murder has already been 'solved' by the police, but I do not believe it to be true. There is still more to learn.

A lot more.

Your first job is to solve the following riddle. I want to see how smart you are. I know you're hungry, but you're used to hunger pangs, aren't you? You are not allowed to ask for help from any of the others. From this point forwards, you are working against them. If they ask you any questions, you are allowed to lie in order to trick them. If you do ask them anything, you must consider that they may also respond with a lie.

Once you have solved the riddle, it will lead you to your next clue and mission.

Good luck.
The Mastermind

> **I am the most common word**
> **I am the same as my sibling**
> **I am a murderer**
> **What am I?**

Christie looks up from reading and sees Andrew and Jane have also taken a seat, their heads bowed over their folders. She catches Andrew's eye and he smirks at her. Arrogant twat. He's enjoying this. He hadn't seemed so cocky a few minutes ago when he'd been cowering on the ground and shaking like a leaf. She wants to wipe that smug grin off his face. She's going to win this.

She takes a deep breath and looks back at the page. She can do this. She just needs to focus. The answer to this riddle will take her to her next clue.

I am the most common word ...

Christie lists some common words in her head; a, to, the, of, and ...

I am the same as my sibling ...

Sister? Brother? If you're the same as your sibling, then you're ... a twin?

I am a murderer ...

Does it mean another word for a murderer? Killer, perhaps? Or maybe ... executioner, or assassin or slaughterer ...

Christie wishes she has a pen. It's difficult doing all of this in her head and not writing anything down so she can see it in black and white, but the folder hasn't come with a pen, and she can't see any lying around the room.

As she glances down at the page again, her mind snaps the answer into place like a key sliding into a lock. She remembers something she's seen on the news about a serial killer who abducted and killed identical twins several years ago. They called them The Twin Killer.

Is that the answer?

Oh God ...

She looks up and this time catches Jane's eye.

Jane ...

Wait ...

There was a woman who'd escaped from the killer. She had never been pictured in the media and hadn't been named officially. They'd called her Jane Doe, which is fitting since half of that name could be correct. Surely not? Didn't the killer brand the woman with a Gemini symbol? And Jane said she's a Gemini ...

Is Jane the one who was abducted?

Does this mean Christie is supposed to investigate the identity of The Twin Killer?

Christie gets to her feet and begins to circle the room. At the same time, Jane is doing the same. Maybe she's solved her riddle too. What is she looking for? Hell, Christie doesn't even know what *she* is supposed to be looking for. 'The Twin Killer' offers no direct clue.

No one knows who The Twin Killer is or was. They've never been caught, and the killings and abductions had stopped right after Jane (if it is Jane) had somehow managed to escape from her torture chamber. Christie can't remember any more details. She'd watched the news briefly, but five and a half years ago she had her own problems to deal with and hadn't paid much attention to the world around her.

The one thing she does remember is the killer apparently wore a strange mask on their face because the woman who escaped had described it to the police when she'd been found, half-dead and in a great deal of pain.

Christie stops and looks towards Jane, who is standing in front of a glass cabinet. What's she looking at? Christie creeps closer and gasps when she sees what's sitting inside the cabinet.

It's a mask.

Christie stands next to Jane, who is trembling. 'That's a freaky-looking mask, isn't it?' she asks.

Jane nods. 'Y-Yes ... Freaky.'

'It looks familiar, don't you think?'

Jane snaps her head around and looks at Christie. They hold eye contact. The kindness in Jane's eyes has disappeared. She looks like a scared rabbit caught in headlights. Christie knows that Jane will now be keeping her mouth shut. If her instructions were the same as hers, then anything coming out of Jane's mouth will most likely be a lie.

'It's the mask of The Twin Killer,' says Jane.

Christie raises her eyebrows. It appears she may be mistaken. 'The serial killer who abducted identical twins?' She's toying with Jane.

'Y-Yes. I don't understand ... What's it doing here?'

Christie shrugs. 'I have no idea.'

Jane breaks eye contact, grasping the folder tighter against her chest. 'Good luck,' she whispers before walking away to the other side of the room.

Christie watches her and then turns back to the mask. This strange-looking thing is her ticket to the next phase of the game. She's going to solve The Twin Killer case, and she'll be rich and famous when she does.

Chapter Twenty-Five
Jane

Jane feels as if she's on a never-ending rollercoaster. She hates rollercoasters, ever since she was a teenager and went to Alton Towers with some friends, drunk too much, eaten too much, and ended up emptying her stomach of its contents on the grass after she'd swiftly exited the ride; *Oblivion.* Her stomach is looping and swirling in the same way now as she watches Christie studying The Twin Killer mask; the mask she's had vivid nightmares about ever since that day.

Why is Christie so intent on looking at it? Why is she asking questions about it out of the blue? Does Christie recognise her as Jane Doe? She'd specifically asked not to be photographed after her escape. They'd kept her last name out of the media. Does Christie know it was her? What does this mean?

She can't worry about it now though. She has her own investigation to do.

Jane finds a corner and backs up into it, holding the folder close to her chest. She knows what she has to do to proceed in the game. According to her folder, she's investigating the death of a man called Shaun Willis. There's no picture of him, but she's been given a brief description: dark hair, six foot two, athletic build. He died approximately six years ago of a supposed drug overdose. The police deemed it an accidental death, so no one has been accused. No one has been falsely imprisoned because of it, so why is she now investigating the case? What's so special about Shaun Willis?

Jane checks the folder again, scanning her eyes over the short anagram she's had to solve. It had been easy enough and she'd got it within twenty seconds.

All Hunk Sum

She waits until the others are occupied and have their heads turned away and then approaches the human skull on the wall; the one with the strange horns sticking out of its head like a weird demon from hell. As she stares into its empty eye sockets, she shudders and then runs her right hand over the top of the skull, feeling for anything out of the ordinary.

Nothing. The only thing that isn't ordinary about the skull are the horns, so she grabs one and tugs. Nothing. She tries again, this time with a little more effort. A crack emanates from the skull and then the wall it's mounted on begins to sink.

At this point, the other three in the room look up.

'Guess I'll see you all later,' she says.

Ryan nods. 'Be careful.'

'Thanks.'

A warm glow makes her stomach settle as she thinks of Ryan and the fact he still cares about her well-being and safety, despite them being competitors. She decides, when she wins the money, she'll give him some. The other two won't like it, but Ryan and his daughters need the money as much as she and Ben do. There are no rules to say what she can and can't do with the money.

Jane ducks as she passes through the wall. As she does, the wall seals itself behind her. She's trapped. The only way is to continue ahead.

Her skin prickles with sweat as she follows the narrow passage. Unlike Andrew, tight spaces don't worry her. At least she can still breathe.

Her phobia is water.

Deep water. Going underwater in general.

Being submerged means she can't breathe and if she can't breathe then, eventually, she'll die. Her fear stems from childhood, a silly game between her and her twin sister which had gone horribly wrong. Annie and Jane had been splashing in the sea, enjoying a particularly hot summer at a beach in Cornwall with their aunt. They always visited her in the summer. They'd turned eight a couple of months before and therefore had been told by their aunt that they were old enough to play in the sea by themselves, as long as they didn't stray from her line of sight. She'd set herself up under a huge sun umbrella on the sand and had her head buried in a book, some cosy romance with a pink cover.

Jane and Annie sprinted into the waves and began to play, splashing each other and shrieking as little girls did. Even now, Jane couldn't remember a happier time …

Until Annie had pushed Jane hard in the chest and Jane stumbled, tripping over a submerged rock. Jane retaliated by shoving Annie back.

There was no reason for it, but they'd started shoving and pushing each other and it had turned rough. Jane slipped again and her whole body went under, and she swallowed a lot of salty water. When she came up, coughing and gasping, her sister was nowhere to be seen.

She shouted for Annie and then spotted her back up on the beach with their aunt. Jane didn't join them, choosing instead to wander to a nearby rock pool. Sometimes she hated her sister. Why had she just left her after pushing her under the waves? She could have drowned.

Jane balanced along some slippery rocks, but a large wave knocked her off balance and she fell into the water, banging her head. That's when the panic set in and she breathed in, inhaling more water. She couldn't seem to find air and kicked out her legs, but the more she fought against the waves, the more they pounded her into the rocks.

She was going to die …

Jane stops walking and puts a hand over her heart to steady her breathing. Even thinking about that day and her fear of water often leads to a panic attack, and this is no place to have one. There is no deep water here. She's safe.

At the end of the passageway, it opens into a small metal room, a stark contrast to the large room she left the others in. This room has no decoration at all, but what it does have is an array of newspaper clippings, notes and photographs adorning the walls.

Jane leans closer to one of the photographs. When she sees the man staring back at her, her heart leaps in her chest, and she lets out a loud gasp.

This is the man whose death she is investigating.

Shaun Willis.

And she recognises him.

Chapter Twenty-Six
Andrew

That bitch, Jane, has disappeared into the wall and he's still stuck here on a chair trying to work out this damn riddle. Apparently, he's investigating the death of a woman who died in a car crash a few years ago. But the folder has given him no other details. He must figure out this riddle first. He has an eidetic memory and can recall things he's seen briefly even years later, but working out a fucking riddle is beyond him. How is this fair? It appears Jane is good at riddles and is already ahead of him.

Turn us on our backs and open our stomachs,
and you will be the wisest but at the start a lummox.
What am I?

Fuck sake, he doesn't have time for this crap. What the hell is a lummox? Everyone else in the room looks to have solved their riddles or puzzles or whatever was in their folders. Jane is gone. Christie has, just a moment ago, opened a hole in the wall after finding some sort of lever behind the freaky mask she was studying, and Ryan is standing in front of a large frame on the wall, which houses a mirror.

Andrew stands up. Maybe moving about will help loosen the cogs in his mind. Why couldn't he have been given a picture puzzle or a number game?

Okay …

He takes a deep breath.

What else is in this room? As he looks around, he sees that the mirror is on the left wall, the mask is on the wall next to the door they came through and the human skull that Jane had been fiddling with is on the right wall, which means the entrance to his secret passageway must be on the far wall. And what's on the far wall?

Books.

Is that the answer to the riddle?

Rows and rows and rows of books of all different sizes, thicknesses and ages. Andrew stomps up to the shelves. But which book?

'There are fucking hundreds,' mutters Andrew. He looks at the folder again, but no further information jumps out at him.

Perhaps he has to pull them all out until he finds one that acts as a lever. He's seen it in many films before. Andrew starts on the left and works his way across the first row of books. They stretch up to the ceiling and down to the floor … He's going to be here a while.

Meanwhile, Ryan has disappeared behind the mirror, leaving Andrew alone in the room. This is ridiculous. How is he supposed to win this game now? Had their puzzles been easier? They hadn't had to search through hundreds of books to find a lever. They'd just had to feel around for a bit.

Andrew pulls book after book out and tosses them to the ground. He's in no mood to replace them all, so the pile of discarded books begins to grow. He even has to climb on some of the shelves to reach the books right at the top. The shelves creak under his weight, but luckily, they hold.

After ten minutes of pulling books off shelves, he's only halfway. He screams and then his movements become more violent and frantic. He grabs a couple at a time and throws them to the ground, their spines breaking, their pages bending.

Fifteen minutes pass and he arrives at the final one. He stares at it. One lonely little brown book on the last shelf.

'No fucking way,' he mutters.

He pulls it off the shelf and there, nestled behind it, is a small silver lever.

'You have got to be fucking kidding me!' he screams. 'How is that possible?' Andrew looks up at the ceiling as if there is a camera there watching him. 'You think this is fucking funny, don't you? First, you make me look weak and pathetic in those dark tunnels, and now this!' He kicks the nearest wall and screams again before pulling on the lever.

A loud click emanates from the bookshelves as they magically sink into the floor, revealing a narrow passageway beyond. Someone is clearly enjoying watching him squirm.

'I'm going to fucking kill the lot of you,' he mutters as he squeezes his broad shoulders through the gap. He takes small steady breaths as he navigates the path, which luckily doesn't go on for very long and he doesn't get another bout of claustrophobia. He ends up in a small metal room with no windows or any other doors. On the walls are dozens of newspaper clippings, photographs and sticky notes.

'Fuck me,' he says as he walks up to the nearest wall.

Someone has been busy collecting all this information. A picture of a heavily pregnant woman is pinned in the centre and her name is scrawled across the top in red pen.

Lisa Neville.

A flicker of recognition ignites inside his head, but the truth doesn't fully settle until he sees the picture of her husband, located next to her with the words 'Did he kill her?' written in red.

'Well, well, well,' says Andrew with a smirk. 'It looks like Ryan Fucking Neville isn't so perfect after all.'

Chapter Twenty-Seven
Ryan

Ryan stares long and hard into the long vertical mirror after figuring out his clue from the riddle. It was straightforward for him, but it seems Andrew has been given a much harder riddle to solve (if he had been given one, or perhaps he's just useless at solving them) as he's stomping around in a huff, seething at the rest of them. Ryan's riddle was: *I make two people out of one. What am I?*

Ryan has read the brief note at the start of the folder. He's to figure out the death of a man called Luke Blake. He was brutally beaten to death with a claw hammer and the folder revealed a horrific picture of the crime scene. Ryan had covered his mouth to stifle a gasp when he'd first seen it, trying his best not to react to the gruesome images. He'd never seen so much blood. It was everywhere, as if someone had taken a huge can of red paint and just thrown it around the caravan he'd been found in. The skull of the man had been pummelled to a pulp. Bone, blood and brain were splattered everywhere, creating a sticky, messy pile of remains on the floor of the caravan.

That's all the detail he has so far.

Luke Blake … who killed you?

The mirror is his way out. He runs his hands along the side, at the bottom and the top and finds a small button on the left side of the mirror, which, when pressed, causes the mirror to slide to the side, revealing a small gap. Luckily, narrow spaces don't worry him, so he sucks in his chest and squeezes through, then must get down on his hands and knees and crawl through a low metal duct. That's what it looks like; one of those huge air vents they often use in movies. His favourite film, *Die Hard*, springs to mind.

Welcome to the party, pal!

Ryan fights a smirk as he reaches the end of the duct and kicks out the grate. It clatters down into a metal room, causing a loud crash, which echoes for several seconds. Ryan jumps to the ground and straightens his shirt, which has ridden up and become untucked. It's also soaked in sweat under the armpits and he's starting to be able to smell himself.

He looks around the room, bare apart from one wall covered in photos, newspaper articles and sticky notes. Ryan approaches and scans his eyes briefly across the headlines.

> *Headless Man Found Beaten to Death.*
> *Man Found with Head Smashed In.*
> *Brother Dead – Sister Alive.*

The last one catches his eye, so he reads further.

Brother Dead – Sister Alive.

The body of a man, Luke Blake, was found in a caravan late last night. His head was completely smashed in by a claw hammer, which had been found at the crime scene. His sister, Laura, was found unconscious and locked in a cupboard, covered in blood, which belonged to her brother. She had no memory of what happened and appeared to be suffering from a mental breakdown. She was taken to a nearby hospital to be treated for minor wounds but then had to be transferred to a mental health facility where she was put under close supervision.

Police say it is possible she beat her own brother to death and then had a breakdown due to her actions, but further evidence was found a few days later to suggest a third party was involved. The police are still searching for a possible female witness whose DNA was also found at the scene. As yet, no one has come forward and the DNA has not been matched to anyone in the system.

Ryan scans the next article, his eyes growing wider as he absorbs the words.

Where is the sister now?

Laura Blake escaped from the mental health hospital several weeks after being admitted for allegedly murdering her brother, Luke. She appeared to have made a miraculous recovery but fled before the police could come and question her about the death of her brother. It is still unclear whether she did kill him, and the female witness has yet to be found and questioned.

Why was Laura spared? What had she seen or done to cause a mental breakdown? And where is she now? Why did she escape and run away if she wasn't guilty? Was she faking her mental breakdown?

Ryan shakes his head. The story itself is an awful crime, but he can't remember it ever being on the news. Granted, he doesn't watch or read the news religiously, but surely he'd have heard something about this. The newspaper articles were dated from 2018, roughly six years ago. Has Laura been found since?

That year was the year he lost his wife, so not only was he trying to recover from her passing, but he was also up to his neck in dirty nappies and wipes with two screaming babies who wanted their mother's arms around them, not his. Maybe he'd missed the news story.

In any case, he must solve it now, but how? All he has to go on are old articles, pictures and headlines.

A photograph catches his eye.

He leans closer and squints. The photo is grainy but clearly shows the face of Laura Blake as she emerged from the cupboard, drenched in her brother's blood. In the picture, she looks deranged. Her eyes are black holes. Her hair is long and plastered to her head and face with sticky blood and sweat. She looks to be a teenager, maybe very early twenties, but there's no mistaking it ...

He knows that woman.

In fact, he's seen her recently.

He's staring at a younger version of Christie Truman.

Chapter Twenty-Eight
Christie

Her eyes grow wide as she enters the metal room at the end of the short narrow passageway that opened after pulling the lever she'd found behind the mask. It made an odd groaning noise as she pulled it, almost like the human skull with horns was coming to life before her eyes. The room she's entered is plain and has no windows or any other exit as far as she can see, but one wall is adorned with rows and rows of articles and information regarding all The Twin Killer cases, not just Jane Doe's. There were several sets of twins before Jane and her sister were captured, none of whom survived.

Jane's sister, the one who was killed, was a police officer called Annie Patterson who'd been investigating The Twin Killer cases at the time.

Only Jane had survived. Barely. Apparently, one of her little fingers had been sliced off. Christie thinks back and can't remember seeing Jane without one of her little fingers, but then again, she hadn't been looking for anything like that, so perhaps she'd overlooked that detail.

According to the police, since Jane Doe escaped capture, the serial killer has stopped abducting and killing victims.

Christie's mouth waters at the prospect of finding out the truth. Is there something Jane is hiding? Did she kill the serial killer? If so, where is the body and why hasn't it been found? Only Annie's bruised, battered and branded body had been discovered in the abandoned warehouse. Jane had escaped, but when the police had turned up, there was no sign of the killer. Were they still out there? There are many unanswered questions to this case, but the police don't seem to have found any new leads on the identity of the killer or their whereabouts for over five years.

Christie scans the information sheet on the wall. The bits she picks out are that Jane's and Annie's blood had been found all over the crime scene, along with unknown DNA that has never been link to anyone. They'd been held in an abandoned warehouse in the middle of nowhere in the Peak District. Annie and Jane had been taken from their homes in London and Birmingham, drugged the entire time. It was the same as the other crime scenes for the other three sets of twins who'd been captured and tortured before Jane and Annie. They hadn't been found in warehouses but in other deserted buildings all over the United Kingdom, including rural parts of Wales and Scotland.

The Twin Killer appeared to target only identical female twins who were born under the Gemini star sign. A very specific MO. What's the reason for that?

Jane was found wandering across the mountainside in her underwear, half-dead and shivering from shock and cold. She'd been covered in her own blood and her sister's. The hikers who found her called the police and Jane had been taken to hospital and then explained where the warehouse was located.

She'd been questioned by the police on how she escaped when no other victim had been able to. Jane said she'd watched The Twin Killer kill her sister by stabbing her in the side with a large knife. Jane had fought the killer and managed to escape. The killer had, apparently, not chased after her and allowed her to go.

Having been satisfied with her story, the police closed the case and were still searching for The Twin Killer, but with no new suspects and no further abductions, the case came to a halt. No new evidence regarding the killer had surfaced since that day.

Annie Patterson had been given a police burial and was remembered as a hero, losing her life during her call of duty. She'd been investigating the cases before being abducted and had made it known she was a Gemini twin herself, as if she'd baited The Twin Killer. Jane hadn't known this and received no warning before being grabbed off the street after work on her birthday.

After being checked over, it was revealed Jane was a few weeks pregnant. The killer had branded her with a Gemini symbol on her side. Also, Jane told the police that the killer was a woman. This had been new information to the police at the time because no one had ever survived to tell them. Jane said she didn't see her face but could tell from the body shape and voice.

So … who is The Twin Killer?

Is she still out there or is she dead?

Those are the questions Christie needs to answer to win this game, but how is she expected to answer them stuck in here? Is she meant to solve another puzzle to continue or is she trapped in this room until she solves the case based on the evidence in front of her? If the truth is buried in these newspaper articles, then surely the creator of this game would have discovered it by now. They're clearly smart enough. Why does Christie have to figure it out?

She tosses the folder on the floor and sighs as she looks up at the ceiling. 'What am I supposed to do now, huh? You're not making this very straightforward.'

No answer, but she doesn't expect one. Because this isn't supposed to be simple, is it? Her mind drifts briefly to the other three and how they might be getting on with their cases. She wonders whose murder they are trying to solve …

Then it hits her smack in the face.

What if they are all here attempting to solve murders relating to each other?

A cold shiver spreads around her body. This won't end well for any of them.

'Shit,' she mutters.

If NV Enterprises has all this information on Jane and her case, then what do they have on Christie and everyone else?

Christie jumps as a distorted voice begins to speak over a seemingly invisible speaker system.

'You will now progress to Stage Two. Please enter the door to your left and wait.'

Christie leaps in fright again as a new door emerges in the wall next to her, revealing a small dark cupboard barely big enough to stand in.

'Are you kidding me? I'm not locking myself in there. What is this? What's going to happen?'

No answer ... again.

Christie huffs out a breath. 'This is mental.' She stands staring at the dark space for several minutes. It feels wrong. All the hairs on the back of her neck are vibrating, telling her not to follow the instructions.

This game no longer feels like a game. They've all been manipulated and blackmailed into coming here. The invitation she'd received had mentioned that her past was known, but she'd taken it to be an empty threat, never paying it any attention. It's always been about the money for her.

'Fuck this,' says Christie. She turns and heads for the door where she entered the room, but it's gone. Sealed up. No handle or anything. 'Let me out!' she screams, but the only sound that echoes back is her own.

She bangs her fists against the wall where the door had been. It's solid. Christie stops and takes a breath before she loses it completely as she turns to face out across the metal room.

Deep red blood pours down the walls and creeps across the floor towards her like an ever-expanding river.

Christie shrieks. They know … just like they knew Andrew was afraid of dark, tight spaces. They know Christie is terrified of blood.

Just as the river is about to touch her feet, her legs collapse underneath her, and she sinks into the floor and into total darkness.

Chapter Twenty-Nine
Jane

The man in the photograph looks the same as she remembers. He hasn't changed at all. Tall, with dark hair, devilishly handsome and a muscular physique. She may have been drunk when she slept with him, and she may not have known his name at the time, but she could never forget the face of the father of her child. Now, almost six years later, she knows his name.

Shaun Willis.

And she's investigating his death. No ... his *murder*.

It makes no sense.

When did he die? Was that why he'd never contacted her? Because he was dead? Why hadn't she seen anything on the news?

Jane's eyes search frantically for an answer until she finds a newspaper article. She yanks it off the wall, tearing the corner of the page, and reads.

Man Found Dead in Own Flat

The body of Shaun Willis was found by his housemate late Thursday night. He had locked the door to his bedroom and was found with a needle in his arm. Police are treating it as death by suicide. When questioned, his housemate, who has asked to remain anonymous, told police that Shaun Willis had a drug problem, and it was only a matter of time before he accidentally overdosed.

Police are not treating his death as suspicious.

Jane frowns as she finishes reading. Shaun died from an accidental drug overdose. That isn't possible. She closes her eyes as she tries to recall the few words they'd exchanged that night. While they'd been kissing at the back of the club, a man had approached them and offered them drugs, which Shaun had turned down. Jane remembers he said he didn't do drugs, only hard liquor and cigarettes because they'd then shared one in the alley before heading back to his house. Had he been lying? Had he been a drug addict?

Granted, she could be misremembering, but she's sure that's what he said, so how had he ended up dead in his room with a needle in his arm?

Jane looks at the date that he'd been found. The day after she slept with him. She doubles over on the floor as a wave of nausea overwhelms her. A strangled sob escapes her lips.

The father of her child is dead.

Maybe he would have attempted to contact her if he hadn't died the next day. She'd left her number for him. Maybe he was going to wait a couple of days before calling her.

Jane clenches her teeth as she pushes herself to stand up. Anger pulses through her veins. Someone took away his chance of being a father to her child, had taken away the chance of her baby growing up with a father. Her life could have ended up so differently had he survived, had someone not killed him.

She scans the wall again, searching for a lead of some sort, and then it hits her ...

The housemate.

Who was his housemate?

She can't remember seeing them when she arrived at the house before they'd gone straight upstairs to his room. And when she left the next morning, she hadn't seen anyone either. There are no leads on the wall to suggest whoever had brought her here knows who he is either, but the word 'housemate' is circled in red in every newspaper article, so it must be the clue she needs.

Okay, think ...

Jane takes a deep breath.

Had she seen any random photos while she'd been in Shaun's house of him and his friends? Not that she can remember. She was so drunk at the time. Had she seen him with anyone the night they'd met? The club had been dark, but yes, when she first laid eyes on Shaun, he'd been standing with a group of men his own age, but she'd only had eyes for him.

He caught her staring and it had made her blush. A few minutes later, he'd found her at the bar waiting for a drink order and offered to pay for it. He hadn't gone back to his friends after that, not even once. And no one else had approached him except for …

The guy with the drugs.

At the time, she'd been pressed up against a cold wall in the back of the club with Shaun's body close to her. She'd felt his hardness against her stomach and her head had been swimming with alcohol and happiness.

'Damn it,' she mutters. She can't force her brain into remembering. The details are blurry and out of order. If only she had Andrew's photographic memory. That would certainly come in useful right about now.

'Oh my God!' Jane gasps as her eyes widen.

There it is. The flicker of a memory.

She knows who the guy with the drugs is. It was the housemate.

He'd been wearing a bright blue T-shirt stretched tight across his torso with a Harley Davidson logo on the front. And she'd seen that same top lying on the floor in the hallway as she'd crept out of the house the next morning. She had to step over it and had wondered why the person who'd worn it hadn't bothered to put it in the laundry bag, which was right next to it.

Jane shakes her head, but as she does, a soft creak sounds behind her, as if someone is walking across an uneven floorboard. She spins around and barely has time to open her mouth to scream before a large black shape descends upon her head, and she falls into darkness.

The first sensation Jane is aware of is the throbbing pain on the top of her head, followed by a sharp sting around her wrists. She recognises that sting. It's the bite of pressure when her wrists are bound together, cutting off the circulation to her hands.

Jane snaps her head up but meets nothing but black. A soft blindfold is covering her eyes. A memorable wave of fear explodes from within because she's been bound before, back when she'd been taken by ...

Oh, God ... no ...

She isn't strung up to the ceiling like last time, but bound to a chair, her ankles tied to each of the front legs and her wrists behind her back, tied to the back of the chair.

A scuffling sound.

'Who's there?' she croaks.

It stops.

Jane swallows and tugs on the bindings around her wrists, but they are too tight to even move an inch. This isn't supposed to happen.

Footsteps echo around her. And then stop again.

'Help me!' she begs.

'Jane?'

'Christie?' Jane sobs. 'Oh my God, Christie! Help me! I'm tied to a chair. I need help. I need you to—' At this point, her blindfold is ripped off and she stares into Christie's wide eyes.

'Christie, what's going—' But she stops again when she sees the newspaper clippings on the walls. She's not in the same room as before.

'I'm sorry,' says Christie, 'but it looks like you're one of the suspects I need to interrogate. I need to ask you what really happened that day you escaped from The Twin Killer.'

Chapter Thirty
Andrew

He can't help the smug grin from spreading across his face while he reads what Ryan has done during his youth. Andrew's done some fucked up shit in his time, but Ryan, apparently, used to take it to a whole other level. He's not sure whether to be impressed or jealous of the dude ... or maybe a little scared. No, he's not scared. Concerned, perhaps. Intrigued.

On the wall are police reports, clippings of newspapers and even school reports going back decades, detailing the mischief and trouble Ryan had been involved in. That twat had waltzed in all high-and-mighty earlier, thinking he was better than anyone else, yet in his teens and early twenties he'd been a proper rebel. In school, Ryan had punched a kid who'd beat him in a foot race, been arrested for drink driving at the age of fifteen and been caught having sex in a classroom by a teacher. He failed the majority of his GCSEs, only finishing with two; a C in English and a D in Maths. Somehow, he'd got into university and had never graduated, bailing at the end of the first year.

Now, he's a father and a widower and has a steady job. But, according to whoever has set this up, he isn't so innocent after all. Maybe he's been hiding a dark secret all along. Ryan has a shady past. Just because he now has kids, it doesn't change who he really is on the inside, does it? A leopard never changes it spots; Andrew's mother used to tell him that.

He rubs his hands together. This is getting better by the second. He reads a newspaper article, which mentions Ryan by name. Apparently, at university, he'd set fire to one of the halls of residence. Well, okay, maybe Andrew is reading between the lines on that one, but there had been a fire in the building where Ryan lived, and it had been caused by a prank that had gone wrong between him and his mates. Then, Ryan had the audacity to say that he'd saved a girl's life by rescuing her from the fire.

'Yeah, right,' mutters Andrew.

He wonders when Ryan started to transform from wild boy to pretty boy. Maybe he'd met his future wife and calmed down. Clearly, she'd been a good influence on him.

It's the car accident that interests him the most. The one which killed his wife and their twin girls several years ago … But wait …

Andrew tilts his head to one side, a piece of the puzzle not quite clicking into place in his head.

Hadn't Ryan mentioned he had twin girls earlier to Jane? He didn't say anything about his wife dying, so that's an interesting twist, but Andrew's certain Ryan said he had twin girls. He forgets their names. So why are there random sticky notes saying *Ryan lied*, *They all died* and *He stole them*?

He stole who? The twin girls?

What the fuck?

That can't be true. Surely, Ryan Fucking Neville wouldn't stoop that low.

Andrew scratches his head. It doesn't make sense. What he really needs to do is question Ryan about it, strap him to a chair and shine a light in his eyes. Maybe slap him about a bit, cut off a finger or two. Then he'd fucking talk, wouldn't he?

What is he supposed to do now?

Andrew paces in front of the wall like a caged lion. He hasn't eaten for hours. His stomach aches and he feels slightly sick. His body is trembling and he's not sure if it's from lack of food and energy or withdrawals from his daily fix.

He hasn't worked out since early this morning. He'd been able to squeeze in an early morning gym session before he set off for Wales. Even in this metal room, he feels constrained because he knows the only way out is back through the dark and narrow tunnel. He's somewhere underground and trapped until he can figure out what is going on and move forwards.

Andrew's mouth turns dry as he looks above him and imagines the hundreds of tons of earth and rock above his head. No, no, no. Not here. Not again.

He takes a deep breath to focus his thoughts.

Right, back to Ryan.

Had Ryan Neville killed his wife and kids and then stolen two kids and pretended they were his own? Why the fuck would he do that?

A heavy weight presses on his chest. Andrew puts a fist to his heart and thumps it, willing himself to get a grip. He needs a drink. In fact, where the fuck is the food and water? Are they supposed to starve to death in here? There was water back in the other room, but he needs some more now. And food. He's never been so hungry before. He has to eat regularly to sustain his energy levels. He's struggling. And it's making him feel … trapped. Weak.

'Hey!' he shouts at the ceiling. 'I need food. You think I'm this big by eating fucking salads? I need protein and carbs, motherfuckers!'

No answer comes.

'This is bullshit.' Andrew slams his fist against the wall. 'Bullshit!'

He takes several deep breaths, reminding himself this situation is only temporary and at the end of it is a big pile of money waiting for him.

He can do this.

He's been in worse situations before.

Andrew chuckles as a memory pops into his head. The irony that he's gotten away with murder himself isn't lost on him.

'Oh, fuck,' he says.

It dawns on him that if he is investigating Ryan for possibly murdering his wife, then is Ryan or one of the women investigating him too?

Is this what the whole game has been about? All four of them have gotten away with murder and must solve each other's cases. Is that what this is?

Now he really does feel trapped. The air is thinner. The walls tremble around him, swarming in and out of focus. They are closing in on him again. There is no way out.

Andrew throws his right arm out towards the wall to steady himself as his legs buckle underneath him. There is something wrong with the air. It burns his throat and eyes.

A cough erupts from his mouth as he bends over on the floor, retching and wheezing.

His visions blurs.

His throat constricts tighter and tighter.

And the air disappears.

A light flickers on and off in front of him. His head pounds so hard it feels like it might explode. He has never gone this long without some form of substance, be it alcohol or otherwise. Andrew coughs violently as his dry throat feels the cool relief of oxygen.

Has he been drugged? He knows what the effects of drugs feel like, or at least some of them, but none he's taken in his life have ever rendered him unconscious in a matter of seconds.

He's on his back on a hard floor. The light is still flickering above him.

'Fuck sake,' he mutters as he pushes himself to a seated position.

A note floats down from his chest. It must have been lying on him. He grabs it and reads. A smirk appears on his face.

'I've got you now, you motherfucker.'

Chapter Thirty-One
Ryan

He's staring at a much younger-looking picture of Christie Truman. It's undoubtedly her, despite the grainy, faded photograph showing her with no hair and bloodshot eyes. Her hair isn't completely shaved off, but at least a grade one all over. It makes the angular shape of her jaw stand out and even emphasises her dark eyes and bone structure. The woman he'd left in the previous room looks nothing like her younger self.

Laura Blake.

The question remains: how and when had Laura Blake become Christie Truman? And why? Because of what had happened to her brother? Had she been sent into the witness protection programme? Or is she on the run because she was suspected of his murder? Is any of it even true?

Ryan can't quite get his head around it. She seems so ... normal, if a little standoffish. If that's even the correct word to use. If she's lied about her name, what else has she lied about?

He knows he must find out who is responsible for killing her brother in order to escape and win the money, but how is he supposed to do that with only a few newspaper articles and photographs to help him? Then he remembers what the cloaked figure had said at the start. When was that? Ryan could have sworn it was yesterday, but it must have been only a few hours ago. He misses his girls so much. His stomach is growling at him. When was the last time he ate something?

Are they going to be fed and given more water while down here? Now that he thinks about it, he needs to urinate too. It's only a matter of time before his head starts to ache and his thirst will become overwhelming, turning to dehydration, which will affect not only his energy levels, but his cognitive ability to solve this murder. He needs to get out of here and home to his girls.

His girls.

Ryan's mouth twitches into a smile as he thinks about them and what they might be up to at school. He hopes they are behaving for Amanda. They are good girls really. The lights of his life. His thoughts drift to Lisa and, without meaning to, he remembers the look on her face the last time he'd seen her alive.

Fire. There had been fire. And heat. And … screaming. Lots of screaming, like tortured souls clawing to escape hell.

Ryan closes his eyes as the horrendous memories flash before him, but the action doesn't help. The memories just continue to play out in his head like a movie, complete with sound effects.

Her screams fill the room.

The fire crackles and hisses.

Ryan opens his eyes.

The sounds are real, echoing around the metal room. They aren't in his head.

Lisa?

'Lisa!' he shouts into the abyss.

'Ryan!'

His whole body freezes at the sound of his wife's voice answering back.

'No ... no ... that's not possible,' he says. He runs to each corner of the room, hunting for the source of her voice, but it seems to be coming from everywhere. All around him. The door he entered through is sealed shut. There's no door handle or a way out now.

'Lisa!'

'Ryan, help me!'

Tears stream down his face as he scrapes his fingernails into his flesh until it hurts. 'This isn't real. This isn't real.' He continues to repeat those words as he closes his eyes and sucks in a deep breath, doing his best to control the rising panic and fear within.

The screaming stops. The crackling of the fire ceases.

Ryan stands in silence.

Is it over ... or has his nightmare only just started?

'What is this?' he shouts into the empty room. 'What do you want from me?'

Sweat soaks into his shirt. He's dripping. Is it getting hotter in here? It almost feels as if someone has cranked up the heat.

Ryan looks up.

A huge fire ball engulfs the ceiling. Flames lick and spread across the area to all four corners of the room, circling him, trapping him.

Ryan screams. He screams so loud that his throat hurts and contracts. But there is no smoke from the fire. It isn't real … is it?

Someone is messing with him, just like they messed with Andrew in the narrow dark passageway. Someone knows his weakness, which means someone knows the truth …

And that makes his insides clench. A wave of nausea takes over him and he dry retches, his stomach clenching in agony. This can't be happening. It isn't possible. Who would know what had happened? Who would concoct such an extravagant game to get the truth from him?

Once he's finished retching, he straightens up. 'I'm not playing your game anymore. I want to leave … now.'

He stands in front of the door, but nothing happens. The fire continues to blaze above him, and the heat keeps increasing. This is how he's going to die … the same way his wife had died: engulfed in flames.

The heat. It's too much.

Ryan collapses to the ground, his vision blurring, his head spinning.

And then he sinks into nothing.

Chapter Thirty-Two
Christie

She stares open-mouthed, unable to believe what she's seeing. Jane is tied to a chair in front of her, her head hanging forwards with her chin almost touching her chest. Her wrists are bound behind her at an awkward angle and her ankles are tied to the front legs of the chair. She doesn't look injured, but how long has she been like this?

What the hell is going on?

This doesn't feel right. Surely she isn't supposed to …

She takes a step forwards, causing Jane to stir. It looks as if she's regaining consciousness.

'Jane?'

'Christie?' Jane sobs. 'Oh my God, Christie! Help me! I'm tied to a chair. I need help. I need you to—' Christie pulls off her blindfold. 'Christie, what's going—' She stops and her mouth falls open. Christie watches as Jane's eyes focus on the information that adorns the walls.

'I'm sorry,' says Christie, 'but it looks like you're one of the suspects I need to interrogate. I need to ask you what really happened that day you escaped from The Twin Killer.'

Jane almost chokes, emitting a sound between a laugh and a sob. 'You … what? What are you talking about? Why am I tied up? Did you do this to me?'

'No!'

'Then why am I tied up, Christie?'

Christie takes a breath. 'I told you ... I think I'm supposed to ask you some questions. I've just found you like this. I don't know who tied you up.'

'B-But ... we've been tricked. We're investigating the deaths of people we all have a connection to. We've been set up, Christie.' Jane's voice has risen an octave or two. She's either a decent actress or close to freaking out. Christie doesn't blame her; she's close to losing it too.

'Whose death are you trying to solve?' she asks.

Please, God, don't say ...

'I ...' Jane stops, and the women lock eyes. It seems Jane may have been given the same brief as her: that they aren't supposed to trust anything anyone says and whatever comes out of their mouths is most likely a lie. 'Untie me and I'll answer any questions you have,' says Jane in a calmer voice. She tugs on her wrist restraints and flinches as they bite further into her skin. 'Please.'

Christie shakes her head. 'The quicker you answer my questions now, the better. I'll untie you afterwards, I promise.' Christie flicks her eyes towards the wall of information. Where is she supposed to start? She's never questioned anyone before, let alone someone who's tied up against their will. 'Do you know who The Twin Killer is?' She thinks she may as well start with the most obvious question.

'No, of course I don't,' replies Jane quickly. 'If I did, I would have told the police.'

'So you admit it. You *are* the Jane Doe who escaped, aren't you?'

Jane blinks rapidly and opens her mouth. Her lips are trembling. 'Y-Yes, it's true. M-My sister Annie was killed by The Twin Killer. I've tried to forget it ever happened. It was ... the worst moment of my life.' Jane's eyes fill with tears, which start streaming down her cheeks and dripping off her chin.

'Did you see her face? The killer, I mean.'

'I ... No, she was wearing a mask, which you obviously know because it's across the walls. Some of it makes no sense. Where did all this information come from?'

Christie ignores her question. 'How did you escape?'

Jane doesn't answer straight away. She appears to be thinking about her response. Her left eye twitches and her jaw tightens. 'I got lucky.'

'Bullshit,' snaps Christie. 'You and your sister were shackled to the ceiling by chains. She died from a stab wound to the stomach still in chains and you escaped with only a severed finger.' Christie circles to the back of the chair and inspects Jane's fingers. The little finger on her left hand is missing from the knuckle up. 'Must have hurt like a bitch.'

'It did,' mutters Jane.

'So ... how did you get free from the chains? It says that The Twin Killer MO was to take identical female twins, but why? Did you talk to them? What did they say?'

'They didn't say anything.'

'Stop lying!'

'I'm not!' Jane shakes the ropes and attempts to stand up, her bottom only lifting an inch or so from the chair.

Christie sighs as she pinches the bridge of her nose, closing her eyes. A headache is forming behind them; the beginnings of dehydration, perhaps? Her senses are weak. It's becoming more and more difficult to focus. 'What happened to The Twin Killer? Why have they never been found?'

Jane stares up at the ceiling for several seconds before answering. 'I managed to escape, and I ran and never looked back. She must have stopped torturing people after that.'

'Yes, but *how* did you escape?'

'She let me go.'

'Why?'

'Why does it matter?'

'Because you're tied to a chair in an underground room, in a building on a remote island with no way of contacting the mainland and no means of getting off. Plus ... the whole point is to solve the murders, right? You say The Twin Killer killed your sister, but you don't know who they are. Here's your chance to find out.'

Jane narrows her eyes while staring at Christie, who holds her gaze.

She's not talking ...

Christie clenches her fists at her sides. That's when her eyes drift to a table in the far corner; a table that hadn't been there before when she'd been in the room alone. On it are a selection of knives and sharp tools. Why are they there? What is she ...

No ... she can't torture Jane. Can she?

That isn't her anymore. She can't let her inner demon be free again, not after last time. Jane will tell her the truth ... eventually. She must be patient and approach her questioning from a different angle.

'Okay,' she says quietly, 'do you want to find out who killed your sister or not? You want to find out who The Twin Killer is and bring them to justice, right?'

'Y-Yes, but if I help you now then I'm helping you win the money.'

'I'll split it with you.'

Jane's eye twitches again. She's considering it. That's a good sign. It means she's desperate. Christie can work with desperate, can use it to her advantage.

'No,' says Jane on an exhale.

'You're kidding, right?'

'I don't trust you, Christie.'

'Likewise.'

'So what are we supposed to do about this? Are you going to keep me tied up and torture me or something?' Jane's eyes drift to the table and the array of tools and knives. Christie follows her gaze and then sighs loudly.

'We're being tested.'

'You think?'

'I don't know what to do.'

'Neither do I, but there's not much I can do tied up to this chair. Will you at least loosen the ropes around my wrists? I can't feel my fingers.'

Christie rubs the back of her neck as a strange tingle makes its way up her spine. Who is she kidding? She can't keep Jane tied up like an animal. Whoever is running things around here is making her paranoid, turning her into someone she doesn't recognise.

'Wait ... first tell me who you are investigating? You are investigating someone, I take it?' asks Christie as she paces in front of Jane.

Jane nods. 'Yes. It seems we've all been led here to solve murders relating to each of us. I'm looking into the death of someone called Shaun Willis.'

'Never heard of him.'

'He's the father of my son.'

Christie's eyes widen. 'Oh, shit.'

'Yeah, that was my response too. I didn't even know he'd died. He was a one-night stand and even though I left him my number, he never called me ... Now I know why.'

'Didn't you know his name so you could look him up when you found out you were pregnant?'

'No, I didn't know his name.'

Christie clicks her tongue. 'Damn, I guess I misjudged you.'

'What's that supposed to mean?'

'I didn't have you down for a drunken one-night stand type of girl.'

'We all have our pasts, and mine wasn't that long ago. I've had to grow up quick since then.'

Christie nods but doesn't respond directly. 'You found out you were pregnant before you got abducted by The Twin Killer, right?'

Jane holds her stare as she responds solemnly, 'Yes.'

'So ... chances are you'd have done anything to protect your unborn child. That's what they say about expectant mothers, isn't it? The whole maternal instinct thing kicks in, not that I'd know anything about that.'

'What are you getting at?'

Christie rubs her chin as she continues to pace back and forth in front of Jane, who follows her every movement. 'I'm just saying ... that maybe you made a deal with the killer, and she let you go so that you could save your child's life.'

'You think a serial killer has the capacity to make deals?'

'How else do you explain your miraculous escape from chains hanging from the ceiling? She could have butchered you like the rest of the twins she abducted, but she didn't. Why? What makes you so special? I'll tell you right now that it has nothing to do with luck or your resilience.'

Jane sighs heavily. Christie can see the turmoil inside her head. She's getting to her, slowly but surely. Soon she'll crack and tell her what she needs to know, and then what? What is she supposed to do with the answers? Does that mean she automatically wins? Is this conversation between them being secretly recorded? Is this about to all come to an end and someone is going to jump out with a party popper and shout, 'Congratulations! You're the winner!' while balloons fall from the ceiling?

Christie flicks her eyes to the corners of the room, but there is nothing there.

'Okay,' says Jane. 'I'll tell you the truth.'

'How do I know it'll be the truth?'

'I guess you'll just have to trust me.'

Chapter Thirty-Three
The Mastermind

It's getting interesting now. I can barely turn away from the screens. Seeing Jane tied up and talking about her abduction by The Twin Killer is highly entertaining. The Twin Killer is a legend. It's a shame they never continued their work, but I suppose all good things must come to an end. I'm looking forward to the big reveal, when they work out who The Twin Killer is.

I'm rather disappointed in Christie though. She hasn't picked up one of the weapons I provided yet. I was hoping for a bit of bloodshed, but it appears I may have to depend on Andrew and Ryan for that. My eyes flick to their screen, but there's no movement from either of them. Maybe I used too much nitrous oxide. Hopefully, they won't be out for much longer. I'm getting impatient. Time is ticking on. They've now been on this island almost fifteen hours. It's just gone three in the morning, and they have no idea. Exhaustion will be well and truly setting in soon.

They have no idea how much work it took to gather all the information on the walls. Countless hours, huge expense and mountains of paperwork. Luckily, I had help and funding, but I am the mastermind behind the whole thing. I'm proud of myself. All these people will finally get what's coming to them.

They can't kill someone and expect to get away with it. They are all bad people, yet I am giving them the chance to repent. Only one chance though. After that, they lose it.

My stomach rumbles, reminding me that I haven't eaten for a few hours, but I dare not leave the screens in case I miss something. It's just too tense and exciting to miss. Leaning forwards, I pick up my phone and press the call button.

'Can you bring me some food?'

'Right away. Anything good happen yet?'

'Not yet, but it's only a matter of time.'

'I'll be right up.'

I hang up, smiling. Food and a show. How lucky am I?

Chapter Thirty-Four
Jane

Her heart is racing so hard she can barely take a breath. Every feeling, every fear, every fibre in her body is on high alert, warning her that something is wrong. Fight or flight. Fight or flight. Make a choice. But right now, she can do neither. Somehow, she must get herself out of this situation, out of these restraints, and her only lifeline is standing in front of her.

Christie Truman.

A stranger. Her eyes hold a familiarity she can't pinpoint. Maybe she's been in the paper once, or maybe she recognises a fellow woman in an impossible situation. Can she bare her soul and tell this woman the truth? Is it worth the risk? It's the only logical option there is, so she takes a chance.

'My sister and I were in our underwear, chained to the ceiling, our arms held above our heads with our feet barely touching the floor. We hadn't spoken in nearly eight years. She was a cop, and she was working The Twin Killer cases. She set up our abductions as a trap because she knew the killer would come for us. We were Gemini twins. She didn't even warn me. I was angry when I found out.' Jane looks down at the floor as she continues while Christie stands motionless in front of her.

'The Twin Killer murdered my sister in front of me because I wouldn't do it myself. That's her game. She wants to watch while one twin kills the other. It's what happened to her in the past. She had a Gemini symbol branded onto her forehead.' Jane looks up to gauge Christie's reaction, which is no reaction at all. Not a gasp, not an eyebrow raise, not even a flinch. 'I made a deal with her. I told her that if she let me go then I'd join her.'

'Join her? What do you mean?'

'There was a twin killer before the one who took me. And maybe even before that. The woman in front of me was destroyed when her own sister was killed. She just wanted someone like her, someone who was just as damaged to join her and be her sister.'

'So ... she's crazy?' says Christie.

'She wasn't always, I don't think. Plus, crazy is a little ambiguous. She was damaged because of what had been done to her. It wasn't her fault.'

'Did she take the deal?'

'She let me go.'

'And?'

'And I overpowered her, knocked her out and escaped. By the time I raised the alarm and was found and the police got there, she was gone. They found Annie, but she was long dead.' Jane looks at Christie, hoping she has bought it. It's partly the truth, but how much more detail does Christie want? All Jane needs is to get free of these restraints, exactly like last time ...

Christie's left hand is twitching.

Come on ...

Christie bites her lip for a moment, absorbing the story. 'Do you think The Twin Killer is still alive? Why haven't there been any other abductions and killings since you escaped?'

Jane shrugs and then flinches as the movement causes friction on her sore wrists. 'I don't have an answer for that.'

'Well, we're not going anywhere ...'

'What do you want me to say?'

'I need more, Jane! I need to know who The Twin Killer is. You haven't really given me anything I couldn't already work out for myself using the information on the walls.' Christie's face flushes red and she begins her frantic pacing again. Up and down. Up and down. Head down, staring at the floor.

Jane's losing her.

'Don't you think if I knew who she was, I'd have told the police five years ago?' asks Jane, a sharp edge to her voice.

'Maybe. Maybe not.'

'You think I'd willingly keep the identity of my sister's killer a secret on purpose? Why would I do that?'

Christie takes a wide stance in front of her and folds her arms. Threatening. 'Maybe because The Twin Killer didn't really kill your sister and you're lying to me.'

'It's not like she stabbed herself!'

'No because that would be ridiculous.'

'Then what are you suggesting?'

Christie stares at her, eyes narrowing. 'You stabbed her.'

A lump catches in the back of Jane's throat. She fights every reflex and muscle in her body not to flinch or tremble. 'Y-You think I murdered my own twin sister?'

Christie grins. 'Say you did, and this is all over.'

'Wait ... now you're trying to bargain with me? Do you think I killed her or don't you?'

Christie throws her hands up in the air. 'I don't know, but someone thinks you did. Maybe you didn't do it on purpose. Maybe it was an accident. Maybe you made a deal with the killer in order for her to let you go, I don't know, but what I do know is that neither one of us is leaving this room until you start speaking the truth and confess.'

Jane's eyes fill with tears. Her body fails her. There is no way out of this. She doesn't have a choice. It's all over.

'Fine,' she says. 'I did it. I agreed to kill my sister so that the killer would let me go. She untied me. I stabbed Annie and then I overpowered the killer and ran away, but it was too late to save Annie. There. Are you happy now?'

Jane drops her chin to her chest and allows the tears to drip onto her lap. She hears Christie sigh in front of her, but then the lights go out.

Chapter Thirty-Five
Andrew

As he enters the room and sees the scene in front of him, his mouth fills with saliva. It's like someone is throwing a party specifically designed for him. The only things missing are some whores, booze and drugs. All the best things in life (except for money). But that will all come later, much later, once he's cracked this guy. He's going to enjoy every moment of this, watching Ryan Fucking Neville squirm and cry like a pathetic mongrel. He's going to make him squeal like a pig.

'Ryan Fucking Neville,' he says.

Ryan is still out for the count, tied to a wooden chair, his head hanging down towards his chest, so Andrew takes his time walking around him; a predator stalking his prey. Ryan's drenched in sweat and looks a far cry from the polished, smart pretty boy who'd walked into the escape room merely hours before.

He'll be lucky if he even leaves with his limbs intact.

An array of knives and tools are laid across the table in front of Andrew. Seeing them sends a tingle of pleasure straight to his groin, which is weird considering it's nothing sexual. Okay, so it would have been more fun to torture one of the women, but Ryan deserves it more. He wants to wipe that posh-boy smirk off his face.

Andrew picks up a large hunting knife. The edge is serrated. He runs his fingers along the edge then licks it, feeling the blade slide across his wet tongue. He then places it back down on the table. All in good time.

A groan comes from behind him.

The prey is stirring.

'A-Andrew?'

Andrew turns just as Ryan raises his head and looks at him. His panicked expression is pure pleasure.

'What's going on?' asks Ryan, looking from one side of the room to the other in quick succession. 'Why am I tied up?'

Andrew laughs. 'Surely you should know that already, *mate*.'

'Untie me right now. Did you do this to me?' Ryan yanks on his bindings, but all he manages to do is wobble the chair back and forth. He gives up and sighs.

Andrew shakes his head. 'No, I didn't tie you up, but it was a nice surprise, I must admit.'

'Untie me.'

'I don't think so.' Andrew laughs again, enjoying this more than he thought he would. 'Because you have something I need in order to win this game.'

'And what's that?'

'The answer to who killed your wife and kids.'

Ryan makes no movement. None whatsoever. But what little colour he does have in his face seems to drain to the bottom of his feet at rapid speed. His bottom lip trembles and he looks as if he's going to vomit.

'What are you talking about? Is that whose death you're trying to solve? You think my wife was murdered? What the hell is wrong with you?'

At his tone of voice, Andrew raises a single eyebrow. Ryan is rattled, on edge, nervous, whatever you want to call it.

'My wife died in a car accident. A car *accident*.' Ryan leans forward as far as he can, but his restraints keep him from moving too far. Andrew stands in front of him, crouching so their faces are the same level.

'That's not what I think happened,' he sneers.

'And what is it you think?' Ryan's voice is not the usual calm demeanour of late. His perfect shell is cracking around the edges and Andrew is determined to enjoy every minute, revealing the layers beneath.

'I think you killed her.'

Ryan stares at him for a few seconds and then replies in a monotone voice. 'You think I killed my wife?'

'And you stole those two kids of yours.'

'What!' Spit flies out of Ryan's mouth. His nostrils flare and his eyes blaze with fire. 'What the hell are you talking about?'

Andrew folds his massive arms across his chest and widens his stance. 'Just look at the evidence on these walls.'

Ryan scans them briefly. 'What evidence? There is nothing here except random speculation and lies.'

Andrew stomps over to the nearest wall and rips off a newspaper clipping, then waves it in front of Ryan's face. 'This says that both your wife and your kids died in that car accident. How do you explain that?'

Ryan's face is deadpan. 'It's a fake newspaper article, you giant idiot. Anyone can make them up and have them printed out. Hell, even kids can make their own newspaper headlines these days. It's all fake. Just like the website Christie told us about. Everything is a set up so that we all turn on each other. I can guarantee none of this is real or true. It's a psychological game to mess with our heads. Nothing more. And worst of all, you're falling for it.'

Andrew lowers the paper in his hand and balls it into his fist before launching it across the room. As it's so light, it barely makes a noise as it lands in the far corner. 'You're lying.'

'No, Andrew, I'm not. Like I said, this whole game appears to have been created especially for us, to mess with our heads, to spread doubt amongst us, to turn us against each other. That's what they want. Don't you see that? Hell, I'm investigating the death of a guy called Luke Blake. Apparently, his sister bashed his head in and was sent to a mental health hospital. Guess who the sister is supposed to be ...'

Andrew stares at him and answers almost straight away. 'Christie Truman.' Ryan nods. 'I knew it. When she told us the amount of water that needed to be in her glass, I knew her name didn't add up to the right amount. Lying bitch,' says Andrew, gritting his teeth.

'But now I know that you're accusing me of murdering my wife and children, and, by the sounds of it, abducting two others to pass off as my own, it could mean all of this has been concocted from the start. Maybe we're being led on a wild goose chase.'

Andrew narrows his eyes, not liking where this is going. 'What do you mean? Why would someone go through all this just to mess with us?'

'Maybe we're here to only solve one murder case, the one that has actually been in the news, the one that's been front and centre of this whole thing.' Ryan lets the words hang in the air for a few seconds before continuing, 'I know for a fact that Jane is the Jane Doe who escaped from The Twin Killer's clutches. It's a case that's never been solved. It took me a while to place her, but it's definitely her. I was fascinated by the case in the papers. They didn't name her officially, nor did they photograph her, but some of the things she said made me think. Plus, the mask the killer wore was in that room back there and I saw a weird brand on her side when her T-shirt rode up slightly.'

Andrew scoffs. 'Taking a good look, were you? I've never heard of The Twin Killer.'

'Probably because you're too busy to take notice of what's going on in the world around you,' mutters Ryan.

'Watch your tongue, pretty boy. You're in no position to accuse me of anything. So, you think whoever set this up has put in red herrings to confuse us, like some sort of sick mind game?'

Ryan nods. 'That's what it feels like to me because to accuse me of killing my family is ...' He stops as tears fill his eyes. He looks away and sniffs loudly. 'I couldn't possibly ... It's too awful to even think about.'

Andrew takes a few slow paces backwards and then turns to the knife table. Ryan keeps his head down. Andrew smiles as he picks up the hunting knife again, running his fingers over the edge.

'I'm afraid I don't quite believe that to be true, Ryan. We're all here to solve different murders. The Twin Killer case. Christie's brother. Your wife and kids. You know how I know that for sure?' Andrew allows the silence to build as he walks towards Ryan, who lifts his head to look at him as Andrew comes to stop in front of him. 'Because I've killed someone too and one of those bitches is trying to find the proof. But there's no way I'm going to let that happen. This game is about to get really interesting.'

Chapter Thirty-Six
Ryan

Ryan stares at the large man standing in front of him flipping a knife over in his hand as expertly as a Japanese sushi chef. Andrew's eyes are huge black orbs, staring at Ryan without blinking. How is this happening right now? Has the guy been possessed or something? Is he seriously going to torture him? He's been drugged and tied to a chair and now this knife-wielding maniac is smiling at the fact he's about to hurt him. And, even worse, he's admitted to previously killing someone. It means all four of them are killers. No, not him. Ryan's no killer. Yes, he admits, he could have attempted to save his wife, rather than cower on the ground, too scared to reach into the flames to pull her to safety, but he didn't, and he'll regret that decision for the rest of his life. But a murderer? No, he's not guilty. Not of that. Lisa was already dead, wasn't she? No, she was alive, but even if he had rescued her, she most likely would have died from her injuries. There was no coming back from that.

He opens his mouth, but the words don't come. He wants to scream for help. He wants to plead to be set free. He wants to shout expletives until he becomes hoarse. He wants to do all of those things and more, but instead, he remains silent as Andrew continues to talk, clearly loving the sound of his own voice.

'So, you see ... it must mean that we're here to solve each other's cases because we've all killed someone, or in your case, three people.'

'I didn't kill my wife and kids. They died in a fucking car accident!' The swear word slips out effortlessly. It shocks him. This isn't him. He is losing his composure too quickly and Andrew knows it because a grin spreads across his face. He wants Ryan to be nervous and make a mistake, but it isn't going to happen. Not now. Not ever.

Andrew bared teeth gleam in the light as he lowers the tip of the knife to Ryan's Adam's apple. Ryan's immediate reflex is to swallow and, when he does, his skin nicks the edge of the sharp blade. A small bead of blood trickles down his throat. It travels down, almost tickling him.

'Okay,' says Andrew, 'now, that's an interesting choice of words you've just used?'

Ryan does a double blink. 'What do you mean?'

'You just said you didn't kill *them*. They died in a car accident, which means your kids did die, so there are two questions that remain. One: who caused the accident in the first place. And two: if your twins died, who are the girls who are living with you as your daughters?'

Shit.

Before he can think of a legitimate response, Andrew continues his interrogation.

'Had you been drinking?'

'What? When?'

'When the car accident happened. You were driving, right? That's what it says in all that information over there.'

'What? No, I don't drink.'

'Well, that's a lie. I've seen what you got up to at university with your mates.' Andrew points a finger at the wall covered in newspapers. Ryan glances over, flicking his eyes to the left. How the hell has someone gathered so much information on him and his past?

'I meant I don't drink anymore,' he says. Every time he speaks, the knife tip nicks his skin. 'Can you get that thing away from me?'

Andrew smirks, pulling the knife away. Ryan takes a deep breath.

'Look, we've all got dodgy pasts, especially when it comes to university stuff.'

'Right ... there was a fire at your halls of residence, right? A girl died.'

Ryan's mouth falls open and he could swear the floor shakes. 'I ... y-yes, it was an accident.'

'It's funny how so many fatal accidents happen around you, isn't it?'

Ryan's bottom lip trembles, but he hides his nervousness with a small smile. Andrew is making ridiculous accusations based on nothing but hearsay and the fact Ryan was in the wrong place at the wrong time when those tragedies happened.

'What's so funny?' snaps Andrew.

'It's funny because you're accusing me of killing all these people, yet you've just admitted you've killed someone yourself. How do you know this isn't being recorded?' Ryan watches Andrew's eyes dart around the room. 'Exactly. You are only incriminating yourself the more you talk. If you torture me or kill me right now, then what? You're not getting out of here with the money, let's face it. None of us are.'

'You don't know that.'

'I do, Andrew. And so do you. We're going to have to work together to get out of here. I saw what you were like in the narrow tunnels ... I know you must have some dark demons in your past, but—'

'Don't! Don't bring my shit into this. You're the one tied to a chair, so you had better watch what you say to me.'

Ryan doesn't let up. Not this time. 'What happened, Andrew? Why are you afraid of dark, enclosed spaces?'

'Stop it.'

'You were like a cowering child in that passageway.'

'Stop it!'

'I've never seen anything like it. Not from a grown man. A child, maybe. Shaking and crying and—'

'I said stop it!' Andrew lunges and punches Ryan in the face. The shock and force of the attack sends Ryan and the chair flying backwards. Blood spurts from his nose and his teeth reflexively bite down on his tongue. The back of his head bounces off the floor. One of the legs of the chair cracks and he feels his bindings around his ankles come loose.

Andrew paces up and down, muttering words that Ryan can't hear properly. Ryan's head spins and it takes several seconds before his vision returns to normal. The lack of food and water is starting to dampen his senses and reflexes, but his plan has worked. The chair has broken enough for the ropes to come loose, and he's able to wiggle his wrists free, but one of his legs is still tied to the chair leg that hadn't snapped.

He has also landed near the knife table and at this point Andrew looks up, noticing his mistake. Ryan lunges for the table, grabs the nearest weapon and scrambles to his feet while unwinding the ropes from his arms and legs.

Andrew shouts and barrels towards him like a charging bull.

Ryan grips the knife tighter.

Chapter Thirty-Seven
Christie

The room plunges into darkness, and she loses all sense of direction. It shakes like an earthquake is erupting and she swears the room revolves in a circle, like a funfair attraction. She stumbles and falls to her knees while she waits for the shaking to stop.

'Christie!' Jane's voice seems so far away in the darkness.

'Jane! What the hell is happening?'

'I don't know,' comes the quiet reply. She can hear the fear in Jane's voice.

As quickly as the shaking starts, it stops. And the lights flicker on.

'What the fuck?' asks Christie.

The room has changed. In fact, they aren't even in the same room. They are back in the extravagant room where they'd last been together as a foursome. Jane is still tied to the chair and her mouth is opening and closing in disbelief too. Christie closes the distance between them and uses her knife to slice through the bindings.

'You're letting me go?'

'Fuck this shit. This place is freaking me out.'

'You and me both.' Jane rubs her wrists as she gets to her feet. Blood rushes to her extremities and pins and needles spread through her at the sudden release. 'What's the plan now? I've just admitted to killing my sister. Does that mean you've solved the case?'

'I don't know.' Christie rubs her arms. 'Why are we back here? And where are Ryan and Andrew?' As soon as she says Andrew's name, a loud shout echoes around the room. It's a male voice. Christie and Jane lock eyes.

'I think Ryan might be in trouble,' says Jane.

'Me too.'

Both women run towards the sound of the shout. As they do, a passageway opens in the wall. They sprint down it, following the shouts and crashes ahead.

Another doorway emerges in front of them and as Christie's eyes adjust to the light in the metal room, she sees blood smeared over the walls. It shines bright red under the florescent lights. Her eyes follow the smears as the cold tingle of fear spreads through her body.

Ryan stands over the lifeless body of Andrew, who has a large knife protruding from his torso, buried up to the hilt. Jane gasps and covers her mouth with her hand, stifling a sob. Christie grimaces as she sees the pool of blood spreading around the body.

Her vision swims. Hot bile bubbles at the back of her throat as she lurches to the side and vomits, but nothing comes up, so she spits out yellow bile on the floor.

'I ... I can't,' she says. The smell of blood overwhelms her, sweet and tangy in her mouth. She can taste it. She can hear Jane and Ryan talking in the background, but the words make no sense. They fizzle and collide together, forming indecipherable sounds.

Her throat constricts. She grabs it with both hands. Why is the air gone? The other two seem perfectly fine ...

'Help me,' she squeaks as she sinks to the floor.

Jane rushes to her side, but there's only static coming from her mouth. Christie hangs on for as long as she can, but the smell and taste of blood is too much.

It's suffocating her.

Chapter Thirty-Eight
The Mastermind

Oh, what a shame. Andrew didn't make it. However, I would have bet good money that he'd be the first to fall. He may be tough-looking and strong, but really, he's a weak little boy who's scared of the dark and tight spaces. It took some crafty research to find out what happened to him. I was going to go with his fear of spiders, but spiders don't make him practically wet himself with fear. I needed something more, something that would reduce him to a scared little boy. Didn't I do a good job?

Andrew was five when his father buried him alive in a coffin as punishment for misbehaving. Scared, alone and trapped in a dark confined space with little air was enough to scar the poor boy for life. He was locked in the coffin for fifteen hours. He never spoke back to his father again. Well, not until he was a teenager, but he was much bigger then and Andrew could defend himself if he needed to, but his father never threatened or mistreated him again. It was just the one time, but it was enough. Then there was the unfortunate incident when he accidentally got trapped in a basement for two days. I'm sure that didn't help matters.

Andrew's father has never been a nice man. In fact, he's downright evil, so it's no wonder his son turned out to be an arrogant, selfish dick. He treated everyone as if they were merely a piece of shit on the bottom of his expensive shoes. And Andrew learned his ways from him. Andrew got whatever he wanted, whenever he wanted it.

Those fifteen hours of mind-numbing fear were enough to create a life-long phobia of confined dark spaces. It was perfect. It's a shame Andrew didn't learn a lesson from that day. He may have never spoken back to his father again, but he lashed out at everyone else, his mother included. His father treated her and every other woman like a piece of meat, so that's how Andrew treated them. When he grew up, he found drugs and alcohol helped to numb the fear and confusion in his head. It helped him forget.

Andrew could still be of use to me. He might be dead, but that doesn't mean it's over for him. I still have a few cards up my sleeve.

And to think it's Ryan who's killed him! I can't say I'm surprised though. I saw it coming a mile away. He got lucky with the chair leg breaking.

Let's see how this plays out, shall we?

Chapter Thirty-Nine
Jane

Christie is on the floor moaning and muttering incoherent words, but as soon as Jane reaches her side, she goes silent and collapses completely, like turning to stone in her arms. She's deathly pale. Despite the fact Christie had almost tortured her, Jane still feels the need to ensure she's okay. Christie's just scared; they all are. And now one of them is dead.

'She's fainted. She said she had a phobia of blood.' Jane makes sure she's in a semi-comfortable position on her side before standing and turning to Ryan, who looks as if he's had some sort of breakdown and been drenched with a bucket of water.

The pool of blood has expanded so much that Jane has to walk in a wide circle to reach Ryan's side. She places a gentle hand on his arm, but he flinches as if he's been burned and yanks his arm away.

'Sorry,' he says, shaking his head. 'I'm not … I don't …' He screams at the ceiling. 'I didn't mean to kill him. He attacked me. You believe me, right? It was self-defence. The man was going to torture me with a knife. He went crazy.'

'Ryan,' says Jane in as calm a voice as she can manage, 'you don't have to explain yourself to me. We all know what Andrew was like. He's a big guy.'

Ryan nods. 'Yes. Thank you. Yes.'

'Are you okay? Are you hurt?'

'No, I don't think so.' Ryan wipes a small trickle of blood from his neck. It looks as if the knife has nicked him a few times.

Jane allows Ryan a few minutes to compose himself while her eyes drift to the array of information on the walls. It's all about Ryan. About his wife and how she died in a car accident. Jane had no idea. She assumed they'd split up and she wasn't in the picture anymore. She hadn't questioned him about the girls' mother when they'd spoken previously because it had felt insensitive to do so. Her heart goes out to him, at the thought of raising his girls by himself, exactly as she's done with Ben.

But ... there's also information here that accuses Ryan of killing his two daughters too, which can't possibly be true because his daughters are alive ...

'It's not true,' says Ryan. Jane jumps as he comes and stands next to her. 'I don't know where they got this information, or how, but it's not true. I've been set up. It's all fake news ... except for the part about my wife dying in the car accident. That's true, but the girls survived.'

Jane nods in agreement, but a slither of doubt drifts into her mind before she can stop it. Ryan is the most down-to-earth man she's ever met. Yes, he looks a state now, but they've all been through a lot over the past few hours.

From what she can gather, they've been set up to accuse one another of a murder, but is any of it true? Granted, she's guilty of killing her sister, but Ryan is the last person who she thought of as a killer, yet … Andrew is lying in a puddle of his blood, his eyes glazing over in his head with a knife protruding from his torso.

And Ryan has done that.

She hadn't seen it happen. It was more than likely self-defence, but what if it wasn't?

'Were you tied up?' she asks him, taking note of the rope and broken chair.

'Yes. I managed to escape.' Ryan looks at her wrists, which still have red marks, and dark bruising is starting to show. 'Were you?'

'Yes. Christie interrogated me.'

'Christie did?' He looks at her passed out on the floor. 'Did she hurt you?'

'No, but I wouldn't have put it past her. She had this weird look in her eye. I don't trust her.'

'Do you trust me?'

Jane looks into his pleading eyes. 'Of course,' she says, but the quiver in her voice tells a different story. However, if Ryan has picked up on that, he doesn't show it.

'We need to get out of here,' he says.

'I don't think that's possible right now.'

'There's only so much longer we can survive down here without food and water, especially water.'

'Maybe we can go back for the water jug and glasses we used earlier?'

'The door back to the water room sealed shut when we entered the main room.'

Jane sighs. 'We can't stay in this room. Let's get Christie back in the main room. I don't want her fainting if she wakes up here and sees the blood again.'

'Agreed.'

Jane watches as Ryan picks Christie up in his arms and follows him back into the main room. She turns and gives Andrew a quick glance, shuddering as she sees the amount of blood pooling on the floor.

What have we got ourselves into?

Ryan lowers Christie to the floor and places her into the recovery position. Jane walks up to him and places a hand on his arm.

'Are you okay?'

Ryan looks at her and shakes his head. 'I've just killed someone ...'

'Right. Stupid question.' She attempts a smile to lighten the mood, but it doesn't work. The truth is that she knows what it's like to kill someone. Her sister. Ryan had killed a horrible man and still felt bad about it. She'd felt, and still does feel, a million times worse. 'I'm sorry, I don't really know what I'm supposed to say or do right now.'

'You and me both.'

'How did everything go wrong so quickly?'

'Maybe when we found out that we're supposed to be each solving a murder case relating to one of us who is most likely the killer,' replies Ryan.

'So, it's true?'

Ryan's eyes widen. 'Is what true?'

Jane swallows, but her mouth is so dry it makes her cough. 'Your wife ...'

'My wife died in a car accident, like I said, but someone is trying to make it look like I killed her and my daughters.'

'But your daughters are alive,' says Jane with a frown.

'Apparently, I stole them when I couldn't deal with what I'd done.'

Jane clamps a hand over her mouth to stifle a gasp mixed with a laugh. She doesn't mean to be disrespectful, but the idea that Ryan has done such an awful thing is ludicrous. Ryan must see her feeble attempt to hide her emotion because he gives her a reassuring smile.

'It's fine. That was the same reaction I had when Andrew accused me. At first, I thought maybe this was all a set-up to solve your case — The Twin Killer case — but now I'm not so sure.'

Jane's heart leaps when he speaks those words. 'What do you mean?'

'I know you're the Jane Doe who escaped from The Twin Killer.'

'Oh, right … How did you …'

'I put two and two together. Maybe whoever has set this whole thing up has been messing with us from the start. They knew exactly what they were doing when they selected us and stuck us all in here.' Ryan takes a deep breath and continues. 'We all need the money. We all have shady histories and have been involved in a death or murder of some sort. Our friend Christie' – he nods at her unconscious body – 'her real name is Laura Blake.'

Jane looks at her on the floor. 'What? How do you know that?'

'Because I'm supposed to be investigating her brother's murder, Luke Blake. She was there when it happened. They found her cowering in a cupboard covered in her brother's blood. I'm taking a wild guess here and saying that might be why she doesn't like the sight of blood.'

'Did she kill him?'

Ryan shakes his head. 'I don't know. She had a breakdown and was sent to a mental health hospital to recover, but she escaped, changed her name and disappeared. Now she's Christie Truman ...'

'Do you think she's dangerous?' They turn their heads to look at the woman on the floor, whose breaths are steady and quiet.

'I don't think we can trust her,' says Ryan.

'I agree. She seemed to enjoy the fact I was tied up. I thought she was going to hurt me.'

'Maybe we should tie her up.'

Jane winces. 'Isn't there a less ... threatening way of doing this?' Ryan stares at her for a few seconds while she wracks her brain for the answer. 'You're right. I'll go and get the rope from the room where Andrew is.'

Ryan grabs her arm. 'I'll do it.'

'No, it's okay. You stay here with Christie. I'll be right back.'

Ryan nods.

Jane walks slowly down the passageway to the metal room where they left Andrew's body. As soon as she enters, the tangy aroma of blood tickles her nostrils, and she holds back a gag. She uses her fingers to pinch her nose as she approaches his body. It's hard to imagine that less than fifteen minutes ago, he'd been alive. She stops at the edge of the pool of his blood. It has spread so far and wide that it now covers almost the entire width of the room. The rope and broken chair to which Ryan had been tied are on the other side of the puddle. There is no way around it except through.

Jane grimaces as she tiptoes across the blood, leaving half-moon-shaped footprints. She lets out her breath as she reaches the chair and begins to unwind the rope from it. Once she's gathered it all, she looks up at the nearest wall, the one with all the newspaper articles about Ryan and his wife's car accident. Her mouth drops open as she reads what Ryan is being accused of.

No, it can't possibly be true.

Ryan is right. Whoever has set this up is more than capable of faking news articles. But if Christie killed her own brother, and Andrew killed Ben's father, and Jane killed her sister, then Ryan is the odd one out because he couldn't have killed his wife.

It was an accident.

She decides to give him the benefit of the doubt. She needs an ally and turning against him now would be a mistake.

Jane begins her trip back across the puddle, but a sudden noise ahead of her makes her lose focus. Her left foot slips out from under her, easily sliding across the blood. She shouts as her body splashes down, landing awkwardly on her side.

The viscous liquid makes it difficult to gain traction, so she has to crawl on her hands and knees out of the puddle until she reaches a clear floor space. The rope is now drenched in blood too. Jane whimpers as she pushes herself to her feet, her body trembling.

She now resembles a horror movie survivor as she makes her way back to Ryan, whose jaw drops open when he sees her.

Chapter Forty
Ryan

Seeing Jane shuffling towards him covered in blood makes Ryan's heart almost beat out of his chest. The blood-covered rope is grasped tightly in her right hand, and she seems to be favouring one leg over the other.

'Are you okay? What happened?'

Jane wipes her mouth with her left hand, but rather than clearing the blood away, she merely smears it further across her face. 'I slipped and fell and landed on my hip awkwardly while fetching this blasted rope.' She hands it to Ryan, and he takes it. He doesn't know what to say to her. There they are: he drenched in sweat and she in blood. Christie, on the other hand, looks comparatively normal, despite lying unconscious on the floor.

'We certainly look a little different than when we first arrived,' he says, trying to inject some humour into the situation.

Janes attempts to wipe more blood off her face. 'Just a bit. How long have we even been here, do you think?'

'Well, considering how tired, hungry and thirsty I am, I reckon we're past the twenty-four-hour mark.'

Jane nods in agreement. 'You feeling okay?'

'I've felt better.' Ryan glances at Christie. 'She started talking,' he says as he kneels by her side.

'What did she say?'

'Just mumbling really, but she did say her brother's name.' Ryan manoeuvres Christie so that her hands are behind her back and winds the rope around her wrists. He doesn't want to do it, but she's the one who has the most to hide and clearly has lied to everyone about her real name. It isn't about working individually to solve the murders now. They need to understand why they are here and, more importantly, find a way to escape with their lives.

Once Christie is tied up, Ryan retreats and joins Jane, who has found a cloth draped over a table in the far corner of the room and is attempting to wipe the blood off her hands, face and arms.

'If Christie sees me looking like this when she wakes up then she'll faint again,' says Jane by way of an explanation for her actions.

Ryan nods as he looks over his shoulder at Christie. 'She's not going to be happy when she wakes up.'

Jane sighs. 'I can't believe this is happening. What did we do to deserve this?' Ryan notices that Jane is shaking as she says it. 'If this is about The Twin Killer case then … the only way for this to end is for me to confess.'

'Confess? Why would you need to confess? I thought you told the police everything.'

'Not everything,' she whispers. 'I told them that The Twin Killer killed my sister and that I managed to escape.'

'That's not what happened?'

'No ... I *had* to kill my sister in order to escape.'

Ryan shakes his head. 'I don't understand. Are you telling me The Twin Killer forced you to kill your sister?'

'I didn't have any other choice. It was me or her. I'd only found out I was pregnant a few days before. I was going to have an abortion, but when faced with the possibility of dying, I chose to save myself to save my baby. The Twin Killer's whole M.O. was to abduct identical twins and find one who was willing to kill their sibling to survive because that's what happened to her.'

Ryan scratches his head. 'But why?'

'Why do serial killers do any of it? Isn't that what psychiatrists and doctors have been researching for decades? She was clearly mentally damaged or groomed by the one who came before her.'

'There was more than one killer?'

'Yes. She herself had a Gemini symbol branded into her forehead.' Ryan winces as Jane lifts her top to reveal the same brand on her side. He'd noticed it before but didn't want to let on that he had. 'She branded me too.' Jane lowers her top and finishes wiping her hands on the cloth, now stained red. 'She freed me. I killed Annie and then I attacked her. We fought and I managed to escape, and The Twin Killer hasn't been seen or heard from since.'

'Why didn't you tell that to the police?'

Jane gives him a look he knows well. It's the same type of look his wife used to give him when he'd asked a stupid question. 'I didn't want to be sent to prison and have my son taken away from me the moment he was born.'

'Right,' answers Ryan. 'Why do you think The Twin Killer has disappeared? Do you know her real name?'

Jane shakes her head. 'No, I don't know who she is. My best guess is that she either has given up or she died from the wound I gave her. I managed to stab her with the knife before I got away. When the police arrived, there was no sign of her, but there was her blood mixed in with mine and my sister's, but there was no record of her in the system.'

'What happened to her after you escaped?'

'She disappeared and now ... now someone wants to know the truth. Someone wants me to confess, so fine ... if confessing gets us the hell out of here, then I'll deal with the consequences once we get out.'

Ryan looks around the room. 'So ... if the whole reason for this was the answer to who killed your sister ... why are we still here talking about it?'

Jane shrugs. 'I'm guessing I'm not the only one who has to confess.'

'B-But ... I didn't do anything.'

Jane locks eyes with him. Ryan doesn't like the look in her eyes, but before he can defend himself further, a moan echoes across the room.

Christie groans as her eyes flicker open.

Chapter Forty-One
Christie

Nausea swells in her stomach as her eyes flutter open. She can still smell the sweet metallic tang and taste it in her mouth. She licks her dry lips and swallows, her throat like sandpaper. She's desperate for water, but then another sensation rises to the surface: she can't move. Christie attempts to pull one hand up to her face to brush her hair away from her eyes, but neither will work.

What the hell?

'It's okay, Christie. We've just had to tie you up for your own safety,' says Ryan. He appears beside her, crouching to her level. She looks up at him and let out a short sharp laugh.

'My own safety! What the hell is this? Untie me right now. What do you think you're doing tying me up like an animal?'

Jane inches closer, looking like an extra in a blood-thirsty horror movie. Christie shrieks and attempts to shuffle away. It's like looking at a younger version of herself. A terrible memory floods her mind, and she can't help it as tears fill her eyes. She sees the blood. She smells it. Everything.

'Get away from me!'

'I'm sorry,' says Jane. 'I fell over in Andrew's blood. I've done my best to get rid of it.'

Christie bites her lip to stop it from trembling as she takes in the blood covering Jane's body. Some of it has dried, leaving random streaks across her bare skin, but her pale top is the worst, having soaked the blood up like dye.

'Let me go,' she squeaks. 'Please.'

'I'm sorry, but not yet. Not until we have some answers,' says Ryan.

'What answers? What are you talking about? If you want answers, I suggest you ask Jane.'

'She's already told me the truth about what happened with The Twin Killer,' replies Ryan, looking over his shoulder at Jane.

'Good,' spits Christie. 'So that means I've figured out who murdered Annie Patterson. I win the game. So let me out of here!' she screams at the ceiling. Christie kicks her legs out and manages to manoeuvre her body until she is kneeling.

'We're clearly missing something,' says Jane, taking a step forwards. 'I'm not sure that—'

'Congratulations. You three have made it to the next stage of The Murder Maze. To escape from this room and continue, you must solve the following riddle. "I was once alive. Now, I am not. I am much larger than any of you." You have five minutes to complete this riddle and leave this part of the maze. Good luck.'

Christie wobbles so much that she collapses back to the ground. Jane's eyes grow wide as she searches for the location of the voice, but Ryan remains still.

'What the fuck!' shouts Christie. 'I solved your shitty murder. Why are we all working together again now?' She tugs harder on the rope. 'Will someone let me go!'

Ryan and Jane swap looks. Ryan shrugs. 'I guess questioning her is a bit redundant now.'

Jane nods in agreement.

'Four minutes and thirty seconds remaining.'

'What's going to happen if we run out of time?' asks Jane.

Christie rubs her wrists as Ryan releases her and scrambles to her feet, ready to bolt at a moment's notice. 'Do you really want to stick around and find out?' She gulps in air too fast, hyperventilating. She places a hand against her heart to steady it.

'Okay, so what is larger than any of us and was once alive but is now dead?' asks Ryan.

There is a five-second beat of silence.

'Andrew,' says Jane and Ryan at the same.

Christie shakes her head. 'Oh, fuck no, I'm not going back in there with all that blood.'

'Fine, then stay here,' says Jane, already turning to run back down the passageway towards the metal room where Andrew is laying.

Christie watches Ryan and Jane run out of the room.

'Four minutes remaining.'

'Fine, have it your way,' she says with a sigh. And then she runs after them.

Chapter Forty-Two

Jane

'Three minutes and thirty seconds remaining.'

'That's really not helping,' shouts Jane as she arrives in the metal room, but she lets out a scream and comes to an abrupt halt, skidding and almost losing her balance on the blood-spattered floor.

It's not possible.

She glances from left to right, searching for the answer to what she's seeing, but there's nothing. It must be true.

Ryan appears next to her seconds later, slightly out of breath, having run to keep up with her. 'Why did you scream? What's going— What the hell?'

The place where Andrew took his last breath is now only a smeared puddle of blood.

His body is gone.

But that isn't the main reason why Jane's blood turns to ice in her veins.

There are no drag marks.

There are large footprints in the blood that lead to the nearest wall and then stop.

'Three minutes remaining.'

'Where the hell is he? Did he just get up and disappear through the wall?' Jane jogs to the wall and runs her hands over it, searching for a join, for a mark; anything.

'He was dead. He lost so much blood. He was definitely dead, right?' says Ryan. He stands at the edge of the blood pool with his hands on his hips, scanning the area for some sort of explanation. 'The riddle was supposed to lead us back to his body, so where …'

'Oh my God,' says Jane. She stares open-mouthed at the ceiling.

An array of symbols are crudely drawn on the ceiling with blood, by the looks of it with someone's fingers. None of the symbols make any sense. They resemble Egyptian hieroglyphics but are also similar to cave drawings.

'I think we're supposed to decipher those,' says Jane, pointing upwards.

Ryan follows her finger. 'How are we supposed to figure out all that in less than—'

'Two minutes and thirty seconds remaining.'

Ryan sighs. 'Yes, thank you!'

Jane holds up her hands. 'Okay, let's think about this. There's no way anyone could possibly decipher symbols like that in such a short amount of time.'

'That really doesn't help.'

'I think they're a distraction.' Jane turns back to the wall. 'I think we're supposed to follow Andrew through the wall.'

Ryan joins her side. 'There is no way that Andrew got up and walked away. He's dead.'

'Okay, so someone moved him and has made it *look* as if he's got up and walked away.'

'Why?'

'To mess with our heads! Don't you get it? This whole thing has been about confusing us, making us face our fears and turn on each other. This is a psychological game now. We have to outsmart it and get out of here alive.'

'Two minutes remaining.'

Ryan glances back at the wall. Christie has just entered the room and is staring at the blood on the floor and ceiling. Her face turns pale and she gags, closing her eyes and muttering incoherently.

'Don't look at it,' says Jane.

'Where the hell is his body?' Christie asks in a whisper.

'We're assuming he disappeared through this wall,' replies Jane.

'Dead bodies don't just get up and walk through walls.' Christie makes a wide circle around the blood pool, tiptoeing around it as if she's stone-stepping across a river. She joins them by the wall. 'What are those symbols above us?'

'They're nothing.'

'How do you know?'

'I don't, I just ... it's just a hunch.'

Christie laughs. 'We're supposed to risk our lives based on your hunch?'

'Unless you have a better idea.' Jane rarely confronts people, but this is no ordinary situation. She has to take control now. She must get out of this place. There is no other option, and she isn't about to trust anyone except herself to get the job done. Even Ryan.

Christie looks down at the footprints that end just before they reach the wall. 'What the fuck ... This makes no sense.'

'One minute and thirty seconds remaining.'

'None of this makes sense. On the count of three, we push the wall,' says Jane.

Ryan nods, understanding her idea. Sometimes the simplest answer can turn out to be the right one. He rolls up his sleeves.

Christie sighs heavily as she gets into position next to Ryan. All three of them line up against the wall with their hands pressed against it.

'One ... two ... three ... push!'

Jane presses all her weight into her hands. Ryan leans his shoulder against the wall for more leverage, but almost immediately slips in the blood on the floor.

Jane stops pushing.

'One minute remaining.'

'Well, that didn't work. Now what, genius?' snaps Christie.

Jane bites her tongue before she shouts something sarcastic back at her. Her heart feels as if it's about to explode. Her mouth is so dry, her tongue like sandpaper. The throbbing pain in her head no doubt caused by the beginning of dehydration is making her brain slower to respond than normal.

Think …

The symbols. The blood. They are there for a reason.

Maybe they aren't a distraction. Maybe they are supposed to be there …

Jane cranks her neck back and memorises the first two symbols. She splashes both hands into the puddle of blood and then crudely begins to trace the symbols on the wall.

'Thirty seconds remaining.'

There aren't many, but her shaking hands and pounding heart make it difficult to focus and see straight.

'Ten … nine …'

Jane is close to finishing drawing the final two symbols. As she draws the last line, the wall on which she's painting begins to recede, revealing yet another dark, empty hallway beyond.

'Seven … six … five …'

Christie shoves Jane aside and sprints through the open doorway.

Jane's feet slip out from underneath her on the bloody floor.

Ryan grabs her arm, yanks her to her feet and pushes her through the hole.

'Three … two … one …'

A loud bang erupts from behind them. The ground shakes and the walls tremble.

Jane and Ryan stumble into each other as the door behind them slams shut just as an enormous fireball engulfs the previous room. Jane sees Ryan's eyes widen as the flames attempt to squeeze between the crack in the door.

He screams.

The roaring inferno continues behind the now sealed door.

But they are safe … for now.

Jane and Ryan remain on the floor, tangled in each other's bodies while they catch their breaths. Christie has disappeared.

'Thanks,' says Jane with a sigh.

'Don't mention it,' he replies. 'Close call, huh?'

'Maybe a little too close.'

'We're not all going to get out of this alive, are we?'

Jane positions herself so she is on her knees and places both hands on each of his shoulders, forcing him to look at her.

'We are going to get out of this alive … because we don't have a choice. Our children need us.'

Chapter Forty-Three
Ryan

Ryan's eyes flood with tears. Jane's words strike him to the core, making him almost double over as if a swift blow has landed to his gut. He feels it in his soul, and he can barely breathe. For a moment, he lets his mind imagine the worst, that he'll never get out of here and see his girls again. They'll grow up without a father. Perhaps Amanda will be able to adopt them. They have no one else.

But Jane is right. There is no other choice. They *have* to escape.

Ryan rolls onto his back and stares at the dark ceiling. His heart is beating hard in his chest, that spike of adrenaline slowly receding, allowing his body to return to a normal rhythm. His ears ring from the loud explosion. The sweat that's soaked into his shirt has now begun to dry, leaving a musty odour that offends his nostrils.

Jane stands up beside him. She extends her hand. He looks at it, still smeared with dried blood, and then into her kind eyes before taking it. She pulls him to his feet.

'You ready?' she asks.

'Not really ... I have to hand it to you; you're handling this whole thing a lot better than I am.'

'Unfortunately, it's not the first time I've been captured and tortured, albeit in a different way.'

Ryan's face burns. 'Right. Sorry.'

'Don't be. It's made me tougher in more ways than one.'

Ryan glances down the passageway where Christie had run only moments ago. 'I guess we'd better go after her.'

Jane nods as she moves forwards to proceed, but Ryan stops her by extending his arm. She bumps into it with her chest. 'Let me go first.'

Jane doesn't argue, but she keeps close on his heels as they creep along the tunnel.

Ryan doesn't like the way his stomach churns as he inches forwards. He doesn't like the way his body is shaking of its own accord either. He feels as if he needs a weapon to hold in front of him, in case something jumps out and attacks; anything to defend himself against an unknown enemy.

The air is damp and rotten, like they are creeping further down into the belly of a blood-thirsty beast. Almost on cue, a low rumble sounds throughout the tunnel.

'What the hell was that?' whispers Jane.

'I have no idea,' replies Ryan, almost copying her whisper. He realises he is being ridiculous by whispering, but it feels like the right thing to do. Really, they should be calling out to Christie to find out where she is and if she's okay. It was rather reckless of her to run off without them into the unknown.

Ryan reaches a T junction and stops. The tunnel is barely light enough to see his surroundings, as if he is walking along a dark path under the light of the moon. He looks up. There is no moon. There is no way of knowing how far underground they are, buried into the rock of the island. Or perhaps they aren't underground at all. Everything is an illusion here.

'Left or right?' he asks Jane.

'Oh God, this is actually a maze, isn't it? Like a proper maze.'

'It might be ... Christie?' Ryan projects his voice a little louder, hoping he'll get a response, but none comes. Not even an echo bounces back.

'Whenever Ben and I go into one of those adventure park mazes, I always tell him to follow one wall and stick to it.'

Ryan shrugs. 'That sounds like good advice to me.' He places his left hand on the left wall. 'Let's go but keep your hand on my shoulder so we don't get lost.'

'Okay.'

The wall is rugged and cold. He's taken back to his childhood when he frequented funfairs or parks with his brother. Once, his younger brother had gotten lost in a maze made of thick hedges. Ryan hadn't been able to get to him and had attempted to retrace his steps to the start and fetch his parents but had then become lost as well. Luckily, his brother had been found by a kind stranger who'd walked him to the nearest exit. Ryan had stumbled out several minutes later, scared and worried for his brother. While it hadn't been a tormenting experience, it doesn't help to quell his anxiety the further into the maze he goes.

At every turn in the path, he keeps his hand against the left wall, never losing touch.

'Stop,' whispers Jane. She digs her nails into his shoulder. 'I think I can hear Christie.'

Ryan stops and they listen for several seconds.

Jane digs her nails into his shoulder again as a garbled cry pierces the darkness. The sound doesn't seem to come from any given direction but all around, as if coming from surround-sound speakers.

'Come on,' says Ryan, pressing onwards as Jane shuffles behind him.

When he reaches the next corner, the passage becomes narrower. Ryan squeezes between the sides of the maze. He feels Jane's hand lift from his shoulder.

'Stay close.' He is silently relieved that Andrew isn't with them. Not only would he have refused to squeeze himself down the passage, but it is highly likely he wouldn't have even been able to fit thanks to his large chest and shoulders.

'Jane!' Christie's pained cry comes again.

'Christie, stay where you are!' shouts Ryan.

'We're coming!' replies Jane.

Ryan increases his speed but finds it more and more difficult to keep the momentum due to the narrow passage.

But then it widens, and a bright light illuminates their path, revealing the true horrors of what surrounds them.

It doesn't appear to be the middle of the maze, but it is a large clearing and Christie is slumped in the middle of it, a metal clamp digging into her right ankle. While there isn't a huge amount of blood, there is still blood around the wound where the teeth of the bear trap have bitten into her tender flesh. Tears stream from her eyes as she catches sight of Ryan and Jane.

'Help me!'

Ryan rushes ahead and kneels next to her, assessing the damage. 'It's okay, I don't think it's hit a major artery or anything.'

'Do you think it's broken?' Christie asks with a sob.

Ryan shakes his head. 'Hard to tell.'

'It really hurts.'

'I'll try and be careful.'

Jane appears above him. 'What happened, Christie? Why'd you run off like that? Do you realise how stupid that was?'

'I panicked, okay?'

'Ryan and I were lucky to have even gotten out of that room alive after you shoved your way past us and knocked me over.'

Ryan looks up at Jane and gives a slight shake of the head to signal to not make things any worse. Jane sighs. It's understandable that she is frustrated.

'After three, I'm going to try and pull apart the jaws of this trap,' says Ryan.

Christie lets out a whimper but nods her head.

'One ... two ... three!'

The scream that comes out of Christie's mouth rattles the surrounding area and makes Ryan's stomach do a back flip. It's animalistic in nature.

Chapter Forty-Four
Christie

Red hot pain floods Christie's body like a tidal wave. Her jaw clenches and her eyes roll back. She's on the verge of passing out. She can't look at what Ryan is doing. It feels like he's sawing her foot off with a blunt, rusty knife. The teeth of the trap are sharp enough to have pierced her skin and surrounding muscle in her ankle, but thankfully not sharp enough to have sliced through her bone. It doesn't make it any less painful though.

Sweat drips down her face as Ryan slowly pries the jaws apart. She shuffles backwards, away from the trap, and sits panting, clutching her injured ankle. Jane kneels next to her and places a hand on her shoulder. As much as Christie despises the woman, she must admit she is grateful Jane appears to care about her well-being, even though Christie almost killed her earlier.

'Thanks,' says Christie to Ryan, who nods in return.

Jane inspects the wound. 'It's cut pretty deep. We need to wrap this up to stop the bleeding.'

Christie swallows the bile in her throat, turning away from the blood as it drips onto the floor. Jane manages to rip a piece of her top, revealing her soft midriff, complete with caesarean scar and the Gemini brand on her side. She begins to rip large pieces of it into strips.

'What happened? We didn't hear any sort of mechanism release. The jaws on that trap should have done a lot more damage to your ankle. You were lucky,' says Jane.

Christie scoffs as she pulls her trouser leg up, revealing a perfect bite mark around her ankle. Blood oozes from the wound. 'Does this look like I was lucky to you?'

'I'm just saying, I've heard of people snapping their ankles in half by stepping on one of those.'

Christie mumbles a few choice words. 'I guess I am lucky then.'

'Perhaps it was designed to just hurt rather than maim,' says Ryan, but no one answers him directly.

Jane wraps the material around Christie's ankle, pulling it tight. 'I'll ask you again ... What happened?'

Christie flinches as Jane tightens the material. They aren't letting this go, are they? 'It was dark. I ran through the maze and fell into the trap. The end.' She watches as Ryan and Jane exchange looks. They are turning against her. Fine. Let them. She doesn't need them on her side. She just needs them to help her get the hell out of here.

'What's the plan now?' asks Jane, turning to Ryan.

He runs his hands through his hair and looks around the clearing. 'I don't think this is the centre of the maze. We need to keep going. Christie, do you think you can walk?'

'Not without help.'

'I'll help you,' says Jane, already taking her arm and draping it across her shoulders.

Ryan moves towards them. 'No, I'll do it.'

'Why, because you're a man and therefore stronger?' Jane snaps.

Ryan flinches. 'N-No ... because ...'

'I'd rather you go ahead of us and lead the way.'

'Okay, fine.'

Christie smirks at the palpable tension between them. Ryan and Jane, once allies, are fraying at the edges, losing their nerve, and beginning to mistrust each other.

Christie leans into Jane as she struggles to her feet. She attempts to put weight through her swollen ankle and flinches when a sharp pain erupts, taking her breath away. She tries again, this time ready for the pain. She nods at Jane, signalling that she is ready.

Ryan walks slowly, keeping his left hand on the left wall of the maze as they manoeuvre through the various twists and turns.

The darkness makes things more difficult. Noises on either side cause Christie to flinch. It feels as if they've been in this maze for days or even longer.

'What time is it?' asks Christie.

'No idea,' replies Jane. 'No watches, remember?'

'I'm starving.'

'Me too. My stomach feels like it's trying to eat itself.'

Ryan holds up his hand and the women stop. 'Anyone feel that?'

'Feel what?' asks Jane.

As soon as Jane asks the question, Christie understands what Ryan is talking about. A cool breeze floats along the tunnel. Christie shivers. 'Are we outside?'

'We can't be. We're underground,' replies Ryan.

They press on further until the passageway in the maze opens into a large open-air clearing. Christie looks up. Stars twinkle above them. The moon illuminates the area like a light bulb and casts shadows all around.

'What the hell is going on?' asks Jane. 'How can we be outside? I thought we were underground, under the house.'

'We're not outside,' replies Ryan. 'It's another illusion.'

Chapter Forty-Five
Jane

Unless somehow Ryan is right and it's an illusion, there is no mistaking the fact they are standing outside in the open. How can they not be? There's even the faint salty smell of the sea. Jane can taste it on her tongue. The maze has led them to a clearing near the edge of a steep cliff, but there doesn't appear to be any way out of the area, except to go back through the maze. A faint breeze blows across the cliffs, bringing with it tiny splashes of sea water as it crashes against the rocks. It whips around them, flicking Jane's hair across her face and making it stick to her skin. She lowers Christie to the ground and then stretches her back, relieved to have the weight off her shoulders. She joins Ryan at the edge of the cliff and looks down. Jagged rocks and white horses are below them.

'How is this not real?' she asks.

'AI and virtual reality have come a long way in the past decade or so,' is the response from Ryan, who stares down below without blinking. Is he watching something or seen something?

'But ... Is any of this real? Did we even come to an island off the coast of Wales, or are we just in some large warehouse or something?' Jane looks up at the night sky. The stars are twinkling. If it is fake, then it's a bloody good show.

'Your guess is as good as mine, I'm afraid. Perhaps we're just exhausted and hallucinating, delicious from hunger.'

It's a possibility.

'No one knows we're here,' she whispers. She knew that before, but now it feels even more real, more ... foreboding. They may never get off this island. They may never be found. She may never see her son again. It's impossible to comprehend. Ryan shakes his head but says nothing. 'Ryan, we *need* to figure this out. I *need* to get off this island, or wherever the hell we are. Please ... whatever it is you did, it doesn't matter now. All that matters is getting away from here.'

'I didn't do anything. I swear to you on my daughters' lives. I didn't kill my wife.'

Jane stares into his dark eyes and sees a terrified father staring back. What is she thinking? Or course he didn't kill his wife and steal his children. He's an honest man. She can see it in his eyes. The way he looks back at her makes her feel safe. She believes him.

Jane glances back at Christie, who is staring at them as they speak. 'Okay,' she says. 'Then we need to speak to Christie.'

'She won't tell us anything.'

'We have to try.'

'And then what? Look around, Jane. We're on our own here. We always have been.'

'Apart from the hooded figure and whoever it is who's speaking to us through a sound system. Quite possibly they are the same person. I think our next course of action is to find out about Luke and whether Christie killed him.'

Ryan sighs as he stares out across the water. 'Okay,' he finally says. There is a hardness to his voice now. Jane had sensed the shift in his character a few hours ago. Her stomach growls at her and she presses her fingers into her side.

She watches him walk back to Christie and sit down on the ground next to her.

'Time to start talking,' he says to her.

Jane joins them. 'I've confessed. Now it's your turn,' she adds.

Christie glances from one person to the next and then laughs. 'You two have no idea what you're doing, do you?'

'Oh, and you do?' snaps Jane. She's had enough of Christie and her holier-than-thou attitude. If she's the one who is holding them back, then it's about time she speaks up.

'Hell, if I knew what I was doing, I'd have been out of here by now.'

'You seem very sure of yourself,' answers Jane.

'I have to be. When you've had no one to depend on your entire life, you have to be sure of yourself. I've had to be strong and do whatever it takes to survive.'

'Is that why you killed your brother?' asks Jane, straight to the point.

Christie bites her lip. 'Fuck you.'

Jane sighs. She has no idea what lies ahead, but it's better than standing around and waiting for something to happen. She needs to keep pushing. Sooner or later, the weird voice will come again and tell them the next phase.

'It's pointless staying here. We haven't reached the centre of the maze yet.'

'So we need to go back inside again?' asks Christie.

'That or tell us what we need to know.'

'I don't know anything.'

'Fine, have it your way.' Jane gets up.

'Come on,' says Ryan. He bends down and helps Christie to her feet. 'Let's go.'

Christie shoots Jane a stern look as she passes her. Jane watches the two of them hobble slowly towards where they entered the outside area and then follows.

Jane doesn't know how long they stumble through the dark. It's hard to tell if they're going back the way they came or are creeping down a new path in the maze. Every turn looks the same. She feels dizzy, which is either due to the constant walking around in circles or the lack of food and water. How long's it been now since she drank anything? A few hours or a few days? Her eyes are so heavy, it's difficult to keep them open as she stumbles through the dark maze, keeping her left hand on the left wall as Ryan and Christie shuffle ahead.

Jane is concentrating so hard on keeping her eyes open that she walks straight into the back of Ryan. 'What the ...'

Jane peers past him. There are three doors in front of them.

'Oh, great,' says Christie. 'What now?'

'Congratulations. You have now reached Stage Three of The Murder Maze. One member of your group is lying. One is telling the truth. And one is innocent. You now must choose who is who and enter the correct door. Good luck.'

'What the fuck?' says Christie.

Ryan lowers Christie to the floor and walks up to the nearest door, which is the middle of the three and coloured bright red. The door on the right is black and the door on the left is pure white. There are no door handles or knobs of any kind.

'So which door is which? I'm assuming black is the lie door, or maybe it's the red and white is either the truth or the innocent door, but which is which?' asks Jane. She approaches the white door and presses her left ear against it. She hears a faint ticking coming from behind it. She does the same thing with the red door and then the black. Each one has something behind it that is ticking.

'But how are we supposed to—' Ryan stops as he sees what Jane is now seeing. In the middle of each door, words slowly appear as if by magic.

Liar appears on the black door. Innocent on the red and Truth on the white.

'What the hell?' She approaches the black door and places her hand on it, but nothing happens. She repeats the process for the red door, then the white. As her hand touches the white door, a loud click sounds and then it recedes into the floor, revealing a white room beyond. From where she is standing, it's hard to see how large it is. The walls are so bright and white that she has to shield her eyes.

Ryan copies her actions, touching the red door, but it stays shut. He sighs and places his palm on the black door, which opens to reveal a dark room.

Christie shuffles over to the red door, and it opens to a red room.

'What does this mean? Do the doors only open for the right person?' he asks.

'I'm not sure,' replies Jane. 'But I guess so.'

'B-But I'm innocent,' says Ryan. 'I should be going into the white room.'

Jane looks at him. She doesn't know what to say. According to the voice, the black door means Ryan is lying. 'I'm guessing we have to go in and find out,' says Jane.

'I don't like this,' says Christie. 'What if we're trapped inside?'

'I think that might be the general idea,' answers Jane.

'It's okay for you. Your room doesn't look as if the walls are bleeding.'

Jane can't argue against that. She's relieved she doesn't have to enter a black room or a blood room.

'Good luck. See you on the other side,' she says.

Ryan nods at her, sweat beading on his top lip.

Jane passes over the threshold. As soon as she does, the door shoots up from the floor, locking her inside. Now, she realises that the room is roughly the size of a car in diameter. And there is nothing to suggest a way out, other than the door she's come in through, which has now disappeared.

It feels as if she's standing on a cloud. She can't distinguish between up or down.

'Now what?' she says to the empty space.

'Welcome, Jane Patterson. Congratulations on making it this far and for telling the truth. You shall now be rewarded with a show.'

'Wait ... What? A show?'

As soon as she's finished speaking, an image appears in front of her, like a television screen hovering in the white space. The image is of Christie sitting on the floor inside the red room. She doesn't look good. She's trembling from head to toe with her eyes closed.

'Oh God,' says Jane. Her throat constricts as she watches Christie on the screen. She's helpless to stop whatever is going to happen. What is going to happen now?

Chapter Forty-Six
The Mastermind

Oh, goody! This is the part I've been looking forward to the most. They've finally reached the doors and by the looks of it, just in time. It means they are very nearly at the end of the game. All three of them are on their last legs. Christie quite literally. Her ankle wound looks pretty bad, but at least she's not bleeding to death … yet.

The outside arena was fun, wasn't it? I almost pissed myself when they kept thinking they were still underground. They must be very disorientated. Perhaps they are hallucinating a bit due to dehydration. I gave them a bit of water at the start, but it seems it wasn't nearly enough to keep their minds and bodies sustained because all three of them are now showing dangerous signs of dehydration. It won't be long before one of them passes out, but I hope that doesn't happen just yet. The best bit is coming up.

I watch Jane enter the white room and laugh as the door seals shut behind her. Leaning forwards, I press the intercom button.

'Welcome, Jane Patterson. Congratulations on making it this far and for telling the truth. You shall now be rewarded with a show.'

And … play.

Chapter Forty-Seven

Ryan

The black room is so dark that not even a pinprick of light can pierce it. Since the door closed behind him, he hasn't been able to see a thing. His eyes haven't adjusted to the darkness. He doubts there's anything to see anyway. He stretches his arms out in front of him and feels his way around, shuffling his feet, until he walks into a solid wall.

He runs his hands across it, finding a corner, then follows it around in a square. It's a small room, no bigger than a large car. But black. Completely black.

'Welcome, Ryan Neville. Congratulations on making it this far. However, you are not telling the truth and shall now be forced to watch a show that you could have prevented had you been man enough to admit what you did.'

The noise echoes around him, loud and eerie and distorted.

'What? I didn't do anything!' he screams. 'I've been set up! I'm telling the truth!'

'Is anyone there?' Christie's panicky voice makes him spin around. A screen has appeared on the black wall showing her inside the red room, shaking on the floor. 'Please,' she begs. 'Help me.'

'Christie, can you hear me?'

'Ryan?'

'Yeah, are you okay?'

'What's going on?'

'I don't know. Can you see or hear Jane?'

'No.'

'Has the weird voice spoken to you?'

She shakes her head. 'No, it hasn't ... I ...'

'Welcome, Christie Truman, or should I call you Laura Blake? Congratulations on getting this far, but unfortunately, despite being innocent, you are to be punished for Ryan's inability to tell the truth. You will now suffer the consequences of his actions.'

'Wait ... What!' she shrieks.

'No!' Ryan lunges towards the wall and pounds his fists against the screen, but it's merely a reflection. 'Stop, please. Don't punish her.'

'Tell the truth, Ryan!' shouts Christie, shaking.

Ryan tilts his head to the ceiling and screams as he drags his fingers down his face, feeling the burn as his nails scrape a layer of skin off.

'I am! I didn't kill her!'

'Wrong answer.'

Chapter Forty-Eight
Christie

The colour of blood burns her eyes. It's like she's underwater. No, under the blood, swimming in it, and she can't escape. She can't breathe. She's breathing in blood, into her lungs, and it's suffocating her, sliding down her throat. She clutches her neck and gags, reaching forwards to grab onto something for support, but there's nothing there.

Christie can't see Ryan, but she can hear him. And the weird voice. She begs him to tell the truth, but he keeps repeating that he is. He is telling the truth.

She doesn't understand. She's not innocent. She did kill her brother, so why …

'*Wrong answer.*'

Fuck!

Christie covers her head with her arms and attempts to make herself as small as possible. It shouldn't be this way. She shouldn't be cowering on the floor like a scared child. She's better than this. When she arrived here, she felt strong, determined. She had a plan and was going to see it through no matter what. Get the money. That had been her plan, but now she's trapped in a blood room, waiting for whatever freaky punishment is coming her way, all because a fucking man won't man the fuck up and tell the truth.

'Laura Blake, it's time for you to tell the truth. You may be innocent, but you've also been lying, haven't you? Here's your chance to come clean.'

Wait ... What?

Christie lifts her head up, sniffing loudly. 'I don't ... understand.'

Silence.

'Innocence doesn't always mean that you are innocent of a crime. You were an innocent girl, and you made the wrong decision. It's time to admit the truth.'

Christie's eyes fill with tears. 'Okay, fine.' She wipes her runny nose with the back of her hand, pulls her knees up to her chest and talks slowly. If the truth is what they want, then that's what they'll get.

'I was thirteen years old when my brother first raped me. He was sixteen. It happened a lot after that because I never said no. I didn't say yes, but I didn't say no. I was too scared. I didn't know what to do and he was gentle and said it was all okay.' She takes a deep breath as tears stream down her cheeks, running into her mouth as she speaks.

'After two years, he stopped because he moved away to university, leaving me at home. Mum left years ago, while I was still a baby, and Dad liked to gamble. Dad even taught me how to gamble, opened bank accounts in my name, forged my signature, faked my age, signed me up to different online betting accounts so he could double his winnings.' Christie bites her lip. 'I joined in too. I couldn't stop. At fifteen, I was a gambling addict, lying about my age with a fake ID my dad got me. But then Dad died in a hit and run. A freak accident. I had no other choice. I had to contact my brother. He was my next of kin and dropped out of university to look after me. But he found out about the gambling, took over all my money and bank accounts, took everything from me. For two years he ruled my life, threatened to hand me into the police. We had to move into a caravan park. It was the only place we could afford. He worked a lot and so did I, just at a bar. Once I was eighteen, I began to use every penny I had to fund my gambling habit again. He found out.'

Christie stops and slowly gets to her feet. She leans against the blood wall and looks up at the ceiling. 'The night he found out, he attacked me. He was going to rape me again, I could tell. I didn't have a choice. I killed him. I smashed his head in with a hammer and hid in the cupboard. I had a mental breakdown and was sent to a hospital to recover, but they were going to charge me with his murder. I ran. I escaped but I wasn't well. I was very confused.' Christie retches again, but nothing comes up. She continues to cry.

'I changed my name and met a man called Trevor, who helped me. Maybe he felt sorry for me, I don't know. He looked after me and we started dating, but ... I began stealing money from him. Eventually, he broke up with me and I went out on my own again, but things just went from bad to worse. I couldn't keep a job. I couldn't open another bank account. I had nothing. I was kicked out of the room I was renting and started living on the streets. Eventually, I went back to Trevor, and he let me stay with him. The next morning, when I woke up, I received the invitation to this place ...'

Christie blows out a long breath. 'So, you see, I *did* kill my brother, but I'm innocent in all this. Yes, I have a gambling problem, and I've done some pretty awful things to fund it, but ... I only killed my brother to protect myself, but no one sees it that way. If the police ever caught up to me, I'd go to prison for life, or be locked up in that facility again.'

She looks up at the ceiling. 'Is that what you want!' She erupts into loud sobs, not even bothering to try and stop them. They rattle her body as she collapses to the ground again and rests her forehead on the red floor. Tears drip down, forming a small puddle.

'Congratulations, Laura Blake. That was quite a show. Thank you for sharing with us. However, it is still up to Ryan whether you live or die. Ryan Neville, you have one minute to decide.'

Chapter Forty-Nine

Jane

She can't believe what she's just heard come from Christie's mouth. She's misjudged Christie from the beginning. The woman has suffered so much torment and abuse and has been alone all this time with no one supporting or believing her. And she's about to die if Ryan doesn't tell the truth.

She knows neither Christie nor Ryan can hear her, but she shouts his name anyway, begging him to do the right thing. But he merely shakes his head on the screen in front of her.

'I'm sorry,' he says as tears stream down his face. 'I can't.' He collapses into a heap on the floor and covers his head with his hands, screaming into the floor. 'I can't. I can't. It's too awful. I can't. It didn't happen. It wasn't me!'

'Ryan! For fuck's sake,' screams Jane. 'Just tell the fucking truth!'

'Thirty seconds remaining …'

Christie is crying, not even bothering to beg Ryan to save her life. Maybe she knows it's over. He won't say it. He won't save her. Jane has misjudged Ryan too, believing him to be the good guy. She was wrong to trust him.

Jane is helpless as she watches the two people on the screen cry, but for different reasons. Time seems to tick by so slowly, but then …

'Three ... two ... one ... Ryan Neville, your time is up.'

Jane holds her breath. Nothing seems to happen for several seconds, but then Christie stops crying and starts coughing, grasping at her throat and scratching at her eyes. Jane blinks back waves of tears as blood spurts from Christie's mouth and she chokes on it, eventually slumping back to the floor, gargling and suffocating on the one thing she's afraid of.

The life drains from her painfully slowly. Jane can't look away. Even though Christie can't see or hear her, she wants to witness her final moments, be there for her even though she doesn't know it. A red-hot anger ignites inside Jane as Christie takes her final agonising breath.

Ryan is weeping on the floor, having buried his head the whole time Christie was dying because of him. He couldn't even watch her die. He's a coward. Jane grits her teeth as she stares at his reflection, promising herself that she'll make him pay for what he's done. She'll get the truth out of him one way or another. No matter what it takes, Ryan Neville will pay for allowing Christie to die for him.

'Congratulations, Jane and Ryan. You are the final two contestants. Please make your way along the path to the final area where you will find everything you need to finish the game. Good luck.'

Chapter Fifty
Ryan

What has he done? He's let someone die because he's too much of a coward to admit the truth. But saying the truth out loud will kill him. It will literally kill him. Destroy him from the inside. He must stay alive for his girls. They need him. He needs to get back to them, keep them safe, raise them and love them. It's awful that Christie is dead, but better her than him.

He must finish this.

Ryan looks up as a door opens in front of him, a few dull lights illuminating the narrow pathway. He sniffs loudly and wipes his runny nose and eyes on his shirt sleeve before limping towards freedom. His body aches as if he's run a marathon up a mountain carrying a heavy pack. There's nothing left in his legs. Every step takes so much effort, he almost passes out. How long's it been since he ate? How long have they been in here? Hours? Days? It's taking every effort to not collapse on the floor and stay there forever, ignoring everything else in the world. Sometimes he wishes he could do that.

It only takes a few minutes before Ryan reaches the end of the path. There's a simple door with a handle waiting for him. He frowns at it. What, no puzzle to solve? No weird trap? Just a door?

Ryan grasps the handle, pushes down and pulls the door open.

No ... way.

His mouth drops open as he enters the main hallway of the house, the first room the four of them had entered, however many hours or days ago it was. How is he back here? Weren't they underground? Or has this been one big illusion from the start?

The door slams shut behind him, making him jump.

He waits ...

The minutes tick by. Jane must be on her way. He's dreading seeing her after what he's just done. He killed Christie. What must Jane think of him? Why does he even care what she thinks? She's practically a stranger. As much as he likes her, he can't think about her or worry about her well-being. If he's given a choice between her or him, he'll choose himself. He has to. For his girls.

A loud click emanates from the opposite end of the room. A door creaks open and Jane appears. They see each other. They stare.

'Jane ... I'm sorry. I'm telling the truth, I promise,' he pleads.

The door slams shut behind Jane. 'If you were telling the truth then Christie wouldn't be dead, would she, Ryan?'

'You don't understand. I can't ... I'll lose them. I'll lose everything.'

'Maybe you deserve to lose everything.' Jane walks forwards and stands in front of him. 'The voice said we'll find everything we need in order to finish the game.'

Ryan nods and looks around. 'But there's nothing here.'

'Except us.'

'Except us,' echoes Ryan.

'Tell the truth. Please, Ryan. It's the only way to get out of here.'

Ryan laughs. 'You don't get it, do you? I can't tell the truth because I don't remember, okay? I don't remember!' he shouts at the ceiling.

'Ryan Neville, let me refresh your memory.'

This time, the voice isn't coming from any speakers. It isn't distorted or eerie, but close by and clear. Jane and Ryan turn and look towards the top of the stairs. The hooded figure is back. It walks down the stairs, taking its time, each step slow and deliberate. Ryan doesn't move. His whole body is frozen. Is it the same figure as before? It's hard to tell. His mind can't even remember that far back.

The figure stops at the bottom of the stairs, reaches its hands up and pulls back the dark hood covering its face. Finally, the face of the figure is revealed.

Ryan shakes his head and almost collapses to the floor.

No ... it can't be.

It's not possible.

Chapter Fifty-One
Jane

Jane's mouth drops open. Ryan's does the same thing. How is this possible? The person who has walked down the stairs, the person who is wearing the black hooded cape, the person standing in front of them now ... cannot be real. She's seeing things. She must be.

Ryan looks as stunned as she does. He's crumpled to the ground, his hands covering his face as if he can't bear to look a moment longer. Does he know this person too? How can he know them?

How does he know The Twin Killer?

Because that's who has pulled back the hood and is now standing at the bottom of the stairs, grinning at them. She looks different than when Jane last saw her. She has a thick dark fringe covering her forehead, shielding what she knows is under there: a Gemini brand. Her eyes are different too.

'Hello, Jane. Hello, Ryan. I should have known it would be you two who reached the end.'

Ryan finally gets a grip of himself and drags his hands down his face, revealing red, puffy eyes and pale skin. 'A-Amanda? What the hell is going on? What are you doing here? Where are Faith and Hope?'

Jane frowns as he says her name. Amanda. Is that her name? 'Isn't Amanda your ...'

'Au pair,' finishes Ryan.

'B-But ... she's The Twin Killer,' I say.

'That's impossible.'

Jane points at her. 'I'm telling you, that woman kidnapped me, tortured me and forced me to kill my sister. I'd never forget her face.'

Ryan opens and closes his mouth. 'It can't be.'

Amanda smiles, showing her perfect, straight teeth. Her eyes are blue, different than the dark brown she remembers. 'I'm sure you both have many questions, but I'm afraid you don't have a lot of time left to finish the game.'

'This is ridiculous,' snaps Ryan. 'Amanda, where are my girls? Are they safe? Why are you here?'

'The girls are both fine. Trust me.'

'Trust you? How can I trust you? Have you been playing me all this time? Did you set all this up? It doesn't make any sense that you're here.'

Amanda remains still and calm. She looks straight at Jane, and her heart skips a beat. Those eyes. They may be blue, but they still pierce straight through her, opening every wound she struggled so hard to close over the past five years. She needs answers.

'Show me,' she says.

Amanda smiles again as she raises a hand and lifts her thick fringe away from her forehead. Jane inches closer, eyes focused on the area. There is no Gemini brand, but there's something that doesn't look quite right. A layer of make-up, perhaps? The skin is slightly puckered and red.

'I've had several skin grafts over the years. It hasn't gone completely, but foundation helps cover the remaining scar tissue,' she says, letting her fringe fall back down. 'Now show me yours.'

Jane pulls up her top and turns to the side, revealing the brand. 'Why?' she asks. 'Why have you waited so long to come after me? Why have you involved all these other people?'

Amanda takes a deep breath. 'Because, Jane, they are all guilty of something. They have all taken something from me, and I wanted to punish them. But this whole thing has never really been about you. It's been about him.' She points at Ryan, who gasps loudly.

'Why me? What have I ever done to you? I trusted you with my daughters. I allowed you into my house to care for them. I ... Why would you do this to me, to them?'

'Because,' she says slowly, 'they are not *your* daughters, Ryan. They are *mine*.'

Chapter Fifty-Two
Amanda/The Twin Killer/The Mastermind

As soon as I spoke to Jane, I knew she was special. There was something different about her; something I could relate to on a physical and spiritual level, but it wasn't recognisable to me straight away. Annie Patterson was my nemesis, the one who had been tracking me down, but I always kept two steps ahead of her. She was weak. But Jane was different. She was like me; she just didn't realise it yet.

After Jane killed her sister, she turned on me, as I expected her to. She was pregnant. I could see the fear in her eyes as she attempted to shield her stomach against the red-hot brand coming towards her. She attacked me with everything she had left, despite the fact I'd chopped her little finger off and she was losing blood. She grabbed the hot brand from me and smashed me over the head with it, then stabbed me in the side with the knife she'd used to kill her sister. Jane then left me for dead. I can't be sure if she meant to leave me alive, or if she genuinely thought I was dead or going to die, but she made a mistake by leaving me. I managed to crawl out of the warehouse and make it to safety before the police showed up and discovered Annie's body. I went into hiding while I recovered. I'd have preferred it if Jane had joined me as my new sister, but it wasn't to be. She made her choice, and I had to survive.

I knew the police would be looking for me, so I didn't take myself to a hospital even though I knew I needed one. I managed to make do with some over-the-counter medications and bandages. I aspired to find Jane again, but then things took a different turn.

Little did I know my life would change forever a few weeks later. My breasts started aching and I was constantly nauseous. I had managed to avoid an infection, so I knew it had nothing to do with my stab wound, which had begun to heal nicely.

They say motherhood changes you, and when I found out I was pregnant, I decided to change my ways. I no longer needed a twin sister in my life. Jane didn't matter to me anymore. No one did. My babies were all I needed. Twins. It was a sign; I was sure of it. I managed to return to normality, hiding the scar on my forehead and dying my hair.

My pregnancy was relatively normal and stress-free. In fact, I'd go as far as to say I enjoyed every minute of it. Even when I was told at the twenty-week scan that my girls both had a high risk of being born with Down's syndrome. The doctors told me they both had a thickening of the back of the neck, bright spots in their hearts and dilated brain ventricles, but I didn't hear any of that. All I wanted to know was if they were healthy.

The father of my babies was someone I had dated for a few weeks, but it wasn't really going anywhere. I decided not to tell him about them. It was better and less complicated that way. I didn't need him, and I was perfectly happy to raise them by myself. They didn't need him either. I would be both their mummy and their daddy.

I gave up being The Twin Killer. I didn't need her anymore.

It was just me and my babies. Them and me. Forever and always.

But then the worst thing happened.

It was worse than killing my sister.

It was worse than being tortured and captured by a twisted serial killer.

It was worse than Jane abandoning me in the warehouse.

My newborn babies were stolen from the hospital when they were merely hours old.

My whole world fell apart. But even worse than that? I never even saw or held them. They'd been born via caesarean, but there had been complications and straight after I'd had to have an emergency operation to stop some internal bleeding.

My babies had been taken to the neonatal unit while I underwent the surgery, and when I woke up, they were gone. The midwives and nurses were baffled. There was no CCTV anywhere that caught the person who did it. The CCTV had been switched off.

The police had nothing.

I was shattered, completely and utterly broken.

But I refused to give up on my babies. I swore I would find them and destroy the person who'd taken them. But my body gave up on me. It was like I couldn't survive without them inside me. I needed them as much as I needed oxygen.

The search for them dried up. The last piece of information the police gained was that one of the hospital technicians had vanished without a trace. He would have had access to the CCTV unit and the neonatal unit. He was on duty that day.

But it was a dead end.

My dream of raising my babies turned into a living nightmare. I was on every medication possible to control my anxiety, depression and suicidal thoughts. I had no one to help me. I spent my days scrolling through Facebook groups and online forums, searching for families who had twin girls with Down's syndrome. Then, when I found one, I stalked them religiously, until I either confirmed or denied the girls' identity. None of them were my babies.

One day, three long years later, I came across Ryan Neville; a single dad who needed help with housework and looking after his twins. I messaged him and asked him various questions. I looked him up online. His wife had died in a car accident, along with his twin girls. Alarm bells signalled that I'd found them before I'd confirmed it.

I provided a few fake references and qualifications, hoping he'd invite me for an interview. He did. As soon as I met the girls, I knew without a doubt they were mine. It was all I could do not to rush forwards, grab them both and run out the door. I had to bide my time.

But I needed to spend time with them, build Ryan's trust and come up with a plan. He hired me and I started asking him about his wife. Slowly, he began to open up, but I knew his story wasn't completely true.

He told me about the car accident that took his wife, Lisa, but the twins had survived. Unfortunately for him, I knew this wasn't the case. I sat and listened as he poured his heart out, wept like a child and lied to my face. Those girls were not his daughters. They were mine.

And he had stolen them from me because he'd been too traumatised to admit the fact his own daughters were dead.

So many times, I wanted to stab him with a kitchen knife. So many times, when I drove the girls to school, I wanted to keep driving and never look back, but I knew he'd come after me, after them. Besides, I wanted him to pay for what he'd done.

Stealing the girls back wasn't enough.

I needed to make sure he was punished.

I decided to bite the bullet and ask my father for help. I never contacted him before because I'd wanted to do everything myself, but I needed help. I needed his expertise, his power, his control and his money.

Nathan Victor.

A wealthy, powerful businessman who didn't know I was still alive. After I was taken by the original twin killer, I never went back to my family. He was overjoyed at seeing me alive and well, but when I told him the truth about what had happened, he was furious and swore to help me get my daughters back and seek revenge.

We discussed several ideas. It was he who suggested we use this opportunity to make the four people who ruined my life pay for their mistakes.

Chapter Fifty-Three
Ryan

He must be dreaming or hallucinating. Perhaps his severe thirst has driven him mad. He can't quite believe who he's seeing in front of him.

He knows her as Amanda Clarke; au pair to his girls, the woman who washes and folds his laundry, who cooks his favourite dinner sometimes when he's had a stressful day at work, who makes his heart leap when she wears a short skirt, who only has to lightly brush his hand with hers to send a jolt of adrenaline to his heart.

But here she is as someone else.

Jane says she's The Twin Killer; a serial killer who kidnaps, tortures and forces people to murder their own siblings.

Now, Amanda's just said something that makes even less sense.

She's the real mother of his girls. But no. That's wrong. His wife – Lisa – she's their real mother. Amanda's lying. She may be the killer, but those girls are not hers. He raised them all by himself. She was there as an au pair and as a help to him. Nothing more.

'You're wrong,' he says. 'They aren't yours.'

Amanda laughs. 'I can assure you, Ryan. They are mine. I have proof. I had a DNA test done.'

Ryan's jaw clenches. 'You what! That's illegal!'

'And kidnapping newborn babies isn't?' she snaps back. Her eyes flame and her nostrils flare like a bull about to charge. She looks nothing like the kind woman he knew before. Has she been faking it all along? What about their feelings towards each other? Was that all fake too? Over the years, he'd come to not only trust her but admire her too. She told him how she looked after her sick mother, but was that all an act? Was her mother even sick? Has he been played from the start by a deranged woman who wanted his twins for herself?

Jane moves forwards. Ryan had almost forgotten she was here. 'Are you saying that Ryan really did steal his daughters?'

'That's exactly what I'm saying,' replies Amanda.

'But it's not true!' Ryan explodes.

'Are you seriously still denying it? I have proof!' Amanda reaches into the black robes and pulls out a sheet of paper, holding it out in front of her, keeping her arm straight, but shaking slightly.

It's too far away for Ryan to see what it says. He's rooted to the spot, but Jane walks forwards and takes it instead, lowering her eyes and reading it. She glances up and stares at him.

'It's true.'

Ryan rolls his eyes. 'Seriously? You believe a piece of paper that could easily have been faked? What about the website? That's fake too. The people who set this up are masters at forgeries. This whole thing has been faked. I'm pretty sure they have the capability to forge a document.'

Jane shakes her head. 'I don't think this is a fake document.'

'I don't care what you think. It's not true.'

'Maybe ... Maybe you are telling the truth,' says Jane quietly. He's about to open his mouth and say 'Thank you!' but she cuts him off by adding, 'But not about that.'

'What are you talking about?'

'Maybe you really believe they are yours. You don't remember, do you? When my sister was alive, she was a cop. We didn't talk a lot because I hated the fact she was a cop, but she told me once that she dealt with a person who couldn't remember the horrible crime they'd committed. They killed their own daughter by shaking her to death when she wouldn't stop crying. The woman couldn't remember what she'd done. She'd blocked it out. Maybe that's what's happened to you, Ryan.'

Ryan doesn't answer. He can't find the words because he doesn't want to find them. Could Jane be right? Could he have blocked it out?

He remembers his wife's face so clearly as he sat on the side of the road and watched her burn to death. But the girls? They were there, weren't they? Safely beside him in their car seats. He can't remember pulling them from the car, but he must have done.

Yet he was alone when the police and ambulance arrived on the scene several minutes later. There were no babies crying beside him. There was just smoke and the crackle from the blazing fire, roaring in his ears.

Ryan looks at the ceiling and screams as he sinks to the floor, pressing his face into the ground as giant sobs wrack his body.

It's true, isn't it?

They had all died that day. All three of them. The girls hadn't even been born. Lisa had been only four weeks away from giving birth. He'd never seen his daughters, never held them, touched their soft heads, stared into their eyes.

He'd fallen apart as he watched his wife's pregnant body be dragged from the burning car. The smell of burning flesh was seared into his olfactory memory. He can smell it now. He retches and vomits up a small about of water and bile.

'Are you quite done, Ryan?' asks Amanda.

Ryan coughs as he looks up at the woman he thought he knew. 'I ... I did it,' he cries. 'I went back to work at the hospital, and I saw them there in the neonatal unit. I saw my daughters ... and I took them.'

'But they weren't yours, were they?'

'No ...'

'Whose were they?'

Ryan gulps back more bile. 'Y-Yours. I'm so sorry. I'm sorry. I'm sorry.' Ryan faceplants the floor again and weeps, covering his face with his hands as he repeats the word over and over.

Amanda clears her throat. 'Well, now we've got that unpleasantness out of the way. It's time for you to meet the man who killed your wife. Although, technically you killed her because you were too much of a coward to save her from the burning car, but as much as I hate to admit it, it wasn't your fault that the accident happened.'

Ryan stops crying and looks up. He can barely see through the tears. 'W-Who? They never found the person who caused the accident.'

A door opens behind Amanda and an older man steps through. But it isn't him who Ryan stares at. It's the large man he is forcing to walk in front of him with his hands tied behind his back.

The man is covered in blood, bending over at the waist as if he's wounded.

'I believe you know Andrew Carter?'

Chapter Fifty-Four
Andrew

It's all a blur; a painful, dizzying blur. He doesn't remember being stabbed, but he does remember the red-hot pain that flooded his body upon regaining consciousness. He hadn't woken up in the same room. Someone must have moved him while he was out for the count. He woke up on a metal operating table, having had his wound stitched up, albeit crudely.

His head swam with whatever drug concoction they'd given him, which wasn't entirely unpleasant. It wasn't any sort of painkiller though because his side was practically on fire. He was tied down to the table, unable to move.

'Ah, you're awake. Finally,' said a female voice.

Andrew craned his neck to look towards the bottom of the table, at his feet, but the movement caused his side to explode.

'Ooh, I wouldn't do that if I were you. You wouldn't want to pull those stitches.'

'Who the fuck are you?' The woman standing at his feet was young, attractive, but he didn't have a clue who she was.

'My name is Amanda.'

'Yeah, so what? Let me the fuck go!'

'I can't do that, I'm afraid.'

'Why the fuck not?'

'Because I haven't finished playing with you.'

The word *playing* sent a tingle of excitement to his groin. Ah, he got it now. This snooty bitch had tied him up because she wanted to play with him. He could work with that. Shame he was in a lot of pain and his side felt like it was on fire. If he ever set eyes on that bastard Ryan again, he was going to kill him, rip him apart piece by piece.

'So, what did you have in mind?' he asked Amanda, licking his lips.

She stepped closer to his head and placed her palms against his cheeks, forcing him to look up into her eyes. 'Do you remember the events of Tuesday the twenty-eighth of March 2019?'

Andrew laughed, regretting it instantly. He coughed and brought up a spittle of blood. 'Lady, I struggle to remember what I did yesterday. I take a lot of shit.'

'Hmm, yes, I'm aware. Let me refresh your memory. That was the day your father gifted you a brand-new Porsche 911.'

'Ah shit, yeah. That baby was sweet.'

'What happened to that car, Andrew?' Amanda increased the pressure against his cheeks. Shit, this chick was strong.

'I scuffed it that same day. Took too much shit and went for a drive. So what?'

'So ... then what happened?'

'Nothing happened. Listen, bitch, I don't know why you're asking me these dumb questions, but either you let me go or start with the kinky shit, yeah?'

Amanda laughed and released the pressure on his cheeks, moving her hands slowly down the side of his body towards his stitches. It was uncomfortable but not unpleasant. 'You were speeding down the motorway at ninety miles an hour, weren't you?'

'Yeah, so?'

'You clipped the back end of another car, which sent it spiralling into the centre reservation, while you merely drove off with only a small dent in your front bumper.'

Andrew paused for a moment, thinking back. 'I don't remember. I was high, okay? Yeah, I may have hit a car, but I didn't stop to check.'

'No, you didn't. And your actions led to my babies being stolen.'

'What the fuck are you talking about!' Amanda's hands reached his stitches, and she poked them with her fingers, sticking them in between the black threads. He flinched and clenched his teeth. 'What the fuck!'

'The car you hit was being driven by Ryan Neville. In the passenger seat was his heavily pregnant wife, Lisa.'

Andrew couldn't help the chuckle that escaped his lips. 'That's unbelievable. Are you shitting me with that?'

'I can assure you, Andrew. I am not *shitting* you. Because of your actions, Ryan lost his whole family. He had a mental breakdown where he then decided to steal my babies from the hospital only hours after they were born while I was still in recovery after almost dying from blood loss.'

'Jesus Christ. That man is a freak show.'

'Is that all you have to say?'

'What the fuck else is there to say? I'm sorry, okay? I'm sorry that freak decided to kidnap your kids, but how is it my fault? What you gonna do, punish the person who made the damn car, my dad for giving it to me? Lady, you need to get over it.' As soon as the words left his mouth, he knew they were the wrong ones to say.

'Get. Over. It,' she seethed as she increased the pressure, this time against the wound in his side.

'Okay, okay. Fuck! Stop!'

'Don't worry, Andrew. You'll have your chance to redeem yourself in time.' Amanda looked up as a door opened. Andrew couldn't move, dare not move in case she pushed her fingers deeper into his side.

'It's time,' said a deep, male voice.

Who the hell was that?

'Well, Andrew, I guess we shall see if you truly are sorry or if you're just full of shit.'

Now he's here, on his knees, in front of Ryan, and Jane is standing just off to the side. He can barely see straight because of the pain in his side. Whatever drug they gave him has begun to wear off, and now he's delirious and in desperate need of a drink of water. He's never felt so vulnerable and weak before. It's scaring him, deep down.

'Andrew, you're alive!' says Jane. She goes to rush forwards but then stops, maybe re-thinking her act of concern.

'No thanks to any of you,' mutters Andrew. He glares at Ryan.

'You ... You killed my family.' Ryan's eyes are on fire, his fists clenched, his whole body vibrating with energy, ready to explode at any moment.

Andrew attempts to stand up, but his hands are tied behind his back. How is this fair? Surely he should have a chance to defend himself in case Ryan attacks? He topples sideways onto the floor, groaning as his side erupts in pain.

'It was a fucking accident!'

Ryan stamps his foot. 'You drove away and left the scene!'

'I didn't know I'd hit you that hard!'

The two men are shouting at each other, only a few feet between them. Amanda and some weird old dude who looks suspiciously like the guy who drove him to this shithole on the boat are standing off to the side, watching like it's a freaking movie, whereas Jane is just standing there, open-mouthed.

Ryan lunges forwards and punches Andrew hard in the face. Andrew's teeth clamp down on his lip, biting through it. Blood and spit fly out of his mouth, and he falls sideways, unable to stay upright. But Ryan doesn't stop. He grabs Andrew's shirt, pulls him up and punches him again, and again.

Andrew can't do anything to stop him. He can't even speak.

Chapter Fifty-Five
Ryan

He can't stop. He won't stop. Ever. Andrew needs to pay for everything he's done. He needs to feel as much pain as humanly possible. Ryan wants him to suffer for eternity. But it's not enough. Ryan can't see anything but pure anger and blood and fire as he pummels his fists into Andrew's face, one after the other. The skin on his knuckles cracks and bleeds as it connects with Andrew's teeth, but he still doesn't stop.

This is for them. His three girls.

All he sees as he smashes Andrew's face to pieces are their sweet faces, moving further and further away, clouded by thick smoke. His wife screaming for help as the flames engulf her and the babies in her womb. He does nothing apart from watch. He's the one who deserves this punishment, not Andrew. Every punch he lands, he wishes it were for him.

Ryan is crying so hard that he can't see through his tears. He collapses to the ground, spent. Andrew gargles something and then spits out blood on the floor, rolling over to his side and coughing more, sucking in short, sharp breaths.

Jane is crying too, but she can't do anything to stop this.

'Kill me,' says Ryan, looking up at Amanda. 'I can't live with what I've done. I forgot the truth, but now I know ... I can't ... Please, just kill me. You have my permission.'

Amanda walks up to him, looking down at his pathetic form on the ground. 'I don't *need* your permission to kill you. No, Ryan. I've changed my mind. I did want to kill you. In fact, I'd planned on doing exactly that, but now I realise that dying is too easy a punishment for you. You now must live the rest of your miserable life knowing exactly what you did. You not only left your wife and unborn daughters to burn to death, but you also stole my babies from me, taking away the first precious five years of their lives. I can never forgive you for that, but you can go to jail and suffer. That's enough for me.'

Ryan's sobs fill the room. He can't even speak, but he blinks and nods. He doesn't blame Amanda for her actions. He remembers now what he did.

After his wife and daughters died, he spent his days in a vacuum of despair, a deep, dark hole that sank into an abyss. The days rolled into one long nightmare, and he felt as if he were constantly swimming upstream and never getting anywhere. Going under the water, nearly drowning and then surfacing just enough to breathe once, and then drowning again in his sorrow.

He couldn't live like that. He thought about ending his life by stepping in front of a car. Something quick. Maybe jumping from a tall building, but while he was at work, in the hospital, he saw them: two beautiful little girls.

He didn't see anything else. They were his babies and they needed him. No, *he* needed *them*.

The next thing he knew they were back home where they belonged.

'Amanda, I'm sorry for what you've been through, but what about Christie? I mean, Laura. Did she really deserve to die? You've killed an innocent woman,' says Jane.

Amanda raises her eyebrows. 'Have I? You see Jane, when I found out I was pregnant, my whole outlook on life changed. I no longer needed to find my new twin sister. I didn't want to continue The Twin Killer legacy. My girls were my new legacy. Without them, I was nothing. When they were stolen from me, I made it my new life mission to find them and right the wrongs along the way, including punishing those who deserved it. Trust me, she deserved her quick death.'

'What about what her brother did to her? He raped her as a teenager.'

Amanda laughs. 'I'll give you this ... Laura was decent at spinning a story. She was a very damaged young girl. She could barely recognise the truth through all her lies. It wasn't her brother who raped her. It was her father. How do I know this? Because Luke Blake told me.'

Jane frowns. 'How did you know her brother?'

'He was the father of my girls.'

Chapter Fifty-Six
Jane

Her brain can't keep up. The shocking revelations just keep on coming thick and fast, like a tennis ball bouncing back and forth across the net. If she's not careful, one may smack her straight in the face and knock her out. Amanda – The Twin Killer – has intrinsically planned all of this from the start, bringing each of them here for their own reasons. Not only are all four of them connected in some way, but they all have been responsible for destroying a part of this woman's life.

Laura/Christie is dead. Andrew is in dire need of hospital treatment. Ryan will be going to prison, and Jane … What about Jane?

'What happens to me now?' she asks timidly. 'I have a son. I can't leave Ben alone. He has no one. Please … please don't take my baby away from me. You know what that's like, and I'm sorry it happened to you, but please don't take mine away too.'

Amanda sighs, as if it's all just boring her. 'Jane, I'm afraid it's no longer up to me. You've told the truth now, and I have it all recorded. All I need to do is send it to the police and you'll be imprisoned for the murder of your twin sister.'

Jane's eyes flood with tears as she sinks to the ground. 'No, please … I beg you. Please. I need my son. I need him!'

Amanda smiles. 'Then you are ready for your final test. The final piece of the maze.'

'W-What?'

'I meant what I said, Jane. There will be a winner of this game. The money I offered is still up for grabs. You could win the money and return to your son. You won't go to jail because I shall keep your secret safe. But you must pass the final test. Are you ready?'

Jane sniffs loudly and wipes her nose with the back of her hand, leaving a clear residue. There's still a chance she can get out of this. The relief is like a breath of fresh air. 'Y-Yes.'

'You must kill the person responsible for murdering your son's father.'

Jane looks over at Andrew, who has managed to sit up. His face is covered in blood, his nose at an odd angle and several teeth are missing. She's surprised he's still conscious.

Amanda continues. 'Let's be honest. Other than Ryan, Andrew is the one who deserves to die the most, don't you think? Plus, he's a complete dick. Did you know he knew exactly what he was doing when he killed his housemate? And why did he kill him? How about you ask him. Get the answer out of Andrew, then kill him and you will be free to leave this island with the money, return to your son and you'll never hear from me again.'

Jane bites her lip. 'What do I kill him with?'

'Use your imagination.'

There is no alternative for Jane. It's either kill a man who deserves it or go to prison and never see or hold her son again. It's an easy decision to make, but not one she takes lightly. She knows she can do it though. She's killed for her child before. She's killed her own sister, so ending a stranger's life won't be any harder than that.

Jane looks around the room, but there's no weapon she can see so she approaches Andrew, who's still on his knees, with nothing in her hands. He stares at her through swollen, blood-shot eyes as blood and spit slides out of his mouth and drips down his neck.

'Why did you kill him?'

'W-Who?'

'Shaun Willis.'

'Pfft, that loser. He deserved it. Tried to swindle me out of my cut.'

'So you killed him over some stupid drugs?'

'I'd do a lot worse for a lot less.'

Jane sees red. 'You're an evil human being.'

Andrew spits blood in her face.

Jane wipes it away. He's just made this a lot easier. She shoves him to the floor. He topples over easily and lands with a grunt.

'You pathetic bitch! I swear to fucking God you'll all pay for this!'

Jane kneels on his neck, pressing him into the ground. The wound on his side is oozing blood, the stitches slightly ripped. She closes her eyes, then plunges her fingers into the wound, ripping out the stitches. Andrew's guttural screams fill the room as blood pours from the newly opened wound. The slippery feel of blood makes her almost gag, but she holds it together as she yanks her fist out from the hole in his side, leaving him to bleed out on the floor. She gets off his neck and moves back. She's not sure how long it will take for him to bleed to death.

In the meantime, she looks up and sees Ryan being dragged away by the older man who appeared. He looks vaguely familiar. Amanda is still standing and watching her with a smirk across her lips.

Andrew coughs up blood and spits more out. 'H-Help me!'

Jane crouches next to his face. 'This is for Shaun, my son's father ... and for Ryan's family.' She uses both hands and covers his mouth and nose, pressing down so hard that she starts trembling from the effort. Andrew attempts to wriggle free, but his life and energy is seeping out of him as fast as the blood from his side.

It won't be long now.

Jane keeps the pressure on as the life fades from his hate-filled eyes.

Amanda slow claps behind her. 'Bravo, Jane.'

Jane stands up and stares down at the man she's just killed. She takes a deep breath. 'Get me out of here,' she says.

'Come with me. Congratulations, you have won The Murder Maze.'

Jane turns and walks up to Amanda, stopping only a foot from her face. 'Fuck off,' she mutters. 'If I ever see or hear from you again, I'll kill you myself. You got that?'

The Twin Killer merely smiles.

Chapter Fifty-Seven
Amanda

Jane is understandably quiet while we make the trip across the island to the small jetty where there's a boat waiting to take us back to the mainland. She looks like a broken woman, compared to the one who arrived here almost three days ago. Yes, three days. Dehydration has well and truly set in, so rather than have her collapse on me, I hand her a bottle of water along with the bag she arrived with and her jacket to help keep the rain and wind away. She stares at the water bottle for several seconds, most likely wondering if I've poisoned it. I haven't, but it's fun to watch her wrestle with her own brain as she takes a small sip. Then she starts chugging it like a beer bong at a university party.

My father handles Ryan, who is in a catatonic state, just staring at the ground, weeping like a child. His hands have been cuffed, but I don't see him as a danger to me or anyone. He's lost the will to live. The light has gone from his eyes, and I'm elated that I'm the one who snuffed it out.

We climb on board the little boat, not saying a word. My father starts the engine, which splutters and coughs several times before finally roaring to life. He is a man of very few words as he drives the boat through the choppy waters while Jane and I sit next to each other at the back on a little wooden bench, with Ryan sitting on the floor in front of us, his knees pulled up to his chest. Due to the noise of the boat, we can't talk to each other, but we don't need to say a word to understand what the other is thinking.

I trust Jane will keep my secret, that I'm The Twin Killer, and all about this island and what happened here. She can't afford to tell anyone. If she does, she'll lose her son. There's no doubt about that. Women change when they become mothers.

I certainly did.

Before I found out I was pregnant, I was obsessed with finding a sister like me to share my life with, but my children brought me more joy than I could ever believe was possible even before they were born. Currently, my babies are being looked after by my mother. I'm dying to get back to them. We always have such fun together when Ryan is at work. They already think of me as a motherly figure, so I know they won't have any trouble accepting me as their true mother. I will tell them eventually, but due to them having Down's syndrome, I may have to wait a few years before they will be capable of understanding me.

No matter how they react, they will never have to go without ever again. They will receive the best care, treatment and help from me and my family. They are finally where they are supposed to be, and once Ryan has been handed over to the police and they see the DNA results, my babies will be transferred to my care once and for all.

My father is very wealthy and powerful and there's nothing he can't do. He has a lot of friends in the police and higher up, even in government. The events on this island never happened. He can control what the papers print and what the newsreaders say if he needs to. It's why I've been able to keep a low profile for all these years and during the time I was acting as The Twin Killer. We may have been estranged, but my father always looked after me. He loves me. No one would ever have caught me, not even Annie Patterson, Jane's sister. She thought she was getting close, but she was only ever a pawn to play with, to show that I could get close to a police officer and still not be caught.

Years ago, back in the 80s, my father opened an escape room, state-of-the-art, but it wasn't to be. It was one of his only failures in life. A kid died. He covered it up, buried it, used his wealth and power to shove it under a rug. He's very extravagant and has a wonderfully vivid imagination, coming up with The Murder Maze and its many twists and turns mostly by himself. I think he was bored mostly. That's why he helped me seek my revenge. I offered a few suggestions, but he handled everything. It's his passion; to build and create elaborate houses and turn them into an exciting adventure. This gave him an outlet to let his imagination run free. And this time, it wouldn't matter if anyone died. No one knew they were here.

Jane has nothing to fear. I keep my promises. She won't ever be bothered by the police regarding her sister's death, or Andrew's death. Her secrets are well and truly safe with me. However, she must hold up her end of the bargain; her freedom to return to her son with the prize money in exchange for her silence.

I have ears and eyes everywhere and I shall know if she decides to squeal like a pig and tell the police about the events that happened on this island.

As the small boat bobs closer to the mainland, I cast my eyes across the water, the island in the distance. It's the early hours of the morning, the light peering over the horizon. A lot has happened in the past seventy-two hours. It almost feels as if no time has passed at all.

Jane stands as soon as the boat is tied to the mooring and moves to step across me. I grasp her arm, my fingers digging into her jacket. She glares at me as I speak.

'Good luck, Jane. Perhaps, one day, you will seek me out so we may become sisters after all.'

She doesn't respond except to shrug me off.

I watch her climb onto the jetty. She stumbles slightly but remains steadfast as she regains her balance and then takes off running. I wait until she's out of sight before turning my attention to Ryan. I almost feel sorry for him.

Almost.

He seems incapable of speaking or moving of his own free will. My father has to drag him off the boat where he then collapses on the jetty, pressing his face into the wood.

'Come now, Ryan. You don't expect my father to drag you the whole way to the police station, do you?' I give him a small shove with my foot. He grunts and proceeds to roll over onto his back, staring up at the bleak sky.

'M-My girls. I want to see my g-girls.'

'That's impossible, I'm afraid. Prison is no place for two innocent young girls.'

'They will want to see me.'

'No, they won't.'

Ryan's eyes are red, on the cusp of crying, but it seems he has no more tears left. 'P-Please ... take care of them. They're all I have. I love them so much. Promise me.'

I sigh and stare down at his pathetic form. 'You have my word. They are my daughters and there is nothing I wouldn't do for them. They will never want for anything. I always keep my promises.'

Chapter Fifty-Eight
Jane

Freedom has never tasted so sweet. She doesn't know what day it is, but when she gets far enough away from the island, from the boat and her captives, her watch and phone spring to life. Dozens of notifications pop up one after the other. It's almost seven in the morning … three days later.

Fuck.

How is that possible? In a strange way, since being on that island, time seems to have stood still for her, yet in the real world, three days have passed. She misses Ben so much. His face and the smell of his clean hair is what has kept her going this whole time. She heads to the train station using the money she has in her bag, which Amanda handed back to her earlier.

Amanda has also provided her some clean clothes, which she changes into as soon as she can before showing her face in public. She has some baby wipes in her bag, which she uses to remove the last traces of blood splatters and grime on her exposed skin.

She spends the next several hours on a train bound for Birmingham.

The monotonous tone of the tracks sends her into a trance, but she doesn't sleep. She can't. Because every time she closes her eyes, she sees blood and Andrew's face as she smothers the life from him. She sees Christie screaming as blood fills her mouth and she chokes to death on it. She sees Ryan crumpled on the floor, a broken man, sobbing like a small child. The same thing happened when she killed Annie five years ago. She couldn't even go to a therapist for help because she wouldn't be able to explain the whole truth. And now, she has two further deaths on her conscience.

Jane's phone finally stops vibrating with all the updates, so she distracts herself from her dark thoughts by scrolling through the missed messages. Her mum has messaged several times to update her on how Ben is and attached some photos of him smiling and having fun at the park. Her heart almost explodes with happiness as she sees his beautiful face. However, the messages and voicemails become more and more frantic and desperate as the hours and days roll by.

She calls her mum back.

'Jane! Are you okay? You haven't answered any of my messages. It's been three days!'

'I know. I'm so sorry, Mum. There was no signal where I was, but I'm on my way home now.'

'Everything okay? Are you hurt? I almost called the police.'

'No, no, nothing like that. I'm fine, really. Can I speak to Ben?'

'Of course ... Benny, your mummy's on the phone.'

Jane listens as her mum hands the phone to Ben. Her heart beats wildly in her chest.

'Hi, Mummy!'

'Hi, Ben! I've missed you so much. How are you? Have you had fun with Granny?'

'Granny let me have chocolate and ice cream!'

'Did she? Wow, what flavour ice cream did you have?'

'Chocolate chip!'

'Wow! Listen, baby, I'll be home soon, okay? I love you so much and I can't wait to see you.'

'Love you, Mummy. Bye!'

'Bye, baby.'

Her mum comes back on the phone. 'He's been as good as gold. He's asked about you a lot. What time will you arrive?'

'My train gets in just after three, so I'll be with you by four. No need to pick me up. I'll get a taxi. There's something I have to do first.'

'Okay, see you later.'

'Bye, Mum.'

She hangs up and then continues scrolling through the phone notifications. One catches her eye. It's from her banking app. Jane logs in and her eyes widen as she sees £1,000,000 in her account.

Holy crap.

Any minute now she'll probably get a call from the bank asking if everything's okay and wondering why she's just been gifted so much money.

She puts her phone away and continues staring out of the window at the countryside whizzing by, wondering if this has all been just a bad dream.

She gets off the train and heads straight for the taxi rank, giving the driver the address she needs. She avoids the usual small talk, having never liked it anyway. When he pulls up outside the graveyard, Jane pays him and gets out, wincing as her stiff muscles click and spasm in protest. She knows she must still look a state, sweaty and pale, but at least she's no longer covered in blood.

The graves pass by in a blur as she briskly walks to her sister's grave, kneeling straight in front of it. She doesn't say anything. She just leans forwards, places her forehead on the cool ground and cries her eyes out. She doesn't attempt to hold back her emotion as it pours out of her like hot liquid. She doesn't care that there's a groundskeeper nearby or a family visiting a grave. Let them stare.

Only when her knees hurt from pressing against the small stones surrounding the grave does she shift position and raise her head off the ground. The other mourners and the groundskeeper have moved away now so she's alone.

She stares at the headstone, gently touching the cool granite. That's when she notices the flowers on the grave. They aren't the same ones she left there a few days ago. Those are still there, but there's a second bunch of flowers, more expensive than hers.

She strokes the gentle pink petals then sees a flash of white hidden behind the leaves.

A note.

Jane pulls it out and reads it.

Till death do us part.

What the hell? She turns it over, but the back of the note is blank. It's written in swirly calligraphy writing, eerily like the handwriting on her invitation. Is this from Amanda? Why would she say that? Jane slips the note into her pocket and leaves the graveyard, eager to see her son.

Jane can barely contain her excitement as she rushes up the stairs of her building. She unlocks the door and calls out for Ben. Her beautiful boy comes charging towards her, dragging his favourite toy bunny, and jumps into her arms. She lifts him up and spins around in a circle, inhaling his scent and planting kisses into his soft hair.

'I've missed you so much!'

'Mummy!'

Her mum appears and watches them embrace. 'Good God, what on earth have you been up to? You look dreadful!'

Jane places Ben on the floor and plants a kiss on her mum's cheek. 'Gee, thanks, Mum.'

'Seriously though, Jane. You look like you haven't slept for a week.'

'It certainly feels that way.'

'I'll pop the kettle on.'

'Mum ... have you visited Annie's grave recently?'

Her mum shakes her head. 'No, not for about a month. Why?'

'No reason.' Jane sits at the kitchen table and Ben climbs onto her lap.

'Mummy, you smell funny.'

Jane laughs. 'Sorry, baby. I'll have a shower in a minute.'

'What exactly did you do while you were away?' asks her mum, placing a cup of tea in front of her. 'You said it was some sort of adventure expedition and team building?'

'I'm not sure you'd believe me if I told you.'

'Oh, I almost forgot. A friend of yours stopped by not long after you left.'

Jane looks up from sipping her tea. 'A friend? Who?' She doesn't have any friends so already her defences are on high alert.

'She said her name was Amanda. She wasn't exactly very pleasant, to be honest, but she didn't stay long.'

Jane feels a cold shiver race up her spine. 'What did she say?'

'Nothing much, but she did say something a bit strange. She mentioned Annie.'

'Mum, what exactly did she say? I need to know.'

'She said, "It must be hard knowing your daughter is responsible for what happened to Annie." What did she mean by that, Jane? How does she know about Annie and what happened to you?'

Jane kisses her son on his cheek. 'Ben, why don't you go and watch the TV for a bit, and I'll be in after I've spoken to Granny.'

'Can I watch Bluey?'

'Yes, of course.'

Ben hops off her lap and runs out of the kitchen. Her mum hasn't taken her eyes off her and Jane can feel her gaze boring into her soul. It's time to tell the truth. If taking part in The Murder Maze has taught her anything, it's that telling the truth is better than living with a lie. She doesn't know what her mum will say or how she'll react, but Amanda has forced her hand. She can't risk her mum finding out another way in the future.

'Mum, there's something you should know about Annie.'

Her mum sits opposite her, leaning forwards slightly. 'How did you find out?'

'What?'

'You said there's something I should know. I already know.'

'You already know what?'

Her mum stares blankly at her for several seconds. 'About Annie and her babies.'

Jane coughs as confusion clouds her mind, which starts races at a million miles an hour again, attempting to piece together the puzzle before she has all the pieces. Or perhaps she does have all the pieces and she's had them all along. She just didn't realise it.

'Her what? What babies?'

'I assume that's what you were about to tell me.'

'Mum, what are you talking about?'

Her mum lets out a long sigh. 'Annie gave birth to twin girls two months before she died. She made me promise not to tell you. She said you wouldn't care anyway.'

Jane swallows hard and sucks in a breath. 'I ... I didn't know that.'

'Then what were you going to tell me?'

'What happened to them? The girls, I mean.'

Her mum's eyes fill with tears. 'They were both born with Down's syndrome, but they didn't survive. Some sort of complication during the delivery. Annie took it very badly, as you can imagine. She threw herself back into her work, but then ... Well, you know the rest.'

Jane slowly rises to her feet and begins pacing up and down in front of her mum. How is that possible? Something doesn't add up. It can't be a mere coincidence.

Could Amanda's girls, the twins who Ryan stole from the hospital … could they have been Annie's children? Which would make them Jane's nieces.

It's all been a lie. Everything Amanda said. Or maybe she doesn't even know and is caught up in her own dream world like Ryan had been, convinced the girls are hers, unable to believe the truth.

Grace and Hope aren't Amanda's children. They aren't Ryan's either.

They were Annie's, her sister's.

Jane needs to get them back.

Whatever it takes.

'They're not dead, Mum.'

'What?'

'Annie's twins. They're alive. I just know it. I have a lot to tell you.'

Chapter Fifty-Nine
Ryan
Three Months Later

He doesn't really know what's happening anymore. The minutes, hours and days tick by, all rolling into one, never giving him any peace from his own mind. Since the events of The Murder Maze, he's barely uttered a single word. His brain has shut down, full of cotton wool and blurry images and memories. The medication he's on warps and distorts his mind further, which is better than living with the truth: that he allowed his family to die and stole two newborn babies from a new mother.

He's not in prison. He's in a mental health hospital along with other patients who require round-the-clock care and attention. Ryan's been on suicide watch ever since he's been here. Any chance he gets he tries to take his own life because living is too painful, too confusing, so they drug him, attempting to numb the pain and his intentions. This is no way to live, like a living nightmare, a ghost of his former self. Why won't they let him die?

Amanda hasn't been in touch. He hasn't seen his girls since before all this happened. In the group therapy classes, he barely speaks about them. Just shakes his head and grunts. How can he possibly explain what happened to him on that island? The police arrested him and charged him with kidnapping, but they quickly realised that he was no longer of sound mind, so he was sent here to live out the rest of his days in a drug-fuelled haze.

The thing is, back then, five years ago, when he'd first taken the twins, he'd felt normal because his mind had blocked out all the bad bits. His wife had died and there was no disguising that fact, but the twins had survived because the truth was just too awful to believe. His mind had protected him all this time, but inside the damage had already been done. It was only a matter of time before the walls came crumbling down and all hell broke loose.

He's in hell now. Eternal hell. He can hear her screaming at night as the flames engulf her body. That's when he thrashes about on the bed, attempting to be free from his restraints. Then, a nurse will rush in and administer more sedative. He welcomes the sedatives. They quieten the screams for a little while longer.

Ryan is sitting in a wheelchair, staring out at the winter snow that started falling last night. He has a wool blanket draped over his hunched shoulders and a string of drool is leaking from the side of his mouth. This is where he likes to sit. He's not often disturbed by the other patients, but a nurse is there somewhere keeping an eye on him. She's sitting in the corner now, reading a book.

A shuffle appears behind him, somewhere out in the hall. Perhaps one of the patients is attempting to escape or overpower one of the nurses. There's no escaping this place. It's not exactly high security, but the people here are safer within these walls. Ryan knows that. He doesn't deserve to be on the outside. Every day he hates himself a little more. Every day a piece of his heart dies and shrivels up. Every day he wishes he would drop dead so he wouldn't have to be in so much pain. Amanda was right; living is a crueller punishment than death.

'Ryan?' The gentle voice of his nurse appears. 'You have a visitor.'

His heart leaps. Surely it can't be Amanda. She wouldn't come here, would she? Has she brought the twins? No, she can't. He doesn't want them to see him like this.

'Hi, Ryan.'

No, it's not Amanda.

He turns his head a couple of inches to look at Jane, who kneels beside him and places a hand on his arm.

A month ago, he wrote to Jane. It was a short letter, but he hoped she'd understood the meaning behind his words. She hadn't replied, nor had she sent any message of any sort. He had assumed either the letter hadn't reached her, or she was ignoring his plea.

But here she is.

She looks good. She's cut her hair short and dyed it blonde. She's lost a little weight, especially around the face and neck.

He nods and manages a weak smile.

'I got your message. I'm sorry it's taken so long for me to visit, but I've been moving house and getting Ben set up in his new school and ... Well, I've adopted Grace and Hope.'

At this, Ryan frowns and opens his mouth, but he's forgotten how to talk. Jane gives his arm a light squeeze.

'I know you're probably confused. Amanda got it wrong. She's not the real mother of Grace and Hope. The woman you stole the babies from wasn't her. It was my sister, Annie. Grace and Hope are my nieces and over the past three months I put together a case and managed to find their real birth certificates and DNA test certificates. Amanda's twins died at birth. Somehow, the two sets of twins were mixed up. I think it was Amanda's father who concocted it all. He has a lot of power and control. I spoke to Amanda about it, made her see the truth, the evidence right in front of her. She was hurting too, like you were. She convinced herself that her twins were still alive and made it her mission to hunt you down and get them back.

'Amanda and I have come to an agreement. Once she calmed down, she realised that she needed to do what was best for the girls, despite them not being hers. They're living with me now and I'm doing the best I can. My mother is helping me out and Amanda is paying for them to go to a special school. She still wants them to be looked after. I know this is a lot to take in.'

Jane stops talking and looks out the window for a while. Ryan turns and they both watch the snow in silence.

'I want you to know how sorry I am about everything,' continues Jane. 'What you did was awful, but ... you'd lost your whole family. I can't even imagine what that must have been like.'

Ryan nods again, blinking his eyes and keeping them closed for an extra second.

'I just wanted you to know the truth about Grace and Hope.'

Ryan smiles.

'What the hell have they got you dosed up on here?' she asks. 'Can you talk at all?'

Ryan gulps and cracks his mouth open. 'Y-Yes, but ... hard,' he manages.

Jane nods.

'B-Bring?'

Jane sighs. 'Yes, I did, but ... I'm not sure ...' She looks behind them at the nurse who is sitting in the corner. Jane leans down and whispers in his ear. 'I hope you find peace.'

Tears fill his eyes, and he closes them. 'T-Thank ... you.'

She smiles as she reaches for his hand, slipping hers into it, and squeezes gently. 'Goodbye, Ryan.' She leans in and kisses him on the cheek before standing up and leaving the room.

Ryan opens his eyes, looking down at the object Jane has left in his palm.

A packet of chewing gum.

He will wait for the right moment to use it.

He's glad Jane was able to work out his coded message. He's never told a soul about his deadly allergy to latex, which most gum is made from.

XLEAT MGU CAILGLRE

Chapter Sixty
Amanda

A few days after The Murder Maze ended, I moved myself and the girls into my parents' large mansion in the countryside, away from prying eyes and ears. I had a private tutor set up who specialised in working with children with Down's syndrome. I had plans to take them on days out to the beach, take them shopping and all the things I've missed out on so far in their short lives.

My girls were everything to me. I loved them so much and I was so proud of how well they coped in their new home with a new routine and new school. There were a few tears when I told them their daddy wouldn't be coming home, but after a few days, they forgot about him. I was their primary carer since they were four years old. They knew me. It was my plan all along.

But then Jane Patterson decided she wanted to rip my heart out.

Again.

My babies were taken away from me.

Again.

My father did his best, but even he couldn't cover up the solid proof that Grace and Hope were not mine, especially when Jane came forward with their original birth certificates and a DNA test that proved, beyond a shadow of a doubt, that they were related to her, not me.

I learned the truth that day. My babies had died during a complicated birth. They'd been suffocated inside my womb and were dead before they even came into this world. My father bribed the doctors and midwives to lie to me and tell me they'd survived.

I had to admit the truth.

When I learned of a set of twins being stolen from the hospital, I convinced myself that they were mine. Years later, when I asked my father to help me get a DNA test to prove it, he faked that too. I had no idea about any of it. I feel so betrayed and hurt by everyone. He told me he did it to save me from myself. He couldn't bear to tell me the truth; that my babies had died. He used his wealth to fund everything, and he kept silent about his knowledge the whole time. He knew the twins weren't mine, but he helped me track down the people I blamed for their death, even though none of it was true. He said he did it because he loved me.

Jane and I came to an arrangement. Together, we took down my father. Now, he's going to rot in prison. I have all his money and power and now I'm using it to help Grace and Hope, give them a decent life by ensuring Jane has whatever she needs to help them thrive. God knows that Jane would never have been able to give them the support they needed throughout their lives without my help. Despite them not being mine, I feel responsible for them. I still love them as if they were my own. In a way, Jane and I have called a truce on our vendetta against each other. All for the sake of those precious girls.

I won't be a part of their lives. How can I be? But I'll be a silent parent in the background. Jane knows I'm always there watching. If she tries to take me down and send me to prison, then she will die, and the girls will get nothing. I have power over her and she knows it.

Nothing has ended the way I imagined.

I'm not sure how I should be feeling about it, but at the end of the day, Ryan Neville, Andrew Carter and Laura Blake got what they deserved. I don't feel guilty for that. I never will.

Perhaps Jane deserves to rot in prison for the lives she's taken, but I suppose it's true what they say after all.

There isn't anything a parent wouldn't do for their child.

Even murder.

****

If you've enjoyed reading The Murder Maze, please consider leaving a review wherever you bought the book or tag me on social media.

Fancy another standalone psychological thriller?

"How to Commit the Perfect Murder in Ten Easy Steps" is OUT NOW and available to read for FREE on Kindle Unlimited. Scan the code below!

Did you like this book?

I really hope you enjoyed reading The Murder Maze.

If you have, please consider leaving me a review on Amazon and Goodreads, share a review on your social media pages and tag me, share my book to any book clubs you may be a part of or recommend my book to friends and family.

Reviews are massively important, especially to self-published authors. They help find other readers who may enjoy the book and spread the word to a wider audience.

For a FREE short story called "You Die...I Die", which is a prequel to The Murder Maze, sign up for my monthly newsletter at:

www.jessicahuntleyauthor.com

Connect with Jessica

Find and connect with me online via the following platforms.

Sign up to my email list via my website to be notified of future books and receive my monthly author newsletter:

www.jessicahuntleyauthor.com

Follow me on Facebook: Jessica Huntley - Author - @jessica.reading.writing

Follow me on Instagram: @jessica_reading_writing

Follow me on Twitter: @jess_read_write

Follow me on TikTok: @jessica_reading_writing

Follow me on Goodreads: jessica_reading_writing

Follow me on my Amazon Author Page - Jessica Huntley

Printed in Great Britain
by Amazon